First Light

The Chronicles of The Sevenths: Book 1

Elvis Lawson

 Press

DXI Press

ISBN 978-0-9977986-0-9

This book is dedicated to the woman that not only helped make this book possible, but nearly every good thing I have done in this life. She is a tireless mother and the most amazing wife I could ask for. She is the yin to my yang.

This book is for Crystal.

ACKNOWLEDGEMENTS

It has been said by people much smarter than me that writing is a lonely thing. The reality is the actual act of writing and putting your ideas on paper is a solitary act, but the entirety of writing a novel requires many people. This book would not be possible without the wonderful help I received from others. Notably my wife, Crystal who read this book far too many times, and Laurie Lawson who helped make sure it looked like I didn't fail grammar class. Any mistakes are mine and mine alone.

Contents

CHAPTER ONE - MARIE

"How in the hell did I let him talk me into this," Marie thought as she was fiddling with the bank deposit slips. As Marie Clarkson stood at the preparation counter in the middle of Junctionville City bank, she kept looking back at the bank's entrance. Junctionville may have been a relatively small town with a population of less than thirty thousand, but it took pride in its downtown. A decade prior, a group of successful residents began a huge renovation project. They were able to convince most of the store owners to invest heavily in renovating their buildings. Those who couldn't afford the renovations were given interest free loans to pay for them. Junctionville City Bank was the crown jewel of that renovation.

The main lobby of the bank had a gorgeous twenty foot high, hand painted ceiling that was held up with large white columns sprouting from a pristine marble floor. The owner and president of the bank was quoted a few years later as saying the remodel was the best idea and investment they had ever made. Apparently, so many people who had visited just to see the ceiling, were swayed by the hometown charm of the bank and changed over from the national chain a few blocks away. So many ended up switching that the national branch closed.

Today, with Christmas less than two weeks away, the columns were wrapped with extravagant garland, and each column had a very large wreath adorning the front. Marie was too busy looking back at the huge arched double doors labeled 'Entrance', to notice the beauty that surrounded her. She couldn't remember ever being this nervous, and she cursed herself again for listening to Darrell. It didn't take long for her to realize that constantly looking back over her shoulder was quite suspicious. She decided to grab a deposit slip and move to the opposite side of the counter. From here she could see the entrance less conspicuously by just looking up. She still had to force herself to slow down and not look up as often as she wanted to.

Marie was, in general, quite an unassuming and non-threatening young lady, especially now that she had purposely dressed down, so as not to attract attention. She knew this was exactly why Darrell chose her to be in the bank, while Darrell and Gavril waited in the coffee shop across the street. Marie was what most would consider quite small. She was fifteen and stood only five feet tall. She never gave her weight much thought, but at her last doctor appointment, she weighed 100 pounds fully clothed and pockets full. She was, however, quite strong and carried a lot of muscle mass for her frame. She usually hid her muscles with baggy clothes to avoid, or at least lessen, the rude comments about her having manly arms and people questioning her sexuality. Aside from her muscles, her hair was the only thing that really stood out about her. Long, thick, and bright red, it was very much like a giant flame, burning bright and hot. She nearly always used her hair as a basis for her Halloween costumes, including recent costumes such as Princess Merida from the movie Brave and Flame Princess from one of her favorite TV shows, Adventure Time.

Her hair was the cause of many conversations with strangers throughout her life. It was quite typical for a stranger to stop her in the store and go on and on about how beautiful her hair was, and how they wished their hair was that nice. The problem with this was that Marie was pretty guarded, and didn't generally like interacting with strangers. If a person wasn't on her very short list of friends, she usually avoided talking to them. In moments of honest reflection, however, she did have to admit that she enjoyed the compliments, and they always gave her an ego boost.

Marie was raised by her father. Her mother died while giving birth to her. She always felt like her father resented her for her mother's death, though he never said it out loud. Her father struggled raising her at times. He was never very good at things that were feminine, though he had tried really hard. Things got much easier for them both when she decided she didn't really like things that were feminine. She liked looking like a tomboy and doing more masculine things, like hunting. She liked her life, but she sometimes wondered how different it would be if she had been into dolls and tea parties instead of hunting and Brazilian jujitsu. Would she be more likely to be hanging out at the mall with other girls? Instead, she spent her time attempting to prove how tough she was. Then there was the pressing question of the moment: would she be gushing at the theater screen as two vampires made out instead of standing in the bank nervously watching the entrance?

Darrell, Marie's best friend for as long as she could remember, had impressed her a few times recently by guessing something before it happened. At first she thought it was some kind of trick, but she couldn't explain away some of the things. He had never guessed something so big and so specific though. When he first brought this idea up two days ago, she couldn't believe it. She figured he was joking. It wasn't until last night when he presented his plan that she began to realize the severity of the situation. She still wasn't sure how he got the map of the bank.

Now here she was, standing in the middle of the bank, the backpack that she wore feeling heavier with each passing minute. The incessant crooning of Nat King Cole and his chestnuts was not helping her nerves. Of all the Christmas songs available, which any rational person would agree was far too many, they had to be playing the one she hated most. She knew there was no way Darrell could be right about his prediction, so she wasn't sure why she was so freaking nervous. Perhaps part of her subconscious truly believed him and knew that if she failed in her task, many people would die. She wanted to call the cops, but Darrell rightly pointed out that they wouldn't believe them.

She glanced up at the large clock hanging above the doors. It read 11:14. Darrell had said that it would happen at 11:15, so she had less than one minute. She watched the second hand as it ticked away, her heart pounding more and more with each passing second. Fifteen seconds to go and she swore that time was slowing down; each second felt like an eternity. She knew that through the music and the cacophony of the banking crowd it was impossible to hear the clock tick, yet she heard each click of the second hand going off like an explosion in her head. Five seconds to go and her head was pounding. Four seconds to go and she felt two beads of sweat, one rolling down each temple. Three seconds to go and her backpack felt so heavy she thought it might topple her over. Two seconds to go and she gripped the table so hard she feared her knuckles might break through the skin. One second to go and she held her breath and stared unblinking at the door. Zero seconds to go and she watched as nothing happened. She kept staring at the door, unblinking and not breathing for several more seconds and no one came through. Darrell was wrong, or maybe it all was a big practical joke to freak her out. Either way, nothing was happening but she couldn't stop her heart from pounding.

Just when she decided she had enough and was about to bail on Darrell's plan, the man walked through the door. When Darrell had described him he had used generic identifiers. Darrell said he would have a slightly dirty trucker's hat with an incredibly sexist restaurant logo on it. He would have a long, dirty blond goatee, and would be wearing an old hair metal band T-Shirt. She asked him to be more specific, but he just said that she would know it when she saw it. Now as she stood here, she couldn't think of a single hair metal band.

Shocked didn't quite describe how she felt when he walked in, just as Darrell described. Well, not exactly as he described, she thought. Sure, he had all the visual descriptors Darrell had used, but Darrell's description hadn't captured how truly creepy the guy was. She couldn't put her finger on exactly what it was about him that she found unsettling, but when his eyes caught hers, every fiber of her being screamed for her to get as far away from him as physically possible. He was almost like a parody of a creepy guy. Marie imagined if people were making some sort of after school special about stranger danger, the makeup department would make a guy that looked exactly like this man, and the director would be upset because it wasn't realistic. They would say that nobody really looked that creepy. Yet here he was standing in front of her, making her skin crawl. She had heard the phrase so many times in her life, but never knew what it actually felt like to have your skin crawling. She actually had to glance down to make sure her arms weren't covered in ants.

Despite all those feelings, she knew she had to force herself to do what she promised Darrell she would do. She still didn't know how he knew this would happen, but she did trust him above anyone else in this world. She would have to take this leap of faith. She slowly slid her backpack off and held it in front of her as she made her way around to the other side of the counter. She didn't realize how much having that counter between her and the creep of the week had helped her nerves. Now that only fifteen feet of well-polished marble floor separated the two of them, she found herself shaking so badly that she wasn't sure if she would even be able to do it.

Luckily, he was focused on something else and wasn't looking at her, or she knew it would be too much. She began to try to open her backpack, but the always annoying buckles combined with her increasingly shaking and sweaty hands, made it seem like an impossible task. She glanced up at the guy and began to panic even more. He had begun to walk further into the bank. He was now only a couple of feet from the potted ferns that Darrell said were the point of no return. According to Darrell, if she didn't pull off the plan before he passed those ferns, people would die. She had tried not to put too much thought into the idea of people really dying, since the entire concept that Darrell knew this was going to happen seemed outrageous. After seeing this guy and seeing the crazy hiding behind his eyes she was sure that Darrell was right, and she had do something quickly, before Mr. Creepy did.

Still having no luck with the buckles, Marie decided it was now or never. She grabbed the front flap and back of her backpack and pulled with all the strength she could muster, ripping the fabric at the seams. Unfortunately, she had ripped the backpack with so much force that she had lost control of it. This sent almost the entire contents of the backpack, about fifteen pounds of marbles, flying in all directions. Luckily, at least half of those marbles had flown where she intended them to go. Dozens of marbles rolled right under the creepy guy's feet. She knew what came next happened in the blink of an eye, but to her it seemed like slow-motion.

The guy stepped on the marbles, just like they planned, and Marie watched in total shock as he began to fall just as he was pulling a big chrome gun out of his coat. He hit the marble floor with a thud she could feel reverberate in her feet. When he fell, his hand hit the ground, sending his pistol sliding across the floor. The pistol came to an abrupt stop as it hit the security guard's right foot. The poor, unsuspecting security guard just stared at the gun in complete shock, not moving a muscle until someone yelled at him to pick it up. Pulled out of his daze, the far too old security guard picked up the gun, looked toward the heap of a man it originated from, turned to the large potted tree next to him and promptly threw up.

Marie shook herself out of her own little daze long enough to look at the guy she had tripped. She couldn't believe what she saw. The guy had apparently hit his head on the floor when he fell, and there was blood everywhere. His hideous hat had been sent flying and she could see the spot where his head had been split open. She was pretty sure that his actual skull had been cracked, but she forced herself to look away before her brain could register anymore specifics. She had never liked the sight of blood, despite enjoying hunting, and this was by far the most gruesome thing her young eyes had ever seen. Nat King Cole was still droning on about his chestnuts. If she hadn't hated that song enough before, now she knew that every time she heard it, she would be reminded of this creepy guy and his blood-soaked head. She couldn't be certain, but with a wound like that, she assumed the man had died. She was not squeamish enough to vomit like the security guard, but she knew the vision of his head would haunt her dreams for quite some time.

She reached down and picked up her backpack, noticing the stun gun was still sitting at the bottom, and thanked God she didn't have to use it like they had planned if the marbles hadn't worked out. She cursed herself for being thankful that a man had apparently died so she didn't have to do something that frightened her. She threw her ripped backpack over her shoulder, and surveyed the madness that had unfolded in front of her. The security guard was now trying to direct all of the customers and employees. He was trying his best to get people to stay away from the body, while at the same time, trying to make sure nobody left the bank. He said that the police would want to interview everyone, and that they needed to stay. Marie knew she wanted no part of a police investigation. How was she supposed to explain why she was carrying fifteen pounds of marbles, much less why she spilled them all over the bank floor?

She watched the guard with a little bit of a heavy heart. She knew he wasn't prepared for this, and try as he might, he didn't have the demeanor necessary to take control. Marie waited for him to be distracted so she could slip away. The guard began arguing with a very old looking lady about leaving. He was demanding she stay so she could talk to the police, and she was telling him that if he didn't get out of her way she was going to wallop him with her cane. Marie was torn. She really wanted to get out of the bank, but a part of her knew that this old lady whacking the just as old security guard with her cane was going to be hilarious. Her good judgement prevailed, and she used the distraction to slip unnoticed out the front door.

When she got out of the bank she had to squint against the mid-day sun and it took her eyes a moment to adjust. In her hurry and blindness, she very nearly was run over by a passing SUV. She stopped to take a breath and get her bearings then headed across the brick covered one-way street to meet up with her two best friends, Darrell Johnson and Gavril Darzi. They were waiting in Dark Brew, a quaint hole-in-the-wall that was downtown Junctionville's best coffee shop. Every bone in her body wanted to break into a run, but she knew there were cameras and the police would be reviewing the footage later. She already looked suspicious by nearly walking in front of a car. The last thing she wanted was to look even more suspicious by full on running out of the bank someone just tried to rob. Having hacked into those same cameras previously, she knew which way they faced.

She made sure to keep her face just out of view without looking like she was trying to. She knew the backpack was going to give her away after what had just happened but she didn't want to give them any reason to think she was anything more than a girl that ripped her backpack. She also didn't want to make it easy to identify her, which is why she made sure to hide her most distinguishable feature, her hair, by putting it into a super tight bun and covering it with a bandana. Sure, it looked horrible and gave her a splitting headache, but she knew it was necessary. If the cops saw her big bright red hair on the surveillance footage, it would take only a cursory pass through her school for the cops to identify her. She was pretty sure now, though, that she wouldn't be identified. At least that was what she convinced herself.

As she entered the coffee shop, the stark aroma of freshly ground coffee mixed with her current anxiety and made her stomach flip. The coffee shop was also playing Christmas music, though admittedly not as annoying. The Squirrel Nut Zipper's Winter Weather played from the overhead speakers. Marie wondered why everyone always made such a big deal out of such a disappointing day. She forced the sick feeling down and quickly found her friends sitting at a table enjoying some iced coffees. She fought a moment of surging anger at the thought of them sitting back like nothing was going on while she had just inadvertently killed a man. She knew it would do no good in the present situation, so she let it go. She made her way over to them, fighting the urge to punch Darrell in his annoying smiling face.

"How did it go?" Darrell asked, still wearing the same smug smile, and staring expectantly with his big brown eyes. Darrell was a large boy by all accounts, both in height and weight. He didn't look overly fat or muscular, just large. He kept his jet black hair a little longer than most boys, but not quite to his shoulders. Marie was always happy he hadn't ever latched on to the awful and annoyingly popular hair style where boys wore their bangs down and swept to the side.

"Not here," Marie said in a barely audible whisper. "Let's go back to HQ." As soon as she said that the alarm at the bank began blaring across the street.

"That sounds like a good plan. This place is going to be swarming with cops soon," Gavril responded. Gavril was in many ways a stark contrast to Darrell. While he also had brown eyes and dark hair, though not as dark as Darrell's, that is where the similarities ended. Where Darrell looked a little nerdy, Gavril could have easily fit in with the most popular of cliques. He was relatively tall and carried a very lean muscular frame. Gavril had a habit of wearing shirts that were a little too small so they accentuated his muscles and Darrell loved to tease him about it. Where Darrell was in constant need of a tan, Gavril had deep olive colored skin. The girls at the school were always swooning over him, which often caused a bit of jealousy from their boyfriends. The boyfriends never did anything about it, at least not after John Sampson had tried to punch Gavril one afternoon, only to wind up being thoroughly embarrassed. It was the only fight Marie had ever seen where the winner never even touched the loser. John kept swinging and Gavril kept dodging until John swung too hard and fell to the ground, hitting his face on a curb and breaking his jaw.

When Darrell had introduced Gavril to her as his new friend about a year prior, Marie wondered if it was a prank. Gavril just seemed too good looking and jock-like to be friends with someone like Darrell. It took less than a minute to change her mind. Gavril may have not looked the part, but he was nerdier than Darrell or Marie.

Darrell and Gavril grabbed their coffees, and then to her surprise, Darrell handed her a cup.

"Two creams and four sugars," he said as she grabbed the cup. "Just like you like it."

Marie was completely shocked. Perhaps even more shocked than she had been in the bank. Darrell had never done anything like that before. In fact, in her mind, he had always shown himself to be incredibly selfish. This never really was upsetting to her, though. He was, after all, the most brilliant person she had ever met, and she understood that quirks came with that. Since she had known him, he seemed to have a tendency to live in his own mind, so she just accepted the lack of thoughtfulness as a by-product of the way his genius brain worked. Was this a turning point to a new, more thoughtful Darrell? She remained lost in that thought as she took a big sip of her coffee.

"What is this?" Marie asked, a little more forcefully than she had intended.

"What do you mean?" Darrell asked.

"It has peppermint in it."

"Marie, it is nearly Christmas, pretty much all of the coffee has peppermint in it," Darrell replied.

"That doesn't make it right. Sorry, I appreciate the gesture and all but I can't drink this," Marie said as she threw away the cup on their way out.

"You are such a scrooge," Gavril said to Marie.

"Gavril, you have no idea," Darrell replied.

CHAPTER TWO - MARIE

The place the trio called Headquarters, or HQ for short, was an abandoned office building they hung out in. About three months prior, Darrell had told them about a great new hangout spot he found. Marie and Gavril assumed he was talking about the new teen club, Conjunction Junction that was all the rage around town. The club functioned much like a real nightclub except for the facts that it didn't serve any alcohol, and the only adults allowed inside were the employees and security guards. The club became big news when the local religious groups began protesting it. There was no law that prevented the club from being built so the religious groups made it a point to tell everyone that entered that they were going to hell. Marie and Gavril were both dumbfounded when Darrell had them sneaking into the broken back door of a foreclosed office building. Marie wondered for a moment if Darrell had been the one to break the door, but then realized how ridiculous that sounded since Darrell was one of the most straight laced people she knew.

Once inside, they had to admit that it was quite nice. Apparently, the office had been previously occupied by the Lowenstein and Wallace law firm. The law firm must have had high end clientele they wanted to impress, because everything in it was posh. As much as Gavril and Marie had been protesting when they were sneaking into the place, it all stopped when they sat on what Marie swore must have been the most comfortable sofa ever made. Sitting on the sofa was like having many huge soft hands holding you up in all the right places. Marie later found out that one of the company's founding partners, John Wallace, had been caught buying off a judge and a couple of jurors in a fairly high profile embezzlement case. After that, the firm went out of business and their office building had gone into foreclosure.

Normally, a place like the Lowenstein and Wallace office building would have been looted or have become a haven for drug users and homeless people. However, it was attached to another high end law firm which had overnight security, and was located in a very high income area with a very low homeless rate. This made it a perfect place for their headquarters. It was only a matter of time before the bank came and took all the belongings but they wanted to milk it while it lasted. Of course, they all knew they were breaking the law, but they made themselves feel better by keeping the place clean. They convinced themselves that it would be easier for the bank to sell if it was kept clean than if it fell into disrepair.

Now that they were in the comfort and privacy of their headquarters, Marie finally let herself freak out. Unfortunately for Darrell, he was first on her hit list.

"What in the hell was that?" she yelled at Darrell, rising up as tall as she could, trying to yell in his face. Part of her knew how ridiculous this must have looked because even on her tip-toes, she only came up to his chest, but she wasn't worried about appearance, she wanted him to know how angry she was. Her heart was still pounding so hard she could feel her pulse throbbing in her temples.

"Whoa. Settle down. What happened?" he replied, putting his hands on her shoulders to try to calm her down. She had also felt him briefly try to push her down from her tip-toes, but apparently realized quickly that he wasn't strong enough to do that and settled for a soothing gesture.

"For starters I'm pretty sure I killed a guy, that's what," she spat, her fury building. She knew she was being mean, but she kept seeing the man's bloody head every time she closed her eyes and her emotions were in a tug of war. She really did most likely save those people, but was it worth taking someone's life?

"Wait, what? What do you mean you killed a guy?" Gavril asked as he put his arms between them and forced them apart. He then put his hands on Marie's shoulders and forced her down. Marie was surprised at how strong he was without really trying.

Gavril was fairly new to the group. It had been just Marie and Darrell as best friends for as long as either could remember. They never needed or even wanted anyone else to hang out with them. Ten months ago, Gavril moved into the house next door to Darrell. This was weird because, according to Darrell, the previous owners never seemed to move out. One day the Fergusons were living there, and the next it was Gavril and his mom. Gavril had told them his mom and the Fergusons were family friends and the Fergusons sold his mom the house. Darrell accepted the explanation but he still thought it seemed strange. Darrell said he never saw any moving trucks. Despite the strange circumstances, Marie, Darrell and Gavril hit it off famously right from the start. Gavril was everything each of them needed or wanted from a best friend, and even seemed to offer the things that each needed from a friend that they weren't already getting from each other. It was only a matter of days before Gavril was cemented into their new circle of friends.

"The guy! The freaking guy Darrell somehow knew was going to be robbing the bank. He slipped on the marbles like we planned, but he hit his head on the floor really hard. I'm pretty sure he's dead. There was freaking blood everywhere and I can't get that picture out of my head of him just lying there motionless while blood just poured out!"

"Pretty sure? So you don't know for certain he's dead?" Gavril asked, now standing in front of Marie, apparently trying to shield Darrell from Marie's wrath.

"No, I don't know for certain," she spat back. Trying to rise back up, but unable to due to Gavril's strong hand. This should have made her angrier, but oddly enough was actually calming her down. "There was a lot of freaking blood, and I'm pretty sure I could see his brain. So yeah, I'm pretty sure he is dead."

"Let's turn on the news and find out for sure, before you freak out any more," Gavril said with a calming look of empathy. He began searching for the remote control to the TV they had moved from the conference room to their new makeshift living room.

"Oh, I am just getting started on the freaking out front," Marie responded, although she could feel her anger ebbing. She turned her attention to Darrell who seemed lost in thought. Why was she the only one that seemed upset? She knew that Darrell and Gavril were very low-key in general, but if there were ever a time to get amped up, it was now. Then again, since they didn't see the severity of the situation, perhaps they couldn't truly grasp how awful it was, she thought. "Let's start by how in the hell you knew that guy was going to rob the bank."

"It's kind of hard to explain," Darrell responded.

"Darrell, you're exceptionally smart. I'm sure your big brain can figure out how to put words together to explain to me how you knew a random guy was going to walk into a bank with a gun, and how a bag full of marbles would stop him." Marie was ranting now, his comment renewing her anger. Darrell learned early on in their friendship it was best to let her finish before he even tried to respond. "I mean, I thought maybe we were just messing around, and you were going to send someone in to mess with me and play along, but I was still nervous, because I thought what if, you know? The moment I saw that creep, I knew that something was up and this was real. By the way, you really undersold how creepy he was. I couldn't believe my eyes when he pulled out a freaking gun! While we are on the subject, let's talk about that gun. Apparently you somehow knew he would be there and people would be in trouble. We can then say it safe to assume you knew he would have a gun. Why, in all your infinite wisdom, did you not think it was important to let me know that he was going to have a gun?"

Darrell just looked at her, not knowing if it was safe to speak or not.

"Are you going to answer me? Or do I need to beat it out of you?" She yelled. Whatever Gavril had accomplished in calming her down, was long gone and she was starting to feel her face go flush with anger.

"I'm not sure where to start," Darrell replied.

"Let me be clear. It is in your best interest to start at the beginning, and tell me everything."

"He's not dead," Gavril interrupted.

"What?" Marie asked, thrown off guard.

"The guy from the bank. The news just said that he was taken to the hospital and is being treated for head trauma, but the doctors expect he will fully recover. You didn't kill him. So you can calm down, everything is going to be okay," Gavril replied, obviously hoping this would ease her mind.

"Just because he didn't die doesn't mean everything is okay. For starters, I expect they might be looking for the girl that dumped a ridiculous amount of marbles on the floor. Secondly, Darrell still needs to come clean on what exactly is going on here," Marie said with a calmer tone, but still glaring at Darrell.

"Remember when my mother died last year?" Darrell asked.

"Of course I remember. What kind of question is that?" Marie asked with a softer tone.

Marie was a bit annoyed that he brought up his mother, knowing that she wouldn't keep up her rage when discussing such a sensitive subject. She really needed to know what was going on though, so she didn't call him out on it.

"A couple of weeks after she died I had a weird dream. The events of the dream were not good, but that isn't what made it so strange. When I woke up I had this weird feeling in my head. It felt kind of like my brain was vibrating. I know that sounds weird, but I don't know how else to describe it. It was one of the weirdest feelings I have ever had. The other thing that was strange about this dream was that I remembered it perfectly. I mean, I sometimes remember a dream, but usually it is only in bits and pieces and it always fades as the day goes on. Do you know what I mean?"

Marie nodded, not wanting to interrupt for fear that he would use it as an excuse to try to change the subject. She looked over at Gavril in fear he would interrupt, and was a little surprised to see him staring at Darrell in rapt attention like he was hearing the most fascinating thing he had ever heard.

"Like I said, this dream never faded. I kept seeing it over and over in my head all day long. In the dream I was walking down the sidewalk toward the bus stop when I notice a woman crossing the street. When she steps into the street, a car speeds by and hits her. She flies over the car and lands on the street. Everyone rushes over and a guy feels her neck for a pulse and says she is dead. So, as you can see, it's not exactly the thing you want running around your head for hours on end," Darrell paused, looking at Marie, obviously wanting to stop his story.

"And then?" Marie could see in his eyes that he really didn't want to continue but with what had just happened, she wasn't going to let him off the hook.

"That afternoon, I was heading to the bus and I noticed that things were happening like I saw in my dream. Small things, you know, like a lady beating a rug in front of her bodega, and a guy in his car honking his horn in a rhythm, trying to get the attention of someone in the building he was waiting in front of. At first, I just played it off like some weird coincidence, and then I saw the lady. She looked exactly like she did in my dream. I started to get really freaked out. I sped up so that I was walking just behind her, but I didn't know what to do. I mean, was I supposed to stop a woman I had never met from crossing the street because I dreamt it? So I just kept following her, and sure enough when we got to the spot I dreamt of she started to cross the street."

"Oh my God! Did she get hit?" Marie asked, almost not wanting to know the answer.

"No. As soon as she started to cross, I reached out and grabbed her arm, stopping her. At first she looked at me like she was surprised and annoyed, until a split second later the car sped by. Everything happened just like I dreamt. She realized that I had just saved her from getting hit by that car and she thanked me then ran away. I guess she was probably freaked out."

"Of course she was freaked out, Darrell. You really suck at reading people," Marie said. Marie's anger was quickly fading away and being replaced with confusion and questions. Could Darrell really see the future? After his story and what he knew about the bank, there could be no other explanation. Darrell could see the future, but how?

"Yeah. Anyway, she ran away and I wasn't really sure what to make of the entire thing. A couple of weeks before, I had seen one of those movies where people avoided death and then death kept chasing them because they were supposed to die. So I got worried that this was going to be like that, and I became obsessed with the idea. I read the obituaries for the next several months, just knowing that I was going to see her in there as a result of some freak accident. There were actually a few that I thought could have been a match for her, since I didn't know her name or anything. I ended up going to those funerals to see if it was her."

"Why would you go through all the trouble, based on a movie that was an iffy idea to begin with even before they pumped out a half dozen sequels?" Gavril asked and Marie silently agreed. Those movies were a bit ridiculous.

"I don't know. I mean, here I was still grieving from my mother, and I had a vision that allowed me to save a woman's life. My entire mind was torn up," Darrell said. Marie could see the emotion he was holding back just below the surface and she felt for him. What a crazy thing to go through. Marie still missed her mother and she had never even met her. Darrell had fifteen years to love and know his mother; it had to be hard.

"That makes sense," Gavril said.

"So, since then, my visions, for lack of a better word, have been becoming more frequent. The others ones have all been very innocuous though. I mean, it would be about Ms. Jensen about to back over her kid's bike, or someone slipping in the cafeteria. Small stuff, you know? Then a few nights ago, I had a vision of that guy robbing the bank. He pulled the gun and shot five customers. Then he had a standoff with the police, where he shot two cops before shooting himself. This vision had the feeling of the first one, not only in the severity of the events, but in the severity of the feelings it gave me. It was different though, in that it was like watching a movie. I have had one like it before, where I'm not there and I can see everything like I'm watching a movie. The point of view changes, like there are multiple cameras, multiple angles, allowing me to see lots of different details," Darrell said.

"Do you have control of the camera in these types of visions?" Gavril asked.

"Maybe. I'm not sure. So far I just let them happen. I haven't tried to alter them, yet. Anyway, in this dream the camera showed me things like people filling out deposit slips, and views where I could see the clock. So this time, I knew exactly when and where it was going to happen."

"So again, you knew that this guy was going to have a gun, and you decided that wasn't information I needed to know?" Marie asked, with a little bit of renewed anger.

"Kind of. You see, the next night I had the vision again, which was the first time I have had the same vision more than once. This time was different though. It was all the same until I noticed you and your backpack full of marbles. I saw you rip your backpack and dump the marbles, and saw his gun sliding over to the security guard as he fell. Is that how it happened?"

Marie noticed Gavril had turned to her, and now focused his intense gaze her way, coupled with Darrell's expectant question, she suddenly felt very flush again.

"Yes, that's exactly how it happened. He fell and his gun slid to the security guard, but that still doesn't mean you were right to hide it from me," she replied.

"I'm sorry that I upset you, but I felt very confident that you were going to be okay. I was worried that if I told you about the gun you might change your behavior and then be one of the people that got shot. I really did it to protect you. I really am very sorry that I upset you," Darrell said with true remorse in his eyes.

Marie always struggled at being mad at Darrell for long and she knew that this would be no different.

"I get where you are coming from but I am going to need some time to try to wrap my head around this entire thing. Part of me says that the entire vision thing sounds like a pile of crap, but then how in the hell did you know about the gun sliding to the security guard? I hadn't told you guys that yet," Marie shifted her gaze. "What are you thinking Gavril?"

"I'm still soaking it in, like you said. I mean, the evidence says it has to be true, but logic says it can't be. How about we all go home and talk again in the morning when we've had ample time to reflect on the day?"

"You are so weird sometimes Gavril. You talk like you are an old man, but that does sound like a good idea. I'll see you guys in the morning," Marie said, and left the two boys as she headed out the back door and toward her house.

CHAPTER THREE - GAVRIL

As Gavril pulled his beat up fire red BMX bike up to his house, he looked over toward Darrell's place. He could see Darrell's disheveled looking dad through the window, sitting in his usual chair with his usual beer in his hand. Gavril wondered how many he had had already. Darrell always told Gavril how his dad was a great father before Darrell's mother died. Gavril wasn't sure if that was something Darrell told himself to deflect what his father was now, but all Gavril had ever seen in the man was an insufferable drunk. On more than one occasion he had treated Darrell so badly that Gavril had wanted to beat the tar out of him. Darrell had always stopped Gavril from doing anything rash, and sadly, often defended his dad's actions at the same time. Once Gavril had asked Darrell if he thought his father acted that way because Darrell was adopted. Darrell was adamant that his adopted father has always treated Darrell like he was his natural child. Gavril locked his bike to the porch column and walked in his house.

"It's about time you got home," Andrea said, looking at him over her book with her fierce hazel eyes that were slightly enlarged by her violet square framed glasses.

"It's been ten months, and you still don't seem to understand that you are not really my mother," Gavril responded with more than a hint of annoyance.

"You know very well that we need to keep up appearances. We can't afford to break our cover."

"I understand that, but you do realize that nobody can see or hear us, right? It's just weird, especially considering I am actually much older than you," Gavril responded.

"I know that you are older than me. You never seem to let me forget, but you seem to forget that I am still your boss. I may not be your mother, but you do still report to me. Let's have your report about what happened today. I am hoping that you will tell me you had nothing to do with what I saw on the news?" Andrea asked as she stood up. Andrea was a tall slender woman who most would consider pretty. She carried an air of formality and nobility that Gavril often found interesting, but at times like this, he just wished she would loosen up.

"Unfortunately, I can't say that."

"Seriously Gavril, you know that stuff like this can't happen. How could you let this occur?"

"There is not a lot to explain really. Darrell had a vision about the bank robbery and how to stop it. We saved seven innocent lives today, so all in all, I think it went fairly well."

"I'm glad that lives were saved, I really am, but how many times do I need to tell you that your job is to get

Darrell to not use his powers? Instead, all you seem to do is go along with him and let him continue to explore his powers. In spite of your so-called attempts at slowing his powers, they seem to be escalating. I don't need to remind you how bad it can get. Am I to assume that what led to today's newsworthy event consisted of multiple visions, considering the amount of information he would have needed?"

"Yes, he said that he had two visions, one of the original outcome and one of how to stop it."

"See, this is escalating far worse than I had even expected. Darrell's powers manifested twenty years too early. His brain hasn't fully formed yet, and you know that excessive visions will change the way the brain develops. Most of the recent studies on the matter have shown that the changed brain development can lead to seizures. This usually leads to the Seventh dying far too early, or at the very least going insane. Gavril, you haven't been an active overseer since World War II. Perhaps you are too out of practice. Do I need to bring someone else in? Perhaps Aida Chang can come in. Maybe Darrell will like her better."

"Of course you don't need to bring someone else in. Besides, Darrell and I get along as well as anybody could. If you think he might find her attractive, Darrell only has eyes for Marie. She doesn't feel the same but I don't see him getting over it anytime soon. I may be out of practice, but let's not forget that my track record is impeccable. No other teen Overseer has successfully repressed more Sevenths than I have in the last two thousand years," Gavril responded.

Sevenths were what most in the Overseer community called the Seers. This was due to their birth line. All of the Seers were the seventh son born from another seventh son. The more generations the Sevenths went back, the more powerful they would become. Overseers like Gavril were inserted into the Seventh's lives to help guide them through the early stages of the powers manifesting and helping them hone the powers. The Overseer's input was vital in the effort to help prevent the new Sevenths from going insane with the sudden ability to see the future, and to guide them to using their powers for good. Overseers are immortal, and since modern Sevenths nearly always develop their powers around the age of thirty-five, most current overseers become immortal around that age to better fit in with the Sevenths they were assigned to. Some Overseers however have a much younger appearance, such as Gavril, to fit in with those Sevenths that develop their powers early.

"The goal for the past three thousand years has been to make sure that the powers are used for the greater good. Today was a prime example of a Seventh using his powers for the greater good," Gavril said. "Besides, Darrell opened up about his powers today. He seems to have figured out that his powers developed after his mother died. It is only a matter of time before I can convince him not to use them."

"Gavril, don't pretend to coach me on our goals. I admit today was a good thing, especially because lives were saved, and him opening up to you is a start. You know very well, however, that our overall primary goal is the health and safety of those we are assigned to oversee. Your primary job as Darrell's steward is to make sure he doesn't use his powers until he is in his thirties, time isn't something you have a lot of. The more he uses them, the more he feels like he must use them. You need to stop him. Is that something you think you can do?" Andrea asked. Her lips were pursed so tightly now that Gavril couldn't even see her pink lipstick any longer.

"Yes. I know, and I will work harder," Gavril replied. He knew she was right, but hated to give her the satisfaction of knowing he knew.

"I have to leave tonight. There is some trouble in Chicago that I need to attend to. Will you be okay here by yourself?"

"Are you serious? I know I am damned to have the appearance, and sometimes attitude, of a teenager but please remember that I am over two thousand years old. I can take care of myself," Gavril responded with some annoyance.

"I know, but it is so easy to forget when I see your cute little face," Andrea said as she pinched his cheek.

"You are hilarious Andrea. You know nobody does that anymore, right? You need to keep up with the times."

"Tell you what, you do your job, and I will catch up on my modern greetings."

Gavril's phone began ringing. He looked down and saw that it was Marie from the Caller ID. He was not looking forward to this conversation. Normally he enjoyed talking to Marie since she was more mature than a normal teenager, in fact he often thought about how lucky he was to have gotten his current assignment. But he really did hate lying, and now he was going to have to ease Marie's understandable concerns and act like he knows nothing.

Most of the teenagers he had been assigned to over the many years acted like normal teenagers and that tended to drive Gavril crazy. While most people thought the world had changed so much in the past several hundred years, Gavril thought teenagers acted pretty much the same they did in the 1800s. Sure they used to have to grow up a little faster and work a little more, but they acted the same and it got on Gavril's nerves. The only big difference was that modern teenagers hid their behavior less often.

It didn't take him long to realize that Darrell and his best friend Marie were different. Not only were they far more intelligent than most he had dealt with, they were much more mature. Sure, they still giggled at fart jokes, but overall they were interested in things other than the latest celebrity gossip and how they looked on social media. Part of Gavril, when he was being honest with himself, thought that maybe he didn't try as hard as he should have to convince Darrell to not use his powers because Gavril secretly didn't want his assignment to end. He really thought of Marie and Gavril as great friends and didn't want to lose that. If he convinced Darrell to not use his powers, he would be reassigned and not be allowed to see them any longer. If he drug his feet, he would be able to be their friends a little longer. He hated himself for thinking that and cursed himself when he realized he might be sacrificing Darrell's health for his own selfish desires.

"Well, are you going to answer that?" Andrea asked, shaking Gavril out of his thought.

"Hey, Marie," Gavril said as he answered the phone. He walked into his room and shut the door. Andrea would flip out if she knew Marie knew about Darrell, luckily the news had apparently kept the mysterious girl out of the bank story. "Hey, Gavril. Sorry for the late call, I just needed to talk to someone about all of this," Marie said. Gavril could hear the uncertainty in her voice. This was a situation Gavril hadn't experienced much in the past. Most Sevenths were reluctant to tell anyone about their powers.

"Yeah, I get that. This whole situation is kind of crazy. Are you sure you are okay with it?"

"I'm not sure. I mean it really doesn't make a lot of sense. How can Darrell really see the future?"

"I wish I knew the answer to that," Gavril replied.

"It all seems so unreal, but at the same time I can't dispute the facts. Darrell knew things about the bank robbery that he simply couldn't have known."

"Unless he was in on it," Gavril said with a laugh.

"That's not funny."

"Sorry."

"The thing is, if I accept the idea that Darrell can see the future, it opens up a ton of other questions and ideas that I usually dismiss. There are lots of people that say they can see and talk to ghosts, which I think is dumb, especially because I don't believe in ghosts, but if Darrell can do what he does, then why can't they do what they claim? You know what I mean?"

"Yeah, what about things like people being immortal, maybe that could happen," Gavril knew he was pushing his luck and didn't even know why he said it.

"Well, that's just silly. But what about the Bible? I mean if people can talk to ghosts that would mean there is something to the afterlife, which could mean that at least some stuff from the Bible is true. I have always been a science over religion person, but this has me all twisted up."

"I don't think we should get caught up in that stuff, especially the religion right now. We can't control what we don't know, so we should only focus on what we do know. Darrell somehow can see the future apparently, and we need to figure out how to deal with it," Gavril replied. He really didn't want to get into the religious aspect of everything. Having lived through many events of the Bible, he had a drastically different view of religion and he found it muddied the waters. Once anyone found out Gavril lived through the life of Jesus Christ, the questions came flooding in, and despite Gavril having actually been there, he still didn't have the answers.

"What do you think we should do?" Marie asked. He thought he heard a little bit of pleading in her voice. The poor girl was so confused and Gavril knew, despite her not mentioning it, that Marie was flooded with questions about her own mother's death. He wanted to tell her, but he didn't know where to start.

"Well, I don't know if Darrell will want to hear it, but I think we should discourage him from using the visions and try to figure out how to stop them. They might not be good for him," Gavril suggested, knowing that if he could get Marie on board, it would make it a heck of a lot easier to convince Darrell.

"Maybe. I don't think that will be very easy though. He seemed pretty happy with himself, that we saved those people. That will be tough to convince him not to do again. If he has the opportunity to save someone and chooses not to, he will see it as the same as killing them."

"I know, which is why we need to figure out how to help him just not have them at all," Gavril replied. He really did know what she meant. Most of his previous assignments didn't have anything remotely as serious or important this soon after getting their powers. It was always a lot easier to convince people to not use their powers when they weren't seeing people die. Gavril knew Darrell would be powerful, but his visions were beyond anything Gavril would have imagined at this point.

"Yeah, that might work. Anyway, thanks for the talk, I should get to cleaning the house, before my dad gets mad. I'll talk to you later."

"Okay, later," Gavril said. He hung up the phone, and walked back out into the living room.

"What was that about?" Andrea asked.

"Nothing. I thought you had left."

"I'm about to. Are you dating that girl?"

"Have you lost your mind!" Gavril shouted. "She is fifteen years old!"

"Calm down, I was just asking," Andrea replied.

"I don't know what kind of guy you think I am, but I don't go around dating underage girls!" Gavril yelled. He stormed back into his room, and slammed the door. He knew he probably over-reacted, but the idea struck a nerve. Being thousands of years old but still looking like a teenager, made dating hard. His best option was to date another Overseer, but that was difficult as well. Most of the Overseers around the world became Overseers when they were grown, and they often found it strange to date someone that looked as young as Gavril.

CHAPTER FOUR - DARRELL

Darrell walked slowly through the early morning fog up to the bus stop and saw, as he feared, that Marie was already there, looking at him expectantly. He had never been more annoyed that he, Marie and Gavril were the only people that used this particular bus stop. Darrell had not been looking forward to facing them and now he had no choice. He had avoided her phone calls and texts for the past day and a half. He knew she had more questions and so did he.

Unfortunately for both of them, he didn't really have any more answers. He had even tried to stay home by pretending to be sick until his father said he had two choices. One was to go to school and the other was to clean the entire house and weed all of the flowerbeds. Darrell wasn't sure if his dad was completely serious but he could smell the alcohol on his breath. As much as he didn't want to talk to his friends, he hated house and yard work ten times more. He decided it wasn't worth the risk. Darrell always hated when his father started drinking so early, but that usually meant he would be passed out by the time Darrell got home, giving Darrell a peaceful evening. He really wished he could convince his father to stop drinking, but each time he brought the subject up, his father would get even angrier than normal. It had only been a year since his mother died, and looking back, Darrell couldn't believe how much his father had changed. Before her death his father had been a great man. He was always there for Darrell whenever he needed and didn't drink. Now he drank nearly every day and had become meaner and angrier with each new day. Darrell knew Gavril hated his father, and Darrell had to stop Gavril from fighting him a couple of times, but Gavril didn't know how good his father could be. Darrell also knew that if his father continued down his current path, Darrell would soon forget how good his father could be as well.

"Good morning," Marie greeted him. "Did you have a good night?" Darrell was a little surprised she didn't start with her questions right away, but at the same time, he knew it fit her personality. She wanted her answers, but she cared about him and wanted to know if he was okay, without coming right out and asking him if he was.

"It wasn't bad. Dad left me alone so I played some video games, ate some microwave burritos and drank some highly caffeinated soda. I would say it was pretty much a perfect teenage boy night," Darrell responded, with a smile. "How are you doing? Are you holding up okay?" Darrell wasn't great at showing his feelings, but knew he should ask her. Not that he didn't really care, it just didn't come naturally to him.

"I'm fine. It's all good," Marie replied offhandedly. "It is typical though. I swear I will never understand why you guys spend so much time playing video games."

"I suppose I should have been playing with tiny pink and purple unicorns like you, huh?" Darrell replied. He didn't need to be good at reading people's emotions to realize that with the way Marie glossed over her well-being, she wasn't doing well, but he let it go for now.

"You do know that I have punched people for less, right?"

Darrell moved closer, so that he was standing right in front of her, his barrel chest right in her face. Darrell towered over her. Darrell was six feet seven inches tall and towered over everyone in the school, including all of the varsity basketball players. Darrell also weighed 250 pounds. He was not overly fat but was in no way muscular. His stature had prevented pretty much all physical bullying throughout his life. He was grateful for that, but always knew that things would have been much different if those potential bullies knew that Darrell would have buckled in the face of most confrontation, and wasn't really as strong as his frame implied. He did however love to mess with Marie since she stood so much shorter than him.

"I don't think you could even reach my face," Darrell said, as he looked down upon her with a huge grin.

"Maybe not, but there are other things I could reach. Things that I think might even hurt worse," She replied, returning his smile.

"Let's not get carried away," Darrell said, covering his crotch as he backed away.

"Good morning guys," Gavril said as he walked up, out of the fog.

"Gavril?" Darrell said with surprise. "You're here."

"Yeah, is that okay?" Gavril replied.

"Of course, I just thought you weren't coming today."

"Why would you think that?"

"No reason, I guess. How was your night? I thought I heard some arguing when I got home."

"Really? Could you hear what we were arguing about?" Gavril asked, with a slight look of concern that he was obviously trying to hide.

"No, I couldn't tell what you were saying, just that your voices were raised. Why, you hiding something?"

"No, not really. It is just a little embarrassing. She found out that I liked Marsha Burns."

"The goth chick with green hair?" Marie asked.

"Yeah. So my mom started going on and on about how she thought Marsha would be a bad influence. Apparently my mom met her mom at some school event and thought she wasn't a good person. You know, typical parent crap," Gavril responded.

Darrell was acutely aware that Marie was not really paying attention to Gavril and was still staring in Darrell's direction. When he looked back at Marie, he thought he could read her expression. She was staring at him partly with pity, and partly with what he assumed to be fear. Darrell was afraid that Marie and Gavril were going to have this reaction, which is exactly why he was avoiding them. He hadn't really even come to terms with his visions himself. He knew it was going to be a very tough pill to swallow, which is exactly why he kept it to himself all these months. Gavril and Marie were both open-minded people, but this was a lot to accept. They were going to think of him as a freak, and perhaps even, as was his biggest fear, stop being his friend. He never would have made it through the hell of losing his mother without the two of them, and he knew that he wasn't going to make it through all of his new problems without them, which is partly why he decided to bring them in. He knew it was a risk, but it was one he needed to take if he was going to keep his sanity. Now he could only hope that they wouldn't desert him.

"Please don't stare at me like that," Darrell told Marie. "It makes me wish I hadn't told you."

Darrell has had a crush on Marie for as long as he could remember. Unfortunately for Darrell, no matter how much he flirted with her, she never seemed to catch on. He knew he should just come out and tell her, but despite having the opportunity nearly every day for the last several years, he could never get the nerve to do so. Today was going to be no different, he thought as he looked at her. Her beauty was nearly blinding despite the odd look she was giving him. He was pretty sure he never even had a shot with her because she never really reciprocated his flirting. He had even begun to think recently that she may not even like boys. He didn't want to sound like one of those jerks that thought someone was gay because they weren't into them, but he was beginning to realize that she never dated, but then again neither did he. Whenever she did talk about a boy being cute, Darrell could tell she wasn't really feeling it. Despite his concerns, he still held out hope, but now he couldn't help thinking he had blown it completely since he had come clean about his visions. Why would anyone, much less someone as perfect as Marie, want to date a freak who could see the future?

"I'm sorry. I don't mean to stare. It's just a lot to take in, you know?" Marie replied.

"That's why I never told you guys. I didn't want it to change the way you felt about me," Darrell replied, feeling a mixture of annoyance and concern. He was terrible about relaying his feelings and didn't really want to get into all of it, but he knew he had no choice.

"I can't speak for Gavril, but it may change how I think about you. I mean, how could it not? Although I don't think it's for the worse. You are still, and will always be, my best friend. You are the person I care about the most in this world," Marie said. Darrell's heart sang a little. Could she really get past this and still be his best friend? He had been expecting the worst, but now was beginning to think it might all be okay.

"I don't know exactly how to follow that," Gavril said. "You don't have to worry about me, big guy. No matter what kind of crazy stuff happens, I still have your back."

"Thanks guys, I really am glad you guys feel that way. I was not sure I was going to be able to go through all this on my own, but you really do need to stop staring at me like that Marie," Darrell said, as the run down but miraculously still functioning bus pulled up. The brakes squealing as loudly as ever.

The trio got on the bus, with Darrell getting on last, so lost in thought that he nearly forgot to duck as he climbed through the doorway. He silently cursed himself for his near misstep. High school was bad enough, but he didn't want to be known as the moron that knocked himself out getting on the bus. They walked down the aisle and just as Gavril was about to sit in their normal seat, Darrell redirected him.

"Not there Gav, let's take the one on the other side." Darrell said, pointing to the seat that was more duct tape than actual seat.

"But we always sit there, and this seat smells like butt," Marie said.

"Your elegance is astounding. Please trust me. Let's get on the other side," Darrell responded.

"Very funny," Marie said. Suddenly, as though the idea just struck her, "Is this because of a vision?"

"Could you have said that any louder?" Darrell responded.

"Sorry, but is it?" Marie asked, in a forced whisper.

"Let's just sit over there. Okay?" Darrell insisted.

They did as Darrell asked, and sat in the seat on the opposite side of the bus. Marie began holding her nose until Darrell took out his cellphone and tried to take a picture of her. Apparently she decided that the smell was bad, but an embarrassing photo was much worse. A few stops later a group of students got on, and two of them sat in the trio's normal seat. Darrell noticed that Marie and Gavril were staring at them. Darrell still wasn't sure he had done the right thing by telling them, but they seemed to be more accepting than he had anticipated. It didn't take long for them to get their answer as to what was going to happen to their seat. A few minutes after the teens sat in the hot seat, the bus drove too close to a van that was carrying paint materials on top of it. The bus struck one of the buckets of paint hanging off the side of the truck and sent the full gallon of beige paint flying through the open window. The wet and sticky paint covered both teens from head to toe, and the entire bus erupted in laughter. Darrell never understood exactly why people were so cruel. Here were two people covered in paint. The paint not only ruined all of their clothing, but he was pretty sure that the cellphones they were holding were going to be ruined as well. Despite this, most of the other people's immediate reaction was to laugh at them instead of show empathy. Darrell felt bad for them. He had known the paint would come through the window, and in his vision the paint had drenched the two of them, but he hadn't had a vision to let him know what would happen if they moved. He had been holding out hope that with the situation changed, the outcome of the paint would have changed too. His hope had been crushed and now these poor people were taking his suffering, and who knew how long they would be teased about it.

"Oh my God!" Marie yelled. "That should have been us," she added, now whispering.

"Yep," Gavril answered.

"You knew this was going to happen?" Marie whispered to Darrell.

"I actually saw it happening to us, so I thought we should sit somewhere else."

"But why did you let it happen to them? You could have done something," Marie said, covering her nose again. The smell of the paint was now overshadowing the smell of the seat.

"And what would you have had me do? The window has been stuck open for as long as anyone can remember, so I couldn't close it. Was I supposed to tell them not to sit there because I had a precognitive vision about it? Tell the bus driver to watch where he was going, because I knew he was going to hit something? I thought about this one all night and couldn't see a good way to prevent it. I was hoping that since we had moved and the paint was meant to hit us that it would just not happen."

"We could have just put some caution tape on it and acted like it was broken," Gavril said.

"I didn't think about that," Darrell responded, silently cursing himself for not figuring out the simple solution.

"That's exactly why you have to keep us in the loop. The three of us can come up with a lot more answers together than either of us could do alone," Marie said.

"Yeah, I see your point," Darrell replied. "But you have to remember that my visions don't always come true." He was elated that Marie was being so accepting. Maybe all of this wouldn't be so bad if he had friends to share his new burden.

"They don't?" Marie asked, with a slightly confused look on her face. Darrell couldn't help think that she looked a little bit like a puppy that turned her head sideways, but he knew better than to mention that to her.

"No. I would say that the vast majority do, but there have been several that just never came true. I haven't been able to figure out why. Also sometimes they aren't exactly like I saw. Today is a great example. When I saw us get hit by the paint, it was only me and Marie, which is why I was surprised when you showed up Gavril. Based on my vision, I figured you weren't coming to school."

"Perhaps it has to do with free will. Maybe those things were supposed to come true, but someone made a different choice than they were fated to, and changed the outcome of your vision. This morning, for instance, I originally planned on staying home, but changed my mind at the last minute, which is why I got to the bus stop late," Gavril said.

"That is a little deep for this early in the morning, but you may have a point," Darrell said. Gavril's idea gave Darrell a lot more to think about, especially the idea that Gavril was missing from his vision, but because Gavril changed his mind, the vision was partially incorrect. How trustworthy were his visions?

The bus finally got to school, the brakes screeching so loudly that the dog across the street began howling in response. The three of them got off, carefully avoiding the still wet paint that covered the seat and floor. Darrell never considered himself a morning person, but it always struck him as funny how the rest of his classmates looked when getting off of the bus. To Darrell they always looked like a zombie hoard shambling across the school lawn. Shuffling their feet, dead look in their eyes and many of them with their mouth's slightly agape.

Their high school, Montrose High, was typical of most high schools in the country, a boxy, brick covered, soul sucking structure. The main difference between their school and most other high schools was the fact that in most situations the different years were separated. There were four main sections of the school, and except for a few less popular electives there was no mixing of the students in different years. Darrell never got a very good answer as to why, but since Marie passed the test to skip her sophomore year and join Darrell and Gavril as juniors, he stopped questioning it.

"Just kill me now. I don't think I can take another day in this God forsaken place," Gavril said, as they headed across the lawn.

Darrell had never met someone that complained so much about school as Gavril, and Darrell could never make sense of it. He could tell that Gavril was very smart, perhaps even nearly as smart as himself, but Gavril's high intelligence was easily over shadowed by his immense knowledge. Gavril was easily the most knowledgeable person Darrell had ever met. Gavril knew everything. He had never given an incorrect answer on any test, and in every class they had together, the teachers couldn't stand him. Darrell was never sure if it was because Gavril could come across as very smug, or the teachers were frustrated that in many instances Gavril was more knowledgeable than they were. It was probably a mixture of both. History was the one that really stood out. Darrell had never seen Gavril study, but he seemed to know everything. Everything. Gavril had even had several brutal debates with Mr. Anderson, their world history teacher, who had a Ph.D. in Middle Eastern history. Gavril could go toe to toe with him on any subject, and it infuriated Mr. Anderson.

"Just keep telling yourself that today is the last day before two weeks off for winter break," Marie responded.

"That's true. Am I the only one that thinks it is really stupid to make us come back from the weekend for only one day before two more weeks off? Why couldn't they just let us be off today and come back a day early on the end?" Gavril asked. Darrell could sense one of his trademarked rants coming on. Gavril was an exceptionally good friend and overall, one of the best people he had ever met. Gavril, however, did have a knack for finding a subject and launching a spectacular rant about it. Marie had tried to get him on the debate team. She said his knowledge and knack for arguing would make him a natural, but he said it would be too much work, which didn't surprise Darrell in the slightest.

"Because that would mean we come back on a Friday, only to have the weekend after. It would be the same thing, just the other way around," Darrell said. "No need to rant about it, we feel the same way. Well maybe not school loving Marie here."

"Seriously?" Marie responded. "I don't love school; I love learning and right now this place provides a space to do that."

"Fine, they could just give us the extra day off. Anyway we need to figure out something cool to do for the break," Gavril said.

"I have a feeling something will find us," Darrell said.

"You know something we don't?" Gavril asked.

"No, just a feeling that this break will be special, that's all," Darrell responded. He really did have a feeling. He hadn't had any specific visions about the break, but he had this weird feeling deep down, that something big was coming.

CHAPTER FIVE - DARRELL

Darrell was, as his father often pointed out when his grades slipped, a genius, and he usually enjoyed learning. He did however, hate history. He knew if he studied he would have no problem learning the dates and places and all the other boring stuff that made up history class, but he could never bring himself to put the effort in. After one particularly bad history grade on a progress report, his father had forced him to study for hours. Darrell hated history so much that he sat there zoned out randomly turning the pages of his history book for hours, until his mother thankfully saved him and said that was enough.

He cheated off of Gavril for a while, but stopped that when he almost got caught. He decided the risk of getting caught and punished by his father was not worth saving the 15 minutes of cramming he needed before each test to squeak out a solid C. As much as he hated history, he was excited for today's class.

"Class, as usual, I was incredibly disappointed in the results of Friday's pop quiz," Mr. Anderson said, as he began walking around the classroom, handing back everyone's graded tests.

"There was one glaring exception however. Mr. Johnson here scored by far the highest grade, with a perfect 100%. If I hadn't created the quiz only a few hours before I gave it to you, I would swear it was like Darrell here somehow knew what questions were on the test," he said as he looked down at Darrell and smiled.

Darrell thought his heart was going to pop out of his chest as he forced a smile in return. He knew that there was no way for Mr. Anderson to know about his vision or powers, but he couldn't stop feeling anxious. He knew he shouldn't use his powers for such trivial things, but when the vision of the test came, he figured if he wasn't supposed to, he wouldn't have gotten the vision. Part of him also thought that many criminals probably had the same thought before committing some big crime. If I wasn't supposed to rob the jewelry store, then I wouldn't have come across those blueprints, he could hear the burglar saying.

"Did you have a vision about that test?" Gavril whispered from behind, as he leaned in over Darrell's shoulder.

Darrell just nodded as he caught Marie's eyes. She was turned around in her seat looking back at Darrell. He couldn't help but feel a little bit ashamed as she gave him a fierce look of disappointment. He hated to disappoint anyone, much less Marie. Darrell just looked back and shrugged his shoulders, trying his best to give her a look that said 'I'm sorry, but I couldn't help myself'. Marie just slowly shook her head and turned back around. Marie had the uncanny knack to make Darrell feel like his moral compass was corrupt whenever he did anything that was against the rules. He was normally a very big rule follower. Maybe that is what made it so bad when she called him out on it. He was determined to not feel guilty about this, but if she kept looking at him like that, it was going to be hard.

"How did I beat you on the quiz?" Darrell whispered back to Gavril.

"I may have gone on a diatribe about the relevance of question seven and not finished the quiz," He whispered back. Darrell barely stifled a big laugh that he knew would have certainly landed him in detention.

"You have a serious problem." Darrell whispered before Mr. Anderson gave the two of them a look that clearly said to be quiet.

Mr. Anderson was back at the front of the classroom, and had begun his lecture on the history of the Dead Sea. Darrell could hear Gavril muttering something about inaccuracy behind him. Mr. Anderson wasn't five minutes into the lecture when Darrell began to feel his head grow very heavy with sleepiness. Darrell didn't always enjoy school but he always made it a point to stay awake. He wasn't sure what fear most drove him to staying awake, the fear of getting in trouble or the fear of Marie's wrath. Neither of those were worth the extra sleep. Today was different though. For starters, he had never been this sleepy in class before. He didn't understand why, since he got plenty of sleep the night before, but he was struggling to keep his eyes open. Every few seconds he seemed to be catching his head as it drooped down, causing him to look like a very slow head banger at a heavy metal concert. Finally, he decided that his perfect score on the pop quiz had earned him a small nap, so he let himself succumb to the sleep.

The young boy playing on the swing set was beaming. A happier boy had never existed. His smile grew each and every time he swung higher and higher, his smile now as broad as the horizon. When it appeared he could get no higher, he let go of the chains and launched himself up and out, flying at least ten feet away from the swing set. He landed with perfect balance, like he had performed the feat a hundred times before.

"That was amazing! You should be in the circus with that act," the man said.

"Thanks, but I'm not supposed to talk to strangers," the young boy replied, nervously shuffling away from the man.

"That's very good. That is a great rule to have. I need some help though. I seemed to have lost my dog Marlowe," the man said as he continued to slowly shuffle closer to the boy. "I was walking him around the park and his leash broke. He ran into those woods over there. I could really use your help finding him. The great thing is you won't have to talk so you don't need to worry about the no talking to strangers rule. We can both be looking and if you find him, you can just whistle and I'll give you a reward. Do you know how to whistle?"

The boy just nodded. He had stopped shuffling at the mention of the dog. He was obviously conflicted between his fear of strangers and his love of dogs.

"Great! Let's go over here and see if we can't find my poor Marlowe."

The man grabbed the boy's hand and led him toward the woods. The boy initially gave a slight struggle against the man's pull, but apparently decided that his desire to find the dog had outweighed the fear of strangers, and he walked willingly toward the woods. Once they were in the woods, the man pulled a rag out of his pocket and after looking around to make sure nobody was watching, placed the rag over the boy's mouth. The small boy immediately began struggling, but he was no match for the strength of the man. It only took a few seconds before the boy stopped fighting and became limp. The man put the boy over his shoulder and began walking.

"No!" Darrell yelled as the school bell startled him out of his vision causing him knock his books on the floor. Darrell franticly looked around and it took him a moment to realize where he was and what was happening.

"I am pleased that you are so heavily invested in the lecture, unfortunately we are slaves to our schedules and must move on. But fear not Mr. Johnson, we will pick up where we left off when you get back from winter break, and I'm sure you will be able to tell us all about the Potash industry in the mid-twentieth century," Mr. Anderson said, causing a few giggles throughout the class room.

Darrell realized that everyone in the class room was staring at him, including Marie, whose disapproving look had been replaced with concern, but Darrell was far too disturbed about his vision to be embarrassed. He needed to tell Marie what he saw, but there were too many people around to risk it in the hallway. He decided to wait until lunch where they could get some privacy, and he could use the time to digest what he had just seen.

"You okay, Darrell?" Marie asked, as they walked out of the class and into the hallway. Several students were still staring at him as they walked by, and he could see many of them muttering under their breath and giggling. They were obviously making jokes at his expense. Marie lightly grabbed his arm as she looked up into his eyes, her concerned look was beginning to change into a look of pity. Darrell hated to be pitied and certainly didn't want it from someone he cared so much about.

"Yeah, I'm fine," Darrell replied, now seeing the expectant look in the eyes of Marie and Gavril.

"You had another one didn't you?" Gavril asked.

"I did, but there are too many people here. I'll tell you guys about it at lunch."

"Okay, but remember, no more hiding things from us," Marie replied, now giving him stern look. Darrell would never understand women and their emotions. How could she possibly feel so many emotions to give him no less than five different looks in less than two minutes? Then again he was so inept at reading people's emotions, she could have been giving him the same look all along and he was projecting his own feelings into her looks.

"I won't, I promise. I just want us to have some privacy."

"Okay, I'll see you at lunch," Marie said, turning and heading to her next class. Darrell noticed her glance back at him after a few steps. She was obviously worried about him and if he was completely honest with himself, he was worried as well.

"You sure everything is okay? You seemed pretty upset when you came out of that vision," Gavril asked.

"I'll be fine. It was pretty bad, but like I said, I'll tell you about it at lunch. That will not only give us privacy, but give me a little bit of time to process it, so I can better explain what I saw."

"Fair enough, see you in a couple of hours," Gavril said and headed toward his next class.

Darrell didn't know what to think. Was it really a vision or was it just a bad dream? It had felt a little different than his previous visions, especially physically, but he wasn't sure what that mattered. It had been more painful, but maybe it had hurt more because it had been more emotional. He definitely felt more scared about a kid being kidnapped than just about anything else. He had always had a soft spot for children. Then again, maybe he just had a headache and a bad dream. He needed to know for sure, but there wasn't really a way to know if something that was going to happen in the future was real, was there? He figured he would have to settle for finding out if it already happened, and if not, maybe Marie and Gavril could help decide if he should be worried.

CHAPTER SIX - DARRELL

Darrell entered the lunch room which reeked of bleach and canned peas and headed straight for his normal table. He was absolutely starving. His stomach had growled so loudly in math class that the entire class had heard and turned to stare at him. That was two classes in a row that he had accidentally been the center of attention. If he kept it up he would take Ron Coursey's place as the butt of everyone's joke. As much as Ron would probably appreciate that, Darrell wasn't keen on the idea so he needed to lay low for a while. Luckily, he thought, the winter break would wipe his fellow teenager's minds as long as he didn't do anything else moronic.

His visions always made him hungry, but he knew it was pointless to try to get decent food coming in twenty minutes late. There would only be salad and broccoli left at this point. He wasn't sure he was ever hungry enough to eat vegetables, so he decided to see what Marie and Gavril had left. As he approached the table, Marie was staring at him so intently that he swore he could feel it making him warmer. What was it with her and the looks today? He sat down and was stoked to see she had a pile of French fries left. He grabbed a handful of Marie's French fries, and promptly shoved them in his mouth.

"What the hell Darrell?" Marie asked.

"Sorry, I'm starving and there is never good food left this late," Darrell replied, barely understandable through his fry filled mouth.

"Not the freaking fries, moron! You obviously had a disturbing vision in history class. You make us wait 'till lunch to tell us about it. Then you show up twenty minutes late and sit down like nothing's going on," Marie said. She was obviously trying to remain calm, despite her annoyance, but her visibly throbbing temple was giving her away.

"Right. Sorry about that. I got caught in math using my phone. I was trying to research stuff from my vision. Mr. Knauth gave me the option of writing 500 lines or calling my father. You both know that wasn't much of a choice, so I had to write the lines," Darrell replied while staring at the corner of the table, avoiding Marie's stare. The laminate had chipped away and someone had carved a dirty limerick into the wood beneath.

"What was so important about your vision that you risked using your phone in Mr. Knauth's class? You know he is one of the toughest teachers when it comes to that rule?" Gavril asked.

"I saw a little boy kidnapped," Darrell replied. "At least I think I did."

"Kidnapped? You think you saw someone kidnap a little boy? What do you mean you think?" Marie asked.

"I'm sure the boy was kidnapped, there was no mistaking that. I'm not sure that it was indeed a vision. It felt like my other visions in a lot of ways but felt different too. I know that sounds weird, but I don't know how else to explain it," Darrell replied, looking back up at Marie.

"We have to stop it," Marie said matter-of-factly.

"I know we do, but it's not going to be that easy. I don't even know if it has already happened or not. This vision was weird though," Darrell said.

"Weird how?" Marie asked.

"Like I said, it felt much different than the previous visions."

"What do you mean it felt different?" Gavril asked.

"For one thing, I was extremely queasy when I woke up. The visions always mess with my appetite, and I usually wake up starving like I haven't eaten in days, but this time I woke up sick to my stomach. I eventually got the hunger I usually do, but it took a while. The other weird thing is, like I said before, the crown of my head usually feels funny like it is lightly vibrating. This time though it was a sharp pain, almost like being stabbed."

"That doesn't sound good. Maybe these visions are really hurting you," Gavril said, in a serious tone, that wasn't really like him.

Did he have a point? Were the visions really harming him or was Gavril overreacting? Either way, Darrell knew it wasn't the time to worry about it. If there was a boy that needed his help, he wasn't going to worry about an upset stomach and a headache.

"I'm sure it was just an anomaly. What we need to worry about right now is this little boy," Darrell replied.

"You said you weren't sure if it happened yet, what did you mean by that?" Marie asked.

"While the majority of my visions are seeing the future, sometimes I have seen the past, like when I saw where my dad had lost his car key. He was looking for it and getting angry and all of a sudden it hit me. I had a quick vision of him stumbling home and dropping it on the front lawn the night before. I went outside and sure enough there it was. That's why I was using my phone. I was searching to see if he had already been kidnapped."

"What did you find out?" Gavril asked.

"Nothing much. I only got a few searches done before I got caught. I couldn't find anything, so I think it may not have happened yet. I think a boy being kidnapped would have made it to the local news website at least, right? I didn't see anything to give me specific times in the vision, but I think it was no more than a couple of hours before or after noon based on the sun."

"What about the kidnapper? We could call the cops and tell them about a creepy guy around the park and give them a description," Marie said.

"That's the other major problem with the vision. I can't give much of a description. I could only see the kidnapper from the back, and I never saw his car. All I can say with certainty is the boy was blond and about ten years old. The kidnapper had brownish hair. It was long and he wore it in a ponytail. Oh and he was carrying a broken leash. That's how he tricked the kid. He told him he lost his dog."

"I can't believe that parents still don't tell their kids about tricks like those. There is no way that in today's world that trick should still work!" Gavril said with a bit of anger that surprised Darrell. "You're right though, that isn't much to go on. Could you tell which park they were in?" Gavril asked.

"I didn't recognize it and I never saw any signs."

"Maybe we can figure out which park." Marie said.

"How can we do that?" Darrell asked.

"If you saw parts of the park, I could find some crowd sourced photos of all the parks in the area and you could go through them until we find a match. Then we could let the cops know the park and give the description of a ponytailed guy carrying a broken leash. That should be enough right?" Marie said.

Marie never ceased to amaze Darrell. Everyone was always quick to mention Darrell's IQ, but Marie was the real genius of the group, he could just never get her to see it. Darrell happened to have a very good memory for facts and formulas and could calculate pretty well in his mind. That just looked good on tests, Marie on the other hand was a technical marvel. She could hack with the best of them and understood computers and technology on a level that was so far beyond a normal person's understanding, that he often thought she was speaking a foreign language. He actually wouldn't be surprised if sometimes she was making things up just to mess with him.

"You're brilliant," Darrell replied. He decided it was best not to make fun of her blushing. "That just might work. What about you Gav, think it will work? Or do you have any other ideas?"

"That does sound like it could work. The other thing I was thinking was that we could use a fake account on Friendly Faces. We could pose as a mother and post on several local mother's pages saying we saw a creepy guy with a ponytail at the park hanging out by the, where was he hanging out?" Gavril asked.

"By the swings, he was watching the boy swing before he approached him."

"Good, we say that we saw a creepy ponytailed guy hanging out by the swings," Gavril said.

"What about when they ask what park?" Marie asked.

"We just ignore it, since we don't know. It's not a perfect plan, but it may make a few mothers a little more observant. Maybe someone will see him, and scare him off," Gavril said.

"I suppose that could work. It's a long shot for sure, but it is better than doing nothing. We have to hope that today is not the day, giving us a chance to work the plans tonight. Marie, when you get home, can you start working on the photos? Gavril, you start posting as a concerned mother," Darrell said. Darrell wasn't sure about their plans, but if Marie said she could do it, then Darrell believed her. Gavril's plan was less of a sure thing, but Darrell couldn't shake the feeling of dread his vision had given him and they had to do something. He had thought about cutting school, but the potential of getting caught by his dad was too scary to risk.

"What are you going to do?" Marie asked.

"I'm going to take a nap, hoping another vision comes that will help us," Darrell responded as he stood up, deciding to get something to eat after all.

"Do you really think that's wise? I mean, you just said the last one hurt you. Maybe we should figure out how to stop these visions," Gavril said leaning in so as not to speak any louder. Darrell figured one of them would say that, and part of him agreed.

"I get what you're saying Gav, but if there is a chance I can help save this little boy, I can deal with a little pain. Like I told you guys before, the visions don't fade, so I keep seeing him being chloroformed over and over again. How in any form of good conscious can I let my pain outweigh his?"

"He was chloroformed? That might be a lead. I'm not certain, but that seems like it might be hard to get, or at the very least leave a paper trail," Gavril replied.

"That's a good idea Gavril. I can look into that later as well, but what if a little pain turns into a lot of pain or even some sort of brain damage?" Marie chimed in.

"I appreciate you caring about me, I really do, but this boy is our primary responsibility right now. We can come back to this after we help catch or stop this creep," Darrell said, then walked away. He didn't want to give them more room to debate and potentially talk him out of what he knew he needed to do. He headed toward the food line. As much as it pained him to realize, he was in fact, hungry enough to eat vegetables.

"Okay, but don't think we are letting this go!" Gavril called out. Darrell just nodded to acknowledge Gavril and kept walking. Darrell knew Gavril was serious and he and Marie wouldn't let it go, and Darrell was silently grateful to have friends that cared about him.

CHAPTER SEVEN - MARIE

Marie rushed into her house, pulled her sticker covered laptop out of her still ripped backpack, and tossed the backpack on the coffee table as she ran toward her room without looking at the pathetic excuse for a Christmas tree her father had put up. She didn't need to see it to know what it looked like. Her father had put the same sad excuse for a tree up for as long as she could remember. The tree stood no more than three feet high and came pre-decorated with ratty tinsel and lights. Every year that went by more lights stopped working, and her father never cared enough to bother replacing them. Last year she counted only twelve working and she wouldn't be surprised if it were under ten this year. The smell of the jasmine potpourri she kept in her room was always a welcome scent, like a breath of fresh air. Her bedroom always stood in stark contrast to the rest of her house. Where her father kept the house very masculine and completely devoid of anything remotely feminine, Marie's room was all things feminine, with lots of bright colors including many shades of pink and purple. She often wondered if she really liked pink and purple, or if she liked them more because her father was so against them.

People never understood her dichotomy. She loved things like baseball and hunting. She also liked pretty things. Why couldn't she be manly and feminine at the same time? Why couldn't she just be herself?

Marie had her laptop up and running in a matter of seconds. Ogre, her giant calico cat, walked in and meowed at her. Marie looked down at him and blew him a kiss. Ogre took this as an invitation to jump up to her lap, and Marie groaned under the pressure of his weight. Ogre weighed around twenty pounds and wasn't exactly a lap-cat, but he never seemed to get that message. Despite the discomfort, she didn't mind; in fact, she found it comforting to have someone show her unconditional love. She scratched Ogre's head for a moment and began typing her code, while awkwardly positioning her arms around the cat.

She was more than halfway through writing the computer code that she was going to use to pull the pictures from the local parks when her father came in. She could tell just by the way he opened her bedroom door that he was angry. Marie loved her father, more than he would ever know, but she struggled to get past his demons. He had raised her by himself after her mother died giving birth to her. She always knew that he held her, at least partially, responsible for her mother's death, but to his credit he always hid it the best he could. Unfortunately he didn't hide his constant anger nearly as well. This time of year was always a little bit worse. Apparently Christmas was her mother's favorite time of year, and thus after her death Christmas became her father's least favorite. She wasn't sure why he even bothered with the tree since he never even talked about Christmas. Maybe it was his way of remembering her, which Marie would have thought was sweet, if he had taken care of it. Instead, at least for her, it was a harsh reminder that she didn't have a mother and her dad became more and more distant each year. Marie was only half an orphan, but at times she felt like it wouldn't have been much different if she was a whole orphan. However, times like this when her father was very angry, she was harshly reminded that she wasn't.

Marie had learned years ago to not even bring up presents. When she was eight years old, she asked him for a Tickle Me Elmo. Her father lectured her for over an hour and grounded her for being selfish. He actually got her the toy a few months later for her birthday. He always made up for the lack of Christmas presents on her birthday, but that never made her hate Christmas any less.

Her father had raised her very much like he would have raised a boy. He always pushed her into typically masculine things, such as martial arts, hunting and baseball instead of softball. She didn't hold it against him but she often wished for help with things like makeup and other girly stuff which was always especially awkward with her father. The real issues for her were always the same though, his anger and his intolerance for people that were different than him.

"You mind telling me what the hell this is about?" her dad asked, as he threw her backpack at her.

"You mean the rip?" she asked as it hit her chest very hard. She didn't dare show how much it really hurt. Marie had her own anger issues, though they didn't even compare to her father's when he was really raging, and having her backpack thrown at her like that was just about too much. She knew it would be bad news to show her anger, so she tried to avoid looking him in the eye, so her eyes didn't give her away. She silently cursed herself for foolishly leaving her backpack in the living room for him to find.

"You know damn well I mean the rip. That backpack is only three months old, and it cost twice as much as the one I wanted to get you. You just had to have this one to carry your precious laptop, and this is how you take care of it?"

"I'm sorry dad. It got caught on a locker at school and then I got pushed before I could get it off so it just ripped open," Marie said, fighting back tears.

She wasn't sure if they were tears from her chest hurting, or tears of rage, but she knew she couldn't let them come out. She would not give him the satisfaction of knowing she was hurt, and her anger would only rile him up further. She really hated lying to him but she didn't see how the truth would go over very well. Darrell and Gavril had helped her come up with the cover story earlier in the day, just in case the rip came up but as she said it, she realized it wasn't a very good lie.

"So that means the person who pushed you needs to replace it, right?"

"I didn't see who pushed me," Marie replied shifting her gaze to the poster of cute kittens hanging right behind her father. Perhaps they could help her calm down.

"I guess that means you get to repay me. I'll expect fifty bucks by the end of the month, and we'll just let you continue to use the torn one as a reminder of how you need to take better care of your stuff. I still don't know why you had to have this one with all the buckles like it is supposed to be fancy. It's pretty gay."

"I really wish you wouldn't do that," Marie said, staring back at her father. She knew he could see the anger in her eyes now, but she didn't care. He knew what he was doing when he said that, and she hated that she gave him the satisfaction of angering her, but she couldn't help it. That was a hot button she couldn't ignore.

"Do what?"

"Use the word gay to mean lame or stupid," she looked down at her backpack, pretending to examine the rip. She was becoming angrier now and thought it best not to let him see that. If he knew, he would push her further just for fun.

"Sweetheart, I wasn't meaning lame, I truly meant gay. It looks like something a homosexual would use, but since when are you so sensitive? You got some homo friends? That Gavril kid looks like he may be one. His shirts are always way too tight. Maybe I should start calling him 'Gayvril', what do you think?"

Marie knew when he was trying to goad her into a fight. He loved to fight. She could tell that with the mood he was in tonight it wasn't in her best interest to fall into his trap. She wanted to lash out at him and make sure he knew how wrong he was. She hated herself when she felt this way. She knew how his anger affected her and she didn't want to have that effect on other people with her own anger, but it was so hard. Often when she was really angry and making a scene, her inner voice was telling her that she was acting stupid and that she should stop, but she just couldn't.

When she was really angry, it was like someone else was in control of her body and she was just along for the ride, constantly telling her body to stop, but it never listened. She took a quiet breath and successfully buried her anger. No good could come from it. Besides, she needed to get back to her code, and that was far more important than letting her father know what an intolerable jerk he was.

"He's not gay, at least not that I know of. I just think it's not very nice." She was trying her best to say her piece and at the same time diffuse the situation, so he would leave her alone.

"As long as I am paying all the bills, you don't get to tell me what I can and can't say, don't forget that."

"Yes sir."

"Damn right yes sir," he replied, and went back to the living room to watch the game, slamming her door and rattling the dozens of magazine pages and band posters she had taped to her wall.

Marie sat for a moment, lost in thought, staring at the giant heart on her wall made out of origami butterflies. She had questioned her own sexuality for the last several years but could never talk to anyone about it. She always thought of herself as a strong woman, both physically and mentally, but this secret was tearing her apart. She often found herself switching from hating herself for being different to hating herself for not being strong enough to handle being different. She knew that she could never talk to her father about it. Even if she fully accepted that she was in fact gay, he would never accept it. She had no idea what he would do if she was still living with him when she came out.

Telling her best friend Darrell was also off the table. They have been best friends for longer than any of them could remember and they shared virtually everything. Darrell was quite tolerable of gay people, having even participated in a few gay pride 5k runs with his gay uncle. The problem with telling Darrell was that he had a crush on her. She had known for the last several years, even though he never told her. She could never bring herself to tell him she wasn't interested, and she certainly didn't want to break it to him by saying that she wasn't even interested in his gender. Part of her sometimes thought her being gay would make it easier for Darrell to accept, but at the same time she worried it could go the other way and devastate him. She cared too much for him to hurt him. She really loved him and she thought he loved her, but could he accept that the love was brotherly? She couldn't imagine her life without Darrell and the thought of him not being her friend if she broke his heart terrified her more than anything else in the world.

She still wasn't sure about Gavril. He was very nice and had shown himself to be quite empathetic, but she wasn't 100% sure he would keep it to himself. As worried as she was about telling Darrell, she knew it would certainly crush him if he heard it from someone else. Marie shook the thoughts out of her mind to focus on the task at hand.

It took a while but she was nearly finished with the code when her cell phone rang. She was annoyed at being interrupted again until she looked down and saw Darrell's name on the Caller ID. She got a sudden pit in her stomach. She didn't think he would call before she had completed running the search, and she couldn't help but think something was wrong.

"Hello," she said as she swiped the screen to answer and pushed the button to send the call to her wireless headset.

"Turn on the news. Channel eight," Darrell's voice was shaky, confirming her intuition that something was wrong. Somewhere deep in her mind it was telling her not to turn on the TV. Maybe if she didn't see whatever it was, it wouldn't be real. She knew she was being ridiculous.

"Okay," Marie responded while she began digging through the mounds of blankets on her bed for the remote control. Her father had always told her she had too many blankets, and at that moment, she thought he may have been right.

"I have Gav on 3 way," Darrell said.

"Hey, Marie," Gavril said.

"Hey, Gavril," Marie responded as she finally found her remote. She turned on the flat screen television, last year's birthday present, and turned to channel eight.

The news had a big red banner at the bottom of the screen 'Boy missing from Palm Court Park.' Marie's heart sank and it took a few moments for her to find her voice, since it had decided to make its way to her stomach.

"Is that him?" she weakly asked. She knew the answer before he said it, but she was trying to will it to not be true.

"Yeah, they showed his picture earlier. It's him. They said he went missing around one thirty this afternoon. If I had seen where it was I could have stopped this," Darrell said. She could hear the anger in his voice. She knew he shouldn't blame himself, but she also knew that wouldn't stop him from doing it. As upset as she was, she didn't have to see it happen like Darrell did. She had been thinking all afternoon, about how much of a burden that would be.

"Don't be so hard on yourself. You can't help what you saw. There was nothing more you could have done. This is not on you," Gavril said.

"Besides, just because we didn't prevent the kidnapping, doesn't mean we can't help catch this dude," Marie said.

"That's a great point," Gavril said. "Let's all think it over tonight and meet at HQ in the morning and discuss our ideas."

"Okay, maybe I'll have another vision that will help. I really want to catch this guy, and I'll need your help guys," Darrell said.

"Don't worry. We've got your back. This guy doesn't have any clue what's coming for him," Marie said emphatically.

"You got that right. See you guys tomorrow," Darrell said as he hung up.

When Darrell hung up the 3-way call ended, so Marie quickly called Gavril. He must have been expecting it, because he answered before she even heard a ring.

"Gavril, I'm worried about him. He is taking this way too personally. I know it must be hard for him, but he can't continue to take on the burden. It's too much," Marie said.

"I agree. We need to find a way to help find this boy. Then we need to convince him to figure out a way to stop these visions. I'm worried they could lead him down a very bad path emotionally, psychologically and maybe even physically," Gavril replied. Marie was glad he was taking her side.

"I was thinking the same thing. I'm going to get back to my research. I'll talk to you in the morning. Good night."

"Night Marie," Gavril said and then hung up the phone.

Marie turned back to the TV and turned the volume up. She knew she needed to do something more about this, but she wasn't sure what. She went back out into the living room, and saw her dad asleep in his ratty old recliner. She knew that when he was this tired he was usually out for the night. Even if he did wake up, he wasn't likely to check in on her. She weighed the potential of getting caught with the ability to work all night without having to worry about being quiet. It didn't take her long to decide. She went back in her room, turned the TV off, and used some dirty clothes and throw pillows to make it look like a body was under the blanket. She couldn't remember this trick ever working in the movies or on TV, but she couldn't come up with a better option. She decided it would have to do. She grabbed her laptop, her cell phone, and her backpack. She slowly snuck past her father in the living room and out the front door. She couldn't for the life of her remember the front door having a squeaking problem before, but now as she tried to quietly and slowly close the front door, it seemed like the squeaks were as loud as air horns. She finally closed the door and peeked back in the window to make sure her father was still sound asleep. She unlocked her bike and rode away as quietly as she could.

It would take her close to an hour to get to HQ, and she would have to pass Gavril's and Darrell's houses to get there. She thought for a moment about stopping by and asking them to join her, but decided against it. She knew she was about to use every bit of computer and hacking knowledge she had, and decided that it would go smoother without any added distractions.

CHAPTER EIGHT - GAVRIL

Gavril woke the next morning with a feeling of dread. He didn't want to make the call, but he knew he needed to do it. He had been an overseer for thousands of years. He was always confident in his knowledge of all things Sevenths, but he couldn't recall anything like the headache Darrell had described, at least not specifically. At first he chalked it up to a normal headache, but the more he had thought about it last night, he decided it couldn't be just a coincidence that the headache happened where Darrell's visions came from. Part of him thought he remembered something about headaches and he felt like he should know it, but couldn't remember. Sevenths had a small node called the node of sight; it of course had a much more scientific name, but nobody ever called it that, unless they were a doctor or were very pretentious. The node grew in their brain, right on the crown of the head. Gavril was concerned that the headache might mean the node was damaged in some way.

He remembered, all too vividly, one of his Sevenths dying in the early first century. When they examined the corpse, they found that the node of sight had burst. The Seventh had never told Gavril about any pains but the Overseer community still held Gavril partly responsible. It was the only time Gavril lost a Seventh before they reached the age of sight. The age of sight, the average age a Seventh developed their powers, has moved over the years as the human lifespan has lengthened. The current age of sight is thirty-five, compared to twenty-eight when Gavril lost his Seventh. Despite the many years since, Gavril was still haunted by the young man's death. Being immortal meant that he buried many friends over the years but it is different when you are in charge of protecting them. The Overseer community didn't help much, since they still brought it up every time he got an assignment. Immortals had a bad habit of treating the distant past like it happened last week.

Gavril always thought it was unfair since ninety-nine percent of the Overseers never even had to worry about losing someone before the age of sight. Usually they didn't even get their assignments till the age of sight had passed. By Gavril's count nearly twenty percent of all older Sevenths died within five years of gaining their powers but nobody ever blamed their Overseer, despite the fact that many of those deaths were because the Seventh went crazy and committed suicide because they couldn't handle the visions. But everyone always placed more concern when minors died, not that Gavril didn't see their point there. Gavril often tried to raise concerns about the high mortality rate of adult Sevenths, since in the vast majority of those cases, the Seventh died before they could have seven sons themselves. With the advent of birth control there are far fewer new seventh sons, although birth control didn't affect those already in the Seventh line. There was no stopping the seventh line, except for death or complete abstinence. Over the centuries many Sevenths have tried every form of birth control they could in an effort to stop their birth line. Unfortunately for them, being a Seventh is a divine power and no matter how hard they tried, if they didn't die or completely abstain, they always had seven sons. Gavril had seen several cases first hand where a Seventh would plan on abstaining after having six sons only to have twins at the end.

Gavril knew he could never live with himself if he lost another ward. He did what he knew he needed to do and picked up the phone to call Andrea. She may not have been around as long as Gavril but she had dealt with hundreds more Sevenths over the years. As much as they didn't get along, he knew she would know what to do, she always knew what to do.

"Hello," Andrea said with more than a hint of tiredness in her voice, she had obviously been sleeping.

"Andrea, it's Gavril."

"Gavril, you do know it is six thirty in the morning here, right? You would think someone as old as you would remember things like time zones." As much as Gavril loved to throw the fact he was older in Andrea's face he sure did hate it when she threw it back when he made a mistake.

"Sorry about the time, but to be fair time zones have only existed for a couple of hundred years, so that's like a couple of years to a normal person. Anyway, I really need to discuss something with you."

"That's fine. I should get up now anyway. What's going on? Since you are calling this early I assume you haven't stopped Darrell yet?"

"No."

"And I assume that something else has happened?"

"Yes," Gavril started. He heard her mumble something to the effect of 'of course' but ignored it. "He had a vision yesterday of a young boy being kidnapped. The news last night was reporting the kid being missing. Now he and Marie are hell-bent on finding the boy."

"Wait! Marie? You mean to tell me he has come out to the girl? You know that is unacceptable. The entire community is at risk when civilians know. Your job is to stop that kind of stuff from happening," Andrea said, her agitation rising. He hated it when she was right, but so many bad things could happen if the world knew that there were really people that could see the future and people that were immortal. They would be dissected, used as weapons and who knew what else. Gavril knew that Marie would never betray their trust, but Gavril also knew it would likely take years to convince Andrea of that.

"I know, but I didn't have a chance, he did it so quickly. She is not a risk though. I am actually quite surprised how easily she adapted and believed him. That is not what I am really concerned about."

"You have an underage Seventh, having serious visions. Visions a boy his age is not remotely equipped to handle by the way, and thinking he is a crime fighter. You have a fifteen year old civilian with knowledge of the visions actively participating in said crime fighting, so tell me what could be more concerning?"

"When Darrell had the vision of the kidnapping, he told me that he came out of the vision feeling sick to his stomach instead of the usual severe hunger. He said that he had a severe headache right where his node is, and said that it felt like he was being stabbed there. I know I have been out of practice but I can't recall ever hearing of this happening. Do you know what it might mean?" Gavril asked.

"Oh. Well that is concerning. Has he had another vision since then?"

"I'm not sure. I'm meeting him this morning. I can ask him then. What does this mean?"

"I don't want to theorize just yet because I am not certain. Let me consult with the council and get back with you. Gavril, this just shows how important it is that you get him to suppress the visions. His body is just not ready."

"I will redouble my efforts, but I'll tell you now that this is one headstrong kid, and it will not be easy."

"I thought you were supposed to be the best, right?"

"I am the best. I said it would be difficult, not impossible. Please let me know as soon as you find out something."

"I will, but it might take a day or so as I am dealing with a little bit of a kerfuffle here too. I'll call you when I can. Bye Gavril," Andrea said and hung up the phone.

Gavril grabbed his jacket and headed out to meet up with Marie and Darrell. He hopped on his bike and headed to their headquarters. The ride was only about twenty minutes but that didn't make Gavril any happier. It really upset him that he had to ride a bike instead of driving a car. Not only was he thousands of years old, his cover ID was actually old enough to have a driver's license. Andrea had decided when they got their assignment that he would not be allowed to drive. She had the notion that by not driving he would come across as more likable. She said this would help him gain Darrell's friendship faster. Gavril thought she was out of her mind. Everyone loved having a friend with a car. It was his first time working with Andrea and she had a reputation for being a real stickler for rules and structure, so he let it go without much of a fight, but now as the near Arctic wind was making his eyes water and then freezing the tears to his face, he was regretting that decision.

Gavril arrived at the building and made his way around the back to sneak in. He was pleasantly surprised that it appeared their neighbor's security guard was nowhere to be seen. He must have been hiding from the weather and Gavril didn't blame him. That always made it easy and quick to get in. As he walked through the office and made his way to their makeshift living room he was surprised nobody was there.

"We're back here in the conference room," Marie's voice rang out.

Gavril pulled off his jacket and tossed it on the couch, and began walking toward the conference room. Someone had apparently turned the heat up as high as it could go because now he was starting to sweat. "I know it's cold outside, but do we have to make it so-," he didn't finish his sentence.

Gavril was in no way prepared for what he saw when he walked into the conference room. There were three large televisions lined up against the back wall, each displaying a separate news channel. There were two local channels, and a national twenty-four hour news channel that had apparently picked up the kidnapping story as well. That didn't surprise Gavril since apparently the kidnapped boy's family was quite wealthy. It had always bothered him that it seemed like the wealthy always got better treatment from law enforcement and the media but it had been that way his entire, very long, life and he expected it would never change. The table was covered in a mixture of computers and dozens of sheets of paper. Gavril counted three laptops and four desktop computers. Marie had her face buried in two of the desktops, looking from one to the other so often and quickly that it made Gavril a little nauseous. Darrell was immersed in one of the laptops, which he recognized as Marie's thanks to the giant purple pony sticker. He was so engrossed in what he was looking at that Gavril wasn't sure Darrell had even noticed his entrance.

"What in the hell is all of this?" Gavril finally said.

"What?" Marie asked as she looked up from her computer monitors.

"This," Gavril said, motioning to all of the equipment. "What is all of this?" he realized that he was waving his arms a little over enthusiastically and was probably looking quite comical so he quickly stopped.

"Oh. Well, I decided to come here last night and get started on finding Kevin," Marie said, obviously quite proud at what she had accomplished.

"Kevin? That's the boy's name?" Gavril asked.

"Yeah. They mentioned it on the news this morning. I just thought if we began using his name it would help us focus."

"In my experience, I've always found that the opposite was true. Making it less personal would help keep you objective. But we all work in different ways," Gavril said. He realized he had said a little too much, but hoped she wouldn't pick up on it.

"In your experience? You're sixteen. Have you been on a lot of kidnapping cases? Anyway, like I was saying, I got here last night because I thought I would work better without having to worry about waking my dad. Once I started, I decided I could use another computer to make things go faster, and a TV to keep abreast of any news. That grew into what you see here. I had to clean them up first. You wouldn't believe the sick things the previous people were into. Also, the computers were so infected with viruses that I'm surprised they still turned on.

Those laptops that Darrell is using are hacked into the police surveillance and traffic cameras. I'm hoping to catch a glimpse of what the guy looks like from the front and hopefully what kind of car he drives. Two of these desktops are running the computer code I wrote last night. The code is pulling all photos that have been uploaded to social media in the past two weeks that were tagged with any of the parks within ten miles of Kevin's abduction. It's also looking for any photos posted to the internet in any fashion that have been geotagged near one of those parks."

"Why worry about all of the other parks?" Gavril asked.

"This guy didn't just wake up and decide to kidnap a kid. He had to have scoped out parks ahead of time. Maybe Palm Court wasn't his first choice. I figured that he wouldn't have strayed too far though, which is why I only went ten miles," Marie replied.

He had to admit it was quite impressive. He had never met anyone quite like Marie before. Of course most of his life technology didn't exist for someone to be good at, but the way her brain worked was on another level. He figured if she had been born in another century, she would have just been amazing at something else. Marie, and others, often pointed out how smart Darrell was, because of his memory, but Gavril felt Marie didn't get near the credit she deserved. He thought she was one of the most brilliant people he had ever met, and he had met a lot of people.

"What about the other two?" Gavril said, almost too scared to ask.

"Ah, the coup de grâce. I have those," she said, pointing at the two laptops in the corner. "Hacked into police databases. One is the local police department who is handling the case, and the other is the federal database. They are scanning through the databases looking for people that were suspects in any kidnappings locally in the past ten years. I then go through those pictures to find anyone with a ponytail. It's not much to go on, but it's all we got."

"Wait. You are hacked into the police and FBI? What are you thinking? They don't screw around with that stuff. We could all go to jail for a long time," Gavril said.

"Relax. You sound like a grown up. For starters, I am running through several access points around the world.

Secondly, I am using a private Wi-Fi from a mile away. Even if they did track it back, it would only lead them to the First National Bank building with well over a hundred employees. They would be tied up in that investigation for days, if not weeks. We would have plenty of time to clear our tracks. Besides, I am only skimming data. I am not actively changing anything. I am also using the login for the person that is assigned to the case. So if they notice the activity it will just look like the assigned person is looking at past cases, which would be a normal thing to do. So again, relax, nobody is going to get arrested," Marie said with a huge smile.

"How are you picking up a Wi-Fi signal that far away? I get outside my house and the signal drops," Gavril asked.

"The bank uses a fairly high powered antenna to send out their signal to make sure that everyone in the building can get a signal. Usually, buildings that big have multiple antennas. This bank is using a newer tech with only one very large antenna in the hopes they can better control access and allow fewer chances for hackers to steal banking info. Couple that with my amplified receiver which piggybacks off of several hotspots hoping from one to another until you get the one you want, my own design by the way, and there you go. It was actually pretty simple to hack into. I sent a few Trojan emails and was on their network in less than thirty minutes."

"So the bank's attempt at making them harder to hack, made it easier for you to do so? Anyone ever tell you that you are kinda scary?" Gavril asked.

"I get that a lot," She replied with a sly smile.

CHAPTER NINE - GAVRIL

"I must admit that this is quite impressive, but what has it yielded? Even though you have reduced the risk, there still is a risk, and it isn't worth it if we can't get something from it," Gavril said. Andrea was already mad at him and if the Overseer council knew that he was helping an underage Seventh look for a kidnapper, he would certainly be punished. If he was arrested doing it, he didn't even want to think about how bad the punishment would be.

"I agree. Let me show you what we have so far," Darrell said, finally looking up from the computer. "We know Kevin was abducted from Palm Court Park while his nanny was busy chatting up some single dad on the opposite side of the playground. We were able to find photos from virtually every angle, and can say for certain that she couldn't see anything from where she was."

"Do you think she is involved, or maybe the guy she was talking to?" Gavril asked. "I hear the parents are really rich, so maybe a ransom is the goal." He cursed himself for not putting a stop to this, but he had to admit it was exciting. He hadn't felt like this since that time back in the old west, and in the end that had worked out okay. Well, mostly okay.

"That is what the feds are focusing on but we don't think so," Marie said. "I ran Mr. Flirty's bank records, and he is loaded. He has nearly twice the assets as Kevin's parents. Also the nanny doesn't have any financial issues. In fact, she has a substantial savings and zero debt. It doesn't appear that either of them had a motive for ransom. At least not that I can see. Both of them have clean criminal records as well. Couple those things with how Darrell describes the vision and I think this is more about the kidnapper's sick mind than about money."

"Tell him about the chloroform," Darrell added.

"Right. Well I couldn't find anything on the sales front so I went with a hunch and checked burglaries and bingo! I found a vet clinic that reported a bottle of chloroform missing when they were broken into last month. I'm not entirely sure they should have even had it or how someone knew to break into the clinic to steal it. The case was never solved and there doesn't seem to be any camera footage so it is a bit of a dead end at this point," Marie said.

"I still think this is best left to the police. We should let them do their job and stay out of it," Gavril said. He knew he didn't sound very convincing and deep down he didn't really want to leave it to them, but it was the right thing to do.

"The major problem with that is that police work takes time. They are still trying to get warrants for the bank records I got hours ago. They are handcuffed by policy. They will-"

"You mean they are handcuffed by laws," Gavril interrupted.

"They will always be behind us," Marie said, ignoring Gavril. "You know as well as I do that time is of the essence when it comes to things like this."

"We also know what he looks like. Well, at least partially," Darrell said.

"We could tell them about the guy having a ponytail," Gavril said, not giving up on convincing them to leave this to the police. As much as he wanted to find the guy, he wanted Darrell and Marie safe more. He also knew that he was fighting a losing battle. He could tell by the way they were looking at him, that they weren't going to give up. Maybe his best course of action was to go along with them and keep them safe that way.

"I tried, but they wouldn't listen," Darrell said.

"What do you mean you tried?" Gavril asked, surprised.

"I called them about an hour ago and told them I saw the back of the guy. They could tell I was a kid. They said that I couldn't have seen him since I would have been in school. They invited me to come in and tell them about what I saw and I could also explain why I wasn't in school. I can't do that since it would be easy for them to prove that I was in school and couldn't have seen him. They also threatened me with things like falsifying a police report. It looks like going to the police is out of the question," Darrell said. "Besides, I can't help but feel responsible. I need to find him. Know what I mean?"

"I know what you mean. I think your guilt is misguided, but I know what you mean," Gavril said. He had seen this a hundred times before with grown Sevenths. They saw such horrible things and since they felt like they could stop them, they often took them personally.

Gavril sat in silence for a moment as Marie and Darrell went back to their computer screens. He had no idea how he was supposed convince Darrell to stop his visions. Normally when Gavril got an assignment it was fairly easy. Most young men that get their sight early are frightened of the visions. It would be much harder to convince grown men not to use their powers since they were more set in their ways. Also, the idea of using the visions to help with women and money was always too strong for grown men to ignore. In addition to usually being scared of their visions, underage Sevenths normally had visions of very little importance. They might see themselves missing the bus, or in the case of one particularly clumsy teenager in the Middle Ages see themselves constantly falling in cow manure. Gavril was able to get that young man to believe his visions were causing the falling into the manure, not the other way around, and getting him to stop after that was easy. Unfortunately he didn't stop falling into the manure. Darrell's visions were way more important than they should have been at this point and it worried Gavril. He knew Darrell was destined to be powerful, but this was unfounded. Darrell's first vision, or at least the first he noticed was a life or death vision. Gavril had seen adult Sevenths go years before having such important visions.

Darrell was already too far down the rabbit hole, Gavril feared. Darrell had far more empathy than Gavril was used to seeing in teenage boys. The fact that he had already had three visions giving him the chance to save people meant that Darrell would not give up his powers without a fight. Andrea was totally results driven though and wouldn't want to hear anything about Darrell's empathy.

"Gavril!" Darrell yelled, pulling Gavril out of his thoughts. "You with us?"

Gavril noticed that Marie and Darrell were looking at a big map on the table, apparently going over some sort of plan.

"Sorry. I was just thinking. What's going on?" Gavril asked as he stood to look at the map with the other two.

"Right now we think our best idea, since we have struck out with all the electronic stuff so far, is to go door to door. We plotted out a grid that covers about ten square miles around the park and about five miles around Kevin's house. We figure we will go door to door looking for men with ponytails. It has been twenty years since ponytails were cool, so how many could there be?" Marie said.

"What is the pretense? I mean, we need to have a reason to be knocking when someone answers, right?" Gavril asked.

"We got you covered. We will just sell that cookie dough we were supposed sell anyway for the school fundraiser. We might even win the free bike," Darrell chimed in, saying the last part quite sarcastically.

"What do we do if a woman answers? How do you get the man to come to the door?" Gavril asked.

"Um, I hadn't thought of that," Marie said. Gavril could see the disappointment on her face.

"I have," Darrell said as he picked up a box at his feet and placed it on the table. "I found all these autographed balls in one of the offices, I think it was the dude that got arrested. Anyway, we ask the wife if her husband is at home and say we are selling them for our college fund."

"Seriously!" Marie said, visibly annoyed.

"What?" Darrell asked, confused. Gavril stifled a laugh. He always loved seeing Darrell dig himself a hole.

"That's seriously sexist."

"What do mean?" Darrell asked.

"You are saying that only a man would be interested in sports and I suppose the cookie dough would be for the woman of the house? Do I need to remind you that I batted .600 this past baseball season and you don't even know how many bases there are?"

"You lost me. What does making out have to do with this?" Darrell asked. Gavril laughed so hard, he knocked over the soda sitting on the table, which spilled on the map they were using.

"Sorry about that," he said as he grabbed some napkins and began to clean it up.

"I don't get it. What's so funny?" Darrell asked.

"Thanks. You've made my point. I will concede though. Despite being sexist, your plan is better than anything I have. Gavril, do you have any ideas?"

"Not anything better," he replied still giggling. "So we may as well go with that. What's the plan for dividing up the grid?"

"We thought that you could take the grid around the boy's house, and we would split up the grid around the park. Darrell mapped out a specific route for each of us that snakes around all of the neighborhoods and allows us to hit each house. We take the special map Darrell printed and mark each house with a special code. 'NM' is the code for no man living there. 'NP' is code for no ponytail, in case there is a man there, but he doesn't have a ponytail. 'CB', for a house we need to come back to for whatever reason," Marie said.

"We figure if there is an issue, another one of us could go to the house to try again. It is also important that you get a picture of the back of all the men with ponytails. If for some reason you can't get the picture, circle the house on the map and I will go back and look for myself," Darrell added.

"That sounds like a plan. I wish that I had worn better shoes," Gavril said as he looked down at his sandals.

"Oh, one last thing. If you see a skull and cross bones on a house, it means that a sexual predator is registered there. If there is a knife, it means someone convicted of a violent crime lives there," Marie said.

"There are an awful lot of skull and crossbones," Gavril said, looking over his map.

"I know. It's pretty scary stuff," Marie said. "So what are we waiting for? Let's go find this creep."

CHAPTER TEN - DARRELL

Darrell was definitely regretting not using his bike. He had no idea how far he had walked/skateboarded, but he had been going for over seven hours and was down to his last house. Despite the major pain in his feet and the massive sunburn on his neck and ears, he couldn't help but perk up when he saw the last house. The house sat on a much larger plot of land than the other houses in the neighborhood. It was at the end of the road, which dead-ended. It sat on the left hand side when you approached it. This made it the last house on the left, which struck Darrell as funny since that was the name of an old horror movie he liked and this looked like a place right of a horror movie. The house and lot stood out like a sore thumb. Not only were the house and land in pretty bad disrepair, it was the only house for blocks that wasn't decorated for Christmas.

Darrell remembered this neighborhood from when he was a child. His mom used to bring him to look at all the huge Christmas decoration displays. People would come from many towns away to see the decorations. A house a block over even had over a million hits on You Tube with its massive display set to music. This house didn't have a single decoration, in fact it naturally looked like it was decorated for Halloween. Darrell wondered how angry the lack of decoration made the other neighbors.

The state of the house had almost made Darrell skip it altogether and assume it was abandoned, until he saw a light in one of the rooms and some movement behind the curtains. Something in Darrell's gut told him that this was the house, and it wasn't just the creepy appearance. He just felt like this was it. He thought about calling Marie and Gavril, but decided it was still premature since he had no proof. Darrell coasted on his skateboard as far as he could, but then had to pick it up since the sidewalk was suffering from the same lack of care. Grass was now covering nearly the entire sidewalk.

The closer he got to the house, the stranger he felt. The house was the creepiest thing he could recall ever seeing in person. If he hadn't known better he would swear it was the scene of the horror movie he and Marie had seen a couple of weeks before. In the movie a group of teenagers have their car break down and end up looking for help from some backwoods hillbillies that end up murdering them all. Darrell knew he had to get this over with before he psyched himself out of it, so he picked up his pace and made it to the front door. He hesitated again, and just stared at the door. Darrell reached his left hand into his pocket and fingered the pocket knife Marie had given him, just in case. He decided to open the knife but still kept it in his pocket with his hand gripping it so hard he was sure the deer figure on the side would be permanently embedded into his palm. He decided it was now or never and rang the doorbell with his free right hand. It only took a moment for the door to open.

"May I help you?" the woman said as she opened the door. Her voice was light and airy and had a strange tone. Darrell thought it sounded soothing and at the same time, projected a hint of nonchalance.

Darrell was thrown. He had been expecting the ponytailed man to answer. He hadn't even considered the possibility of someone else answering, much less such an attractive woman. Darrell put her at around twenty-five to thirty years old, and she was quite striking. Especially her bright green eyes.

"May I help you?" she repeated, shaking Darrell out of his stupor.

"Um, yes, I was wondering if anyone would be interested in buying some of this really cool autographed sports memorabilia?"

"You are selling autographed sports memorabilia? That's an odd thing to do door to door."

"Yeah, I guess it is but I got it all from an inheritance. I am trying to earn money for college. My parents don't trust teenagers on the internet, so this was my only other option."

"I guess that makes sense, though these days are door to door sales any less dangerous than the internet? I'm sorry but I'm not into sports."

"What about anyone else? Maybe your husband or father would be interested?"

"I'm afraid I'm the only one that lives here. Sorry I couldn't have been more help but I really need to get back to my cooking. Have a nice day," she said as she closed the door, not waiting for a response from Darrell.

Darrell was really unsure what to think. He had no reason to doubt her, but it didn't seem to fit. She was so far from the person he expected to live there. Her appearance was such a stark contrast to the house. Also there was something a bit off about her demeanor. He decided not to mark it off as completed because he still had a weird feeling about it. He made his way back down the sidewalk and hopped on his skateboard. He turned back to take one last look and the next thing he knew he was flying off his skateboard. He landed on the front lawn of one of the neighbors, knocking over their inflatable Santa. He looked up to see a very large man standing over him. The guy gathered up the things he had apparently been carrying when they ran into each other. Once the guy had finished picking up his stuff, he began walking away.

"Watch where you're going," the guy said over his shoulder.

Darrell barely heard what the guy said. A sudden sharp pain in Darrell's head brought him back to his knees. He wasn't sure what he hit his head on during the fall but it must have been hard. The headache was immense. Darrell looked back at the man he ran in to and noticed he had stopped and leaned against a car that was parked against the curb. Darrell began to think they had bumped heads when they collided because the man was also rubbing his head and looked to be in a lot of pain as well. The man was staring at Darrell now and was giving him a pretty intense glare. For a moment Darrell thought the man was going to come back and confront him, but the man just kept rubbing his head as he turned to walk toward the creepy house. Darrell felt the top of his head, knowing it was going to be covered in blood, but was surprised to find it dry. Thank heaven for small miracles, he thought. As he tried to get back on his skateboard he got dizzy, so he sat back down on the ground. The world slowly began to get back into focus, so he looked to see what the guy was doing. He was surprised to see the man walking up the front steps of the creepy house. As the man reached for the doorknob, he looked back at Darrell again and gave Darrell a look that made the hairs stand up on Darrell's arms. Darrell was not sure what to think. He tried to make sense of it all. Had the woman been lying to him, or was the guy just a guest? Something sure did seem off about the guy but he had short hair, which meant he probably wasn't the guy from Darrell's vision.

The journey back to HQ was not an incredibly long one, but Darrell was in such pain from his feet and head, that it felt like forever. The intensity of his headache began to mellow but he couldn't get this weird guy out of his head. Something about the man was just off. Darrell double checked his map and remembered that he had two more houses to hit on the way back because nobody had been home. His legs were angry and in heavy protest about the detour, but he knew this was important and forced his way through.

CHAPTER ELEVEN - MARIE

Marie sat at the command desk, flipping through more pictures of past criminals in the federal database. It was such a tedious task and such a long shot that she wasn't sure exactly why she was doing it. She felt like she had to do something and couldn't sit back twiddling her thumbs, but she wasn't convinced this was the best use of her time. All she had to go on was a ponytail. Any picture over a couple of years old was a long shot at best. She may have already passed him and not known it because he grew the ponytail after the mugshot.

She had decided to expand her search after she struck out with her initial run through. She knew it was even more of a long shot, but she thought maybe the kidnapper would have started with lesser crimes. She was now about halfway through men with animal cruelty charges. Gavril sat at the other end of the table, watching more video footage. Marie had expanded the parameters of that search as well. Gavril was now looking at footage from last month. Gavril had insisted it was a waste of time going back so far but he couldn't come up with anything else to do, so he finally agreed.

Marie had been back from her grid search for nearly an hour by the time Gavril got back. Now, it had been nearly another hour and Darrell still wasn't back. He had called about twenty minutes prior, complaining about a headache and his feet hurting, so at least she knew he was on his way. Still, she was becoming impatient. She just picked up her cell phone to call him back when he finally walked into the conference room.

"Hey, guys," he said as he plopped down in one of the chairs surrounding the table.

He grabbed a slice of pizza and bottle of water that Marie had picked up on her way back, since she knew neither of the boys would put any thought into what they were supposed to eat or drink. She knew he must have really been worn out since he didn't even mention the black olives on the pizza. He just sat there staring off into space, slowly eating the black olive covered pizza. That wasn't a good sign, and Marie became concerned.

"Darrell?" Marie asked.

"Yeah?" he replied, still staring off into space.

"You okay?" Gavril asked, apparently noticing his weird behavior as well.

"Yeah, I'm fine. Let's talk about what we found. Who wants to go first?" he asked, shaking off whatever he was thinking about.

"I guess I might as well, since I don't really have much to report," Gavril said as he rolled out his map on the conference table.

Marie was surprised to see how thorough he had been in marking his houses. She knew he was extremely knowledgeable and smart, but she didn't expect him to be so thorough. As she looked at his map, he had gone well beyond the codes she had come up with. There were times listed by each house to show when he had been there and separate notes by each of them. All of the houses seemed to have one note that was some sort of code that wasn't initially clear. Some had a second note that was clearly a file name that Marie assumed correlated with a picture on his phone.

"Wow, looks like you were pretty thorough. What are these extra codes?" Darrell asked what Marie was thinking. She always loved that they were on the same wavelength.

"These," Gavril said, pointing to the one Marie assumed was a filename. "Are the filenames of the pictures I took. I have to say that I was quite surprised at the number of dudes that still sport ponytails. I figured it would be mostly Goth or metal dudes, but those weren't even a third of them."

"I know, right?" Marie chimed in.

"This code here, means that they had a lot of Christmas decorations."

"How is that supposed to help?" Darrell asked.

"I figured that someone that was planning a kidnapping, wouldn't spend all that time putting up decorations," Gavril replied.

"Or maybe they put the decorations up to lure children," Marie replied.

"I thought that too, but figured that was more likely for Halloween decorations than Christmas. Anyway, these," Gavril said pointing to the simpler code that was just a series of numbers followed by a letter. "Are indicators of where my journal entry for each house is. This way I can find my notes on each place."

"See," Gavril said as he laid his journal out on the table.

Marie picked up the journal and opened it to the first page:

1010 Apricot Ave- single mother of two small boys. Asked about suspicious men around the park, but she said her boys never played there since they had a swing set in the backyard. Bought 2 cookie doughs.

"Wow, this is pretty impressive stuff. Several of these you mention asking them about suspicious men, that wasn't part of the plan. How did you go about it?" Marie asked.

"When I got to that first one and realized she had small children, I thought she might be the type to look out for creepy dudes. I decided to go with the story that I knew the boy that was kidnapped and asked her. Some women told me to let the cops do their job, but most seemed to feel sorry for me and told me what they had seen. Most of the women bought cookie dough too. I guess they thought selling cookie dough would make me feel better. I sold two cases by the end. Unfortunately though, I didn't get much on suspicious men. I had a couple point out sexual offenders that were already on our list. One lady told me about a guy that hung around at the park. That guy turned out to be a mentally and physically handicapped man that just liked playing with children. He had short hair and didn't appear to be physically able to pull off what you described. His mom was super sweet though. I think the woman that told me about him was just uncomfortable with his handicaps."

"That's sad that people are like that. How did you fair on the ponytail front?" Marie asked.

"I got a lot of old hippies, but do have a couple of possibilities," Gavril said as he pulled out his phone.

"Put them up on the TV, so we can see better," Marie said.

"Um, I'm not sure how to do that."

"Just hand it here," Marie said in exasperation.

Marie took Gavril's phone and enabled the TV share feature, making his phone's screen mirrored on one of the big televisions on the wall. It took Marie only another second before she had the first picture up for all to see. It was a picture of the back of a ponytailed man who was obviously closing the door on Gavril.

"That's not him," Darrell said.

Marie swiped to the next photo. This one was a photo of a ponytailed man about to get in a car. There were some green out of focus objects that Marie was pretty sure were leaves.

"Nope," Darrell said.

"Okay, seriously. What is up with this picture? It looks like you are hiding in the bushes," Marie said.

"I was hiding in the bushes," Gavril said. "I couldn't figure out how to take the photos so I just did it on the sly.

I'm pretty sure the next one coming up I took through his kitchen window."

"The goal is to find a criminal, not be arrested like one," Marie said, laughing.

Marie swiped through the rest of Gavril's pictures, which were more of the same, all of which were discarded by Darrell.

"How many could you not confirm?" Darrell asked.

"None, really." Gavril said "Any houses where nobody was home, I just looked through their windows at their family photos to see if anyone had a ponytail."

"Jesus, you really are going to get arrested. What if the photos were old, before they grew their hair out?" Marie asked.

"Crap, I hadn't thought of that. I'll mark them on the map so we can go back tomorrow," Gavril said as he grabbed his map and began marking.

"Okay. I'll go next," Marie said.

Marie disconnected Gavril's phone and had hers connected in a matter of moments. She pulled her first photo up on the screen and opened her map, placing it on the table. Her first photo was a stark contrast to Gavril's. Where Gavril's were taken without the subject knowing, Marie's were obviously posed. Her first photo was a picture of her and a mystery man with a ponytail taken from behind, with their arms around each other.

"What is that?" Gavril asked pointing at the screen.

"It's a ponytailed guy, obviously," Marie said.

"No, I mean it looks like he is posing for the photo, how did you swing that?" Gavril asked.

"Oh, that was easy. I just told them that the new teenage craze was reverse selfies and you had to take the picture of your back. Then I told them it would be super awesome if I could have their sweet ponytail in my reverse selfie. Most of them were so into the thought of someone interested in their hair that they were glad to take the photo," Marie said.

"You mean they were into a hot young girl complementing them?" Darrell said.

"You may have a point, but I doubt all the woman that bought cookie dough from Gavril were buying it out of the goodness of their heart," Marie replied.

"No, they thought he could use the money to buy a bigger shirt," Darrell added, laughing.

"Ha ha," Gavril replied, placing emphasis and each word.

"By the way. I also sold ten cases of cookie dough," Marie said.

"Ten cases! You have got to be kidding me. Girls can get away with anything if they are good looking," Darrell said.

"Whatever, talk to me in ten years when I am making twenty percent less than you for doing the same work, and tell me then how girls get a better deal. Darrell, is this him?" Marie said, trying to get back on track.

"No, that's not him."

"This one?" Marie asked, swiping to the next picture. "That's a chick," Darrell said.

"Yeah, but she was really manly. I thought, hey, you never know, maybe it was a really manly chick in your vision."

"No, it was definitely a man."

Marie went through the rest of her photos with no better luck than Gavril's. She was disappointed as she disconnected her phone from the TV and put it in her pocket. She had really hoped that their plan would produce some results and help them catch this guy, but the only thing to come out of it was her selling what she was pretty sure was enough cookie dough to win the bike.

"Obviously you didn't have much luck with the ponytailed man either, Darrell?" Marie asked.

"No, not with the ponytailed guy. But there was something else," Darrell said. "I went to this one house that totally looked like it was straight out of a horror movie. I was sure that it was going to be it, but the woman there said nobody else lived there. Then when I was going back down the street, I ran into this really creepy guy and he knocked me off my board. I think we must have bumped heads because my head hurt pretty badly, and when I looked over to him, he was rubbing his head as well. When I got up and started to get my bearings back, I saw the guy go into the house. It was really weird too, because right before he went in he looked at me and gave me this really creepy stare. He gave me the willies and actually made the hair on my arms stand up."

"You think it could have been him?" Marie asked with a little hope on her voice.

"No, I don't think so. He had short hair. There is something off about him though, and why did that lady say she lived alone?"

"Maybe she did. He might have been visiting," Gavril said. "You said you hit your head?"

"Yeah, it hurt like a son of a gun." Darrell said, reaching up to the crown of his head.

"Did it feel anything like when you had that vision the other day?" Gavril asked.

"Kind of, I guess, but this was much more painful. Luckily, no blood though. And strangely no knot yet either."

"You should look into this guy, Marie. Find out who he is, and maybe run a back ground check?" Gavril said.

"I could try, but I don't have anything to go on. I don't even know his name. I guess I could see who owns the house but even if it is a man, I couldn't be sure it was him."

"I know, but please try," Darrell said.

"Okay, I'll see what I can do."

"Thanks," Gavril said. "I need to get home, my mom is expecting me."

"Sure thing. We should meet back here in the morning and try to decide our next plan."

"Okay, see you guys in the morning," Gavril said as he walked out of the room.

Marie picked up Darrell's map and began to study the marked house.

She made note of the size of the lot. It was much larger than the surrounding houses. She was pretty sure that meant it had been there much longer. Perhaps it used to be a farm and when the urban sprawl of subdivisions reached it the owner refused to sell. She had seen a documentary about a similar situation in another city and they just built around the land the man refused to sell. Maybe this was the same type of thing. She was worried about finding the owner though, since the house from the documentary had been passed down through generations and not sold. If this was the same type of situation, it would make finding the current owner difficult.

"I have a lot to do here, so I'm just going to stay the night. I'll tell my dad I'm staying at a friend's house, so you might as well go home and get some rest," Marie said.

"I don't think I'll get any more rest at home, besides it could be dangerous here overnight. I'll stay to protect you," Darrell said, smiling.

"Darrell, we both know I could wipe the floor with you. You won't be much protection. I could use the company though, as long as you won't get in trouble," Marie replied.

"I won't get in trouble. My dad usually goes to sleep early and wakes up late. He won't even know."

"Cool."

Marie sat in front of her laptop. Some of the other computers they gathered were more powerful, but she felt more comfortable with her own. She always felt there was a nice synergy between her and her laptop. They have been through a lot together over the last few years and she knew it wouldn't let her down. She pushed the power button. She wasn't sure exactly where to start, but she knew if anyone could do it, she could.

CHAPTER TWELVE - GAVRIL

Gavril couldn't recall the last time he was so thankful to arrive home. His legs felt like jelly from the many miles he had ridden on his bike. The spell that made him immortal kept his body thin and in relatively good shape, but that was mostly because of a good metabolism. It didn't help at all with cardio or muscle fatigue. When he was younger and living through the middle ages he was in excellent shape. Not that a young man in the middle ages had much choice. Modern times led to a far more lackadaisical mindset, and he was more than happy to go along with it.

Gavril made his way to the kitchen, tossing his house keys on the table next to the mini two foot Christmas tree that Andrea put up before she left. Gavril didn't really celebrate Christmas and neither did Andrea, but he was sure she put it there for his benefit. He found it funny that she insisted on mothering him, despite his age. He had worked with a lot of bosses over the years and Andrea was easily the strictest in terms of following rules, but she also had the most heart. Being an Overseer manager was a tough job, and they usually chose no nonsense kind of people, but none as no nonsense as Andrea. Gavril usually found them to be mean. Andrea was the opposite of that. She would yell at someone if they messed up, but she really seemed to care about them. However, Gavril learned early on that her caring was not something to be talked about it. She seemed to see it as a weakness at times, so it had become the unwritten rule that they didn't' talk about Andrea's feelings.

He was pleased to see there was still a six-pack of his favorite soda in the fridge. Being an Overseer didn't have a ton of perks, but being able to have your favorite local soda flown in from thousands of miles away was a nice one. He grabbed one of the bottles, twisted the cap off and tossed it into the trash can in one fluid movement. He then headed into the study. As he looked around the very impressive, very full, library it struck him how lucky he was that nobody ever asked to come over. It is one thing to have a full library in your house but as he looked around, he realized how crazy it would seem. The average age of the books in Gavril's library was probably close to eight hundred years old, and almost all of them were covered in symbols. Many of those symbols had become associated with witchcraft and Satanism over the years, despite having innocuous meaning in Oromatic language, the official Overseer language. Luckily the official Overseer symbol, which was a double infinity sign made to look like there was an eye in the middle with two crossed letter T's below, had never been picked up by the public.

Oromatic is a logographic language with alphabetic elements. It is quite similar to Egyptian hieroglyphics, though the two share no common symbols. Over the millennia, many Overseers had lobbied to have the official language changed to something more modern. They usually wanted the language changed to whatever their native tongues happened to be, and usually because they had difficulty learning the ancient language. These requests never got very far though, because the Overseer Council always fell back to security. The fact was that all the texts, at least all the ones Gavril had, were written in a language that was not only dead but one that no non-Overseer linguist on the planet even knew existed.

About seventy years ago, someone got a copy of an Overseer's log and it ended up with a Harvard professor that specialized in dead languages. The professor began trying to decipher the log. Gavril had been the one assigned to get the journal back and destroy the professor's notes. The mission had been an easy one, but part of him always felt sorry for that professor. A man dedicated to studying and teaching a subject that so rarely had anything of the magnitude of the journal happen, came into possession of something that would send shockwaves through the language community, and unbeknownst to the professor, shockwaves through the world when he found out what it was about. Gavril had ruined that for him. Gavril had to keep tabs on the professor for several years after that to make sure that he didn't still have something on the journal and didn't find anything else on the Overseers. Gavril was saddened to see that the professor's life spiraled downward. All the professor cared about was finding more evidence of the Overseers. The professor lost his job a few years after Gavril took the journal, because he wasn't teaching effectively. The professor became even more obsessed and after losing his job, he traveled all over the world in search of proof of the language. The professor had actually gotten close a couple of times and Gavril had to make sure he came up empty handed. In the end the professor lost his drive to live and was checked into a nursing home until he died. Gavril still thought about the professor. He knew he had done the right thing, because it would be catastrophic if the world found out about Sevenths and Overseers, but he felt bad for the professor whose life was altered so much because he happened to be given a thoughtless Overseer's journal.

So now Gavril sat looking at the massive amount of books, all of which were his. He wasn't sure exactly where to start. He knew he had heard something about the headaches that Darrell described, but couldn't place where. It couldn't be a coincidence that Darrell had the headache near his node right after his vision. He decided to start with a book about Seventh health concerns. He took the book out to the living room and placed it on the coffee table. He walked over to the record player and put on the Charlie Parker album 'Bird and Diz'. In his immense lifetime he had heard countless forms of music but none came close to the perfection that was Charlie Parker on vinyl, and this album was the best of all. Charlie Parker, Dizzy Gillespie, Buddy Rich and Thelonious Monk on one album, it didn't get any better. He picked the book back up, stretched out on his chaise lounge and started reading. The book read like the world's most boring grocery list. It was so boring, that he couldn't help but read it in monotone, which was driving him nuts. He made it through the first chapter and checked the time. What had seemed like an hour had only been ten minutes. The most boring ten minutes of his life. It was going to be a long night.

He was on his third soda and fifth book before he found anything. According to the book, a headache similar to the one Darrell described would often happen when two Sevenths were interacting with each other. Gavril was annoyed at himself. As soon as he read it, he remembered it. He guessed it didn't occur to him because it never really came up. Sevenths were never supposed to be in the same town. Gavril couldn't believe it. Was there actually another Seventh in town? If bumping into the Seventh had given Darrell the headache, why had he gotten it from his vision? Did having a vision about another Seventh count as interacting? The book didn't mention anything about Sevenths having visions about other Sevenths, so Gavril checked a few more books, but still couldn't find any mention anywhere about it. He even called Gloria Ford, the researcher at the Overseer Headquarters library to see if she could find anything about it, but she came up empty as well. Gloria was one of the brightest researchers he had ever met. She reminded him of Marie in many ways. If she couldn't find anything, that didn't strike Gavril as good news. Gavril still didn't have the answer he wanted, so he decided to again swallow his pride and call Andrea.

"What is it now?" Andrea asked, picking up on the fifth ring.

"I have a question," Gavril said.

"Spit it out. I am in the middle of something," Andrea replied curtly. Gavril found this quite strange. Andrea was always very matter-of-fact in her tone, but seldom curt. She must have been dealing with something very serious to be this worked up.

"Are there any other Seventh's in town?"

"Not that I'm aware of, why?" Andrea asked curiously.

"Darrell ran into a guy today and got a vicious headache near his node. I did some research and remembered that is an indicator of two Sevenths interacting with one another."

"Research? Color me impressed," Andrea replied. Gavril couldn't tell if she was being sarcastic or not.

"Seriously, I think the guy may have been a Seventh."

"I'm glad that you did some research, but I would have hoped you would have been able to remember that fact without having to look it up. Did you do anything but waste time since your last Seventh assignment? If you would have kept up on your knowledge, you would have known that yes, the headache is one of the side effects of interacting with another Seventh. You would have also known that the side effects of the interactions are the primary reason we don't let Sevenths generally live in the same town as one another, especially a town as small as the one you're in. We always keep them separate, and if two Sevenths end up too close, we convince one to move. Since Sevenths almost always die before their own seventh son develops powers it is usually easy to accomplish. Your Seventh being adopted made it even easier."

"But that doesn't mean that there isn't another one here though. Right?"

"You're right. I guess it could be possible. Don't forget that if there was another Seventh in town his Overseer would fall into my territory and work for me, so I would know. I will, however, look into the possibility of someone vacationing there. I will also talk to the council and see if I can find anything out."

"There is one more thing I was thinking about. Remember I mentioned that Darrell had that pain after waking from his vision?"

"Sorry I haven't been able to ask about that yet. It has been pretty crazy here," Andrea replied. "Are you thinking they are connected?"

"Yeah. Since Darrell got the pain in the same spot when he had a vision and when he ran into the man, could that mean that he was having a vision about another Seventh? This kidnapper might be a Seventh."

"That is an interesting idea. I can't recall ever hearing about a Seventh having a vision of another Seventh, but I don't think it is impossible. I'll bring that up to the council as well. I certainly hope that the kidnapper wasn't a Seventh. That would be awful. In the meantime, how are you doing in subduing his powers?"

"I'm getting closer. Don't worry about me. I'll get the job done," Gavril replied. He tried to sound sure of himself, but he could tell his voice was failing him. Gavril knew he was falling down the rabbit hole with Darrell and was worried if he would be able to do his job.

"I am worried Gavril. This is turning into the same thing you did with Willie Stoddard. We can't have that again."

"This is not the same as Willie and besides that situation worked out okay, all things considered," He replied. He hated to admit it, but this was turning out an awful lot like Willie.

"It worked out, but I wouldn't go so far as saying it worked out okay, many people were seriously injured or killed. If my memory serves, you were nearly killed yourself, well as close to being killed as an immortal can be," Andrea replied.

"Whatever," Gavril replied. He was very annoyed. First at Andrea for dwelling on the past and then at himself for sounding and acting like a teenager, despite his age. Since when did he go around saying things like whatever? "That was a couple of hundred years ago. I swear you guys never let anything go. I'll talk to you later." Gavril didn't give her a chance to reply before he hung up the phone.

Now that Andrea brought it up, Gavril began to dwell on the similarities between this and Willie Stoddard. Of course there were more differences that similarities, but Gavril couldn't help but focus on the similarities, Gavril knew that he couldn't make the same mistakes he made with Willie. He had to be better this time.

CHAPTER THIRTEEN - DARRELL

Darrell was in a very deep sleep when the vision came to him. A young girl was kneeling down by her bright pink bike. Her chain had come off of the main sprocket and was dangling down, touching the ground. She obviously had no idea how to get it back on and was becoming visibly distraught, shaking her head vigorously, causing her long sandy blonde pig-tails to whip through the air violently. Then she flopped to the ground, sitting with her legs crossed. She put her head down and covered her face with her hands. Her shoulders were now moving up and down in a shaky rhythm. She was crying. He walked over and kneeled down beside her, placing his hand on her shoulder.

"That doesn't look like my hand," Darrell thought.

"It's going to be okay," he said. Darrell now realized that while he was seeing the vision from the point of view of the man, the man wasn't Darrell. He was seeing through someone else's eyes. Once he realized that, the entire thing felt a little disconcerting. Darrell couldn't be positive but the voice sounded like the voice of the man he ran into earlier. Was he really having a vision of him, or was this just a dream, and Darrell was just projecting his concerns over the man?

"If I don't get home soon my mom is going to be very mad at me, but I can't fix it," The little girl said, her words broken up by sobs she was struggling to control.

"Can you call her and let her know what happened?"

"I don't have a cellphone. She says I am not old enough for one. Do you have a phone I can use?" she asked.

"I'm sorry, I don't. I can try to help you fix your bike though."

"That would be great, thanks," She said wiping the tears from her face and perking up a little.

"Sounds like a plan," The man said. This definitely wasn't a dream. Darrell could feel the man's pulse rise as he knelt down. Darrell tried to scream out and tell the girl to run away, but he couldn't. Darrell wasn't in control. All he could do was watch. Part of Darrell's mind screamed at him to wake up, thinking that if he woke up it wouldn't happen. Darrell knew this wasn't true though. As awful as it was, Darrell knew he had to watch and hopefully see enough to stop it from happening in the real world.

The man began working the chain on the sprocket while turning the pedal.

"Can you hold the back of the bike up sweetheart?" he asked.

"Okay," she responded, grabbing the seat and pulling the back wheel off the ground.

The man worked the chain and pedal a little more, finally getting the chain on. He spun the pedal a few times to show her it was fixed. She put the back tire down again, and he took the opportunity to move the chain slightly off the sprocket. The man's pulse grew even faster.

"Let's see how she does," he said.

She got on the bike and made it only a few feet before the chain came off again. She fell over, and landed in the grassy lawn. Darrell could tell the man smiled but quickly suppressed it. He could feel the man forcing himself to stay calm and not get overly aggressive. Darrell had never had a vision quite like this before. He was not just seeing the events take place, he was living them. Darrell could feel the man's emotions and it was sickening.

"Oh no. Looks like it might be really broken," the man said.

"My mom is going to be so mad," she said, fighting back tears again.

"We can't have that now can we? How about I give you a ride home so you are not late, and then I can tell her I broke the chain so you won't get in trouble," she said.

"You would do that for me?" she asked. Darrell tried again to scream and tell the girl that she should run, but nothing happened.

"Of course I would! That's what friends are for. My car is right over here; let's go," he said as he put his hand on her shoulder and began guiding her.

The vision began to change. The point of view began to shift from Darrell seeing things through the kidnapper's eyes, to pulling back so he could see the back of the man and the girl. Darrell's mind frantically began searching for ways to identify the man and where this was happening, but in the end he didn't need to. After taking a few steps, the kidnapper stopped and turned around so that he was facing Darrell's point of view. It was the guy from earlier that went into the creepy house. The man looked right at Darrell, smiled and then winked.

Darrell sat straight up, waking with a start. It was early morning and he could see the first rays of sunlight coming through the window.

"It's him! It's him!" Darrell yelled as he got up and headed toward the conference room, knocking over a lamp and nearly tripping over the large wingback chair.

He found Marie asleep with her head down on the table next to her laptop. She had obviously fallen asleep while researching. He couldn't help but think about how beautiful and peaceful she looked, but it only lasted for a moment before he grabbed her shoulder and began shaking her awake.

"It's him! It's him!" he repeated.

"What the hell are you going on about?" she asked, trying to rub the sleep from her eyes.

"The guy from the house, he is the kidnapper."

"Wait, what? You said the kidnapper had long hair, but that guy had short hair," She was suddenly wide awake.

"He must have cut it. I just had another vision and it was him. He kidnapped another kid," Darrell said as he reached over, grabbed a nearby trash can and vomited into it. What was going on? Why was he getting sick to his stomach after visions now? This time was much worse than last time, and he couldn't remember ever feeling this nauseous before.

"How can you be sure it wasn't just a dream, and why are you vomiting?"

"That's how I know it wasn't just a dream. Remember before, when I told you that when I had that vision about the original kidnapping I woke up feeling queasy with the headache? Well, I feel that way again, hence the throwing up and proving it was not a dream. I guess that is a new side effect of the visions. This is our guy. What were you able to find out about him?" Darrell decided not to tell her how he really knew it wasn't a dream and how he had felt the emotions of the kidnapper. He wasn't quite sure why he felt the need to hide this information, but something told him that he should keep it to himself.

"Not much, I'm afraid. I didn't have much to go on. The house was bought by a man named Laurel Franks in the sixties. He died recently but I haven't been able to find his will yet to see who he left the house to and the deed hasn't been transferred yet. I'm sure I can get the info, but I have never looked into wills before, so I'm still not sure where to find them digitally. I need to know this guy's name to really start the ball rolling. Tell me about the vision; you said he kidnapped another kid?" she asked.

"In the vision he kidnapped someone else, but I am not sure if it has already happened yet. This time it was a little girl."

"Let's go through the vision and see if we can figure out something. Where did it happen?"

"It was in a neighborhood. A little girl's bike was broken. He helped her fix it, and then he sabotaged it again to give himself an excuse to drive her home," Darrell replied, closing his eyes to concentrate on remembering the vision.

"The neighborhood, did you recognize it? Your grid had his house in it, so maybe you were in the girl's neighborhood today."

"No. I don't think I recognized it. The houses were much larger and more expensive than the ones I went through today," Darrell concentrated to try to think of anything that could help identify the area.

"What about his car, did you see his car?"

"No. I woke up before they got to his car. Wait!" Darrell said, coming to a sudden realization "I think I may have seen it. This vision was very different. I saw just about everything from his eyes." Darrell hadn't meant to say that part.

"And you saw his car?"

"I'm not sure, but there was a point when he glanced around and I saw a car not far from him that didn't fit."

"What do you mean, it didn't fit?"

"Like I said, all the houses were expensive, so it was a high income neighborhood. All the cars in the driveways were high end as well, like BMWs and Mercedes. This car was an old beat up Ford Taurus, and it was parked on the street. I bet none of those residents would be caught dead in that car. So it had to have been his," Darrell said.

"That's a start. How about the license plate, could you see it?"

"I only saw part of it. There was a bush blocking the other part. The first three were a C a J and a 4," Darrell said after some concentration.

"That's more than enough to get me started. Get Gavril over here while I start digging," Marie said as she pulled her laptop toward her and immediately began typing.

Darrell went back out to their makeshift living room to give Gavril a call. Part of him felt bad for not telling Marie about how the vision was different and how the kidnapper smiled and winked at him at the end of his vision. He still wasn't sure exactly what to make of it, and he didn't need Marie or Gavril being sidetracked worrying about him or what it meant. They still needed to find this guy. Darrell was already concerned about them worrying about his nausea and headaches. He wished he could hide it, but vomiting in front of Marie meant that ship had sailed. Perhaps he could get Marie to agree to not say anything to Gavril about it since Gavril was the one that seemed most concerned. Gavril seemed dead set on convincing Darrell to stop using his visions. Darrell still couldn't figure out Gavril's motive on that front. Was he truly concerned for Darrell's safety, or was the motive more selfish? Perhaps Gavril was jealous. Darrell didn't really believe that was true, but he did find it strange that a guy he had known for only ten months would be so concerned for his safety. Gavril had always been a little bit weird, but that was downright strange.

"Hello?" Gavril asked as he answered the phone.

"Gav, I need you to get down to HQ."

"Dude, it's like five in the morning. Don't you guys ever sleep?"

"This is important. I had another vision."

"Really? What happened?"

118

"I'll explain everything when you get here, just make it quick."

"Okay, give me a few minutes to get ready and I'll be on my way," Gavril said as he hung up the phone.

"Anything yet?" Darrell asked as he made his way back into the conference room.

"A couple of things, but I want to wait until Gavril gets here."

"Why can't you just tell me now?"

"Because I only have so much time. If I have to explain everything twice, that is less time I have to research. Less research could lead to missing an important piece of information, so please let me work."

"Fine, I just hope he hurries. By the way, it is probably best if we keep the vomiting to ourselves. No need to make Gavril worry, okay?"

"Sure, but you may want to clean out the trash can," Marie said as she went back to her laptop and began typing furiously.

CHAPTER FOURTEEN - GAVRIL

Gavril hung up the phone and stretched, trying to shake the cobwebs of sleep out of his head. He had been up until at least two a.m. researching, and although Overseers needed less sleep than normal people, two hours after the days he had been having was not enough. Unfortunately, he had the sinking feeling that things were going to get worse before they got better. He was still trying to find more examples of Sevenths having the headaches Darrell described, and he was only able to find a few examples from Seventh journals.

Each adult Seventh was asked to keep a journal of all their visions, and what happened in the real-life events of the vision, so the Overseer Council could try to decipher why the visions didn't always match, though in several thousand years they were no closer to understanding this flaw. Overseers usually encouraged the Sevenths to record their daily life and feelings as well. This would not only help give more insight, it would help the Sevenths cope with the severe mental and psychological strain being a Seventh brought. A few of the Seventh journals that Gavril owned had mentioned the headaches, but Gavril figured there must have been more mentions that were left out in the copying process. All of Gavril's journals were copies. One of the superficial things that Overseers always competed against each other with, was the size of one's library. This was followed by how many original journals you owned. The original journal almost always went to the Overseer that worked with the Seventh once that Seventh died. That reduced the potential number of Gavril's originals right off the top since he naturally had overseen fewer Sevenths. Gavril never placed much importance on the library thing anyway, so he had sold off his originals years ago, and had been paid handsomely.

Gavril almost always preferred copies, since they were always annotated and had appendices that made it easy to scan for just the information you needed. He had never been as pleased at that ability as he was last night. One of the downsides though was that sometimes the person copying the original text would leave out or miss things. Particularly when it came to the Seventh's margin notes. Without the benefits of the copies, it would have taken him days, if not weeks, to get through all of those journals. Gavril and one of his peers, Othos, had petitioned the council to begin transferring all of their knowledge to a digital format to allow all the Overseers to have easier access to everything, not just what they had in their library. There was a process to submit research requests to one of the central libraries and an in-house researcher would do the research and get back to you. Gavril has used them several times over the years and found their results hit or miss. Recently he began calling the best researcher, Gloria Ford, directly. She wasn't supposed to do that and depending who was around she couldn't always help him. He would greatly prefer to be in control of his own research rather than leave it up to chance on whether or not you got a good researcher, especially since some of the researchers were in place as a punishment, not because they had research skills.

Unfortunately, since Gavril and Othos were both teenage in appearance, they were always treated as such. Their combined age was over five thousand years old but they were only ever seen as children. In general though, Gavril never complained about it since it often meant he was not asked to do things that were important. Unfortunately, it also meant he was never taken seriously. The only reason he got the assigned the Harvard professor was because he could pass for a college student.

Gavril was still getting dressed when his phone rang again. Andrea's eternally frowning face showed on his Caller ID. She always hated that picture, which made him want to keep it all the more. This can't be good, Gavril thought. Why is she calling here so early, which is even earlier for her time zone?

"Hi Andrea, what's going on?"

"Gavril, sorry for the early call but I am still up from last night and wanted to call before I fell asleep."

"You are still up? What is going on over there?"

"Trust me, you don't want to know."

"I'm pretty sure that means that I do want to know.

Anyway, what is so important that you needed to call?"

"After our conversation, I started to dig into whether or not another Seventh could be there."

"And did you find one?"

"Maybe."

"Maybe, what do you mean maybe? The Council knows where everyone is."

"Usually you would be right but there is one situation going on that has them uncertain. The Seventh's name is Gary Franks. By most accounts he was a bad person long before he developed his powers."

"How so?" Gavril asked.

"Gary has been in and out of juvenile hall or jail since he was fifteen years old. His father began having children at a very early age with several women. Because he started so young and had multiple women pregnant at the same time, his seventh son, Gary, was born when his father was only twenty. Gary was his father's last child, and his father actually stayed with him and his mother for a while. In fact his father stayed until his father began developing his powers. Gary's father struggled with his new powers and took off. Gary didn't handle the abandonment well and went kind of crazy, for lack of a better word. His first major arrest was for beating the mother of two of his older half-brothers until she was in a coma. Gary had blamed her for his father leaving town for some reason or another. Before the cops found Gary, those two brothers did, and despite outnumbering him, Gary put both boys in the hospital. One of them even suffered permanent brain damage."

"That's awful," Gavril said.

"Like I said, that was only the beginning. The council

had of course paid attention to him since they knew he was going to develop powers. The council even had a controversial vote when Gary was in his mid-twenties of whether or not to kill him before he developed his powers. Some council members were terrified of what a man with such problems would do with them. Obviously, in the end, they voted not to but it was a very close vote," Andrea said.

"Wow. It must be pretty rare that the council even thinks about killing someone before their powers develop," Gavril replied.

"I have only seen it once personally. If you had seen this man's list of crimes, the vote would come as no surprise, although the outcome of the vote might. It seems like Sofia Amaya, the head of the U.S. Council campaigned heavily against killing him and persuaded some other members to vote her way."

"Weird. That doesn't sound like her at all. I would have thought it would have been the other way around actually."

"I thought the same thing," Andrea replied.

"So how do they not know where he is?"

"Gary developed his powers last year, and as was feared, he went off the rails. His Overseer had been planted for a couple of years to try to make sure he was on a good path when his powers finally came. His Overseer was a woman named Eilana Isidora." Andrea said.

"I know Eilana. I worked with her on a couple of occasions in the past. She is really good," Gavril said.

"I have always heard great things about her. Like I said, she was planted years ago. The council decided against her being open with him and had her go in undercover. By all accounts she did a great job. They became very good friends. She was able to keep him on the straight and narrow by redirecting his aggression. The two of them did every adrenaline junkie sport you could think of and it really seemed to help him avoid criminal behavior. I get the feeling that several people on the council were secretly hoping he would just kill himself doing that stuff. Everything changed when he got his powers. His first vision that he told Eilana about was about a woman falling in front of a subway train. So she was a little concerned right away, since normally he would have had several small visions for many months or more likely years before having such an important vision, and he had kept them secret. She believed they were closer friends than that."

"That's interesting. Darrell's first important vision was of a woman stepping in front of a car and it was after only a few months. Pretty similar."

"That is quite interesting. Anyway, his vision showed him the time and date, so he was set up for success. He confided in Eilana about the vision and how he felt compelled to go there. Eilana followed him to see him save the woman, because she was so excited that he seemed to really be turning the corner. The time came and Gary positioned himself right next to the lady, but when the subway came, he just let her fall," Andrea said.

"He knew she was going to die and he went there to watch it happen instead of saving her?" Gavril asked.

"Yes. Worse than that, is that during the commotion, he picked up the woman's purse and cellphone that she dropped and took them home."

"That is crazy. I have heard of a few Sevenths going crazy over the years but nobody doing anything so psychotic."

"Me either. Anyway, after that Eilana decided hiding the fact that she was an Overseer wasn't the best idea. She came out and hoped that she could get him to good things with his visions. Well, no one is quite sure what happened next, but the general consensus is that he became enraged that she had been lying to him about who she was and he killed her. Of course her being immortal, we would expect her to report back in when she came back to life. Unfortunately though, nobody has heard from her. We think he may have killed her in a way that prevents reanimation. There are people searching for her body as we speak."

"How would he even know to do that? It isn't like we go around advertising it."

"Who knows? Maybe it was by accident."

"Wow, I can't believe Eilana is missing. So why do you think he might be here?" Gavril asked.

"After Eilana's boss lost contact, they began to search for Gary. They found that he had inherited a house in Junctionville from a distant relative. The council is apparently taking a slow approach though as they don't want to risk losing any more people, so they haven't even looked to see if he is in the house. For all we know at this point, he could have fled the country. I really am quite surprised how Sofia and the council are handling this case. It seems like it would be a top priority, but they seem to be treating it like it is no big deal. In fact it was very hard for me to get this information. I got it from Landon Williams. He said that Sofia told them not to talk to anyone about Gary, but you know Landon. He will always do what he feels is right."

"That is so strange that she would want it secret. Maybe she is worried about a scandal and losing her position. I know what you mean about Landon though, without even meaning to, he makes me feel like I need to be a better person. For the record, I don't think Gary has fled. I think he is right here in Junctionville, and I think he is the guy kidnapping these kids."

"Kids? I thought it was only one?" Andrea asked.

"Darrell just called and said he had another vision. I am assuming there was another kidnapping from the way he sounded."

"Another vision? You are supposed to stop them," Andrea said.

"Andrea, you know as much as I do that once a Seventh focuses on something so big, there is virtually no way to stop them. Besides, we need to stop this monster before anyone else gets hurt."

"I have tickets on a flight in a couple of hours so I'll be there in about six hours or so."

"That really isn't necessary," Gavril replied.

"Of course it is."

"Really it isn't. We can handle this. You take care of your situation up there."

"Are you sure?" Andrea asked.

"I am."

"You need to at least get the police involved so they can catch him and keep everyone else safe until the Council can get involved and take care of Gary," Andrea said.

"He will see the police coming a mile away."

"Perhaps he will. But don't forget that he will also see

Darrell coming. I am responsible for you and Darrell, not the police officers. I need you to promise me you guys will stay away."

"Andrea, as much as I respect you, you know that I can't promise that."

"You know despite being thousands of years old, you still act like a teenager."

"Just playing the part, Andrea. I know this may get you in trouble but this is something I have to do. Knowing that he may have done something to Eilana makes me even angrier. I have to catch this guy." Gavril hadn't felt this way in a couple of hundred years and part of him knew from that experience that Andrea was right and the best thing for everyone would be to let the police handle it. He wished he could turn his emotions off and do the right thing, but having seen so much death in his lifetime, nobody treasured life more than Gavril, and this man spat in the face of Gavril's ideals. Being a Seventh was a divine calling and was such a wonderful gift. This psychopath was using his gifts for harm and for harming kids no less and Gavril couldn't sit idly by and let him continue.

"I know," Andrea said. "There is one more thing I think you should know."

"What's that?" Gavril asked.

"According to the Landon it isn't a coincidence that Gary inherited that house in Junctionville. Junctionville is where he is from originally," Andrea said.

"You mean?"

"Yes, Landon says that Gary is Darrell's father. Apparently Gary moved away shortly after Darrell turned five because he was wanted for questioning in a jewelry store robbery. Darrell's mother gave him up for adoption not long after Gary left."

"I guess that explains the similar visions. This really is not good. Darrell will be devastated by that. His adoptive parents have always told him his father was a war hero that died in a firefight while fighting in the Middle East. They said his mother was killed in a car crash."

"You can't blame them, the truth is not very pretty. I don't think you should tell him, at least not until this is all over," Andrea said.

"Yeah, I agree. He is going to hate me for keeping this from him, but telling him could send him into a downward spiral. I'll tell him when the time is right, although right now, I can't think of when that might be. Thanks for the info Andrea, but I need to get to Darrell and Marie and see what his new vision is about," Gavril said.

"Please keep me updated on any new developments, and please keep them safe until the Council gets there," Andrea said.

"I will. Talk you later," Gavril said, and hung up the phone.

Gavril wasn't sure how to take it all in. On the one hand, he was glad he had a decent lead on the person he was now sure was the kidnapper, but at what cost. Going against another Seventh was a daunting task under any circumstances. Going against one that was as vicious as Gary seemed to be was a very scary proposition. He needed to figure out what to say and how to guide them toward Gary Franks without blowing his cover. He knew he would eventually have to come clean to Darrell about being an Overseer, but now wasn't the time. Darrell was already struggling with his visions. To add that one of his best friends was actually a two-thousand year old immortal assigned to spy on him, and that the psychopath they were trying to catch was his father, was likely more than a young man could handle. Not to mention that Gavril was pretty sure the girl Darrell was in love with was gay. If Gavril wasn't carful, Darrell's entire world would come crashing down around him.

Gavril threw his jacket on, grabbed his phone, and headed out the door. He still didn't know what he should do, but he did know that he needed to help make sure Darrell, Marie and the kidnap victims were safe. He hopped on his bike and headed to HQ. As he rode his bike down Main Street, which was lit up by streetlights wrapped in garland and made to look like giant candy canes, he thought that in all of his assignments over the years, he couldn't recall ever being so nervous.

CHAPTER FIFTEEN - GAVRIL

Gavril walked into the HQ conference room and for the second time in as many days, was taken aback. Marie was standing in front of a giant whiteboard on wheels that looked like something straight out of an episode of CSI. She had taped dozens of pages on the board. Some were pictures, others maps and a few even seemed like police reports. There were many lines of string that Gavril assumed were showing that some of the things were somehow connected. None of it made immediate sense to Gavril but one thing stood out above all others, the name Gary Franks in big bold letters across the top middle of the board. Marie's talents never ceased to amaze him. How on earth did she figure out who Gary was? One thing is for sure, he was glad they had made the connection to Gary on their own. He still wasn't sure how he planned to steer that boat.

"So what's the big news?" Gavril asked.

"Darrell had another vision, and we are pretty sure we know who the kidnapper is," Marie said.

"Really? Let's hear it," Gavril said, feigning surprise.

"The short version is that I had a vision last night and saw this guy," Darrell said as he pointed to the mugshot of the man that Gavril assumed must have been Gary, right in the middle of the board. "He was kidnapping a little girl, and he is definitely the same guy from the creepy house yesterday. Marie did some digging and once we had a starting point she was able to work her magic. She found not only his name but darn near his entire life story, which by the way is a pretty bad one," Darrell said.

"I also was able to get this," Marie said, pointing to another photo on the board. The picture was obviously taken from a traffic cam and showed Gary Franks driving.

"You certainly weren't overselling the creep factor on this guy Darrell," Gavril said. Gavril found himself wondering how Eilana was able to do it for all those years. Gary had such a bad history and really did look extra creepy. Gavril had met many people over the years and had been surprised many times when a person's personality didn't fit what society said their appearance showed. He tried to never judge a book by its cover. This guy was different though. It only took one look to see that something was off with him. Gavril also decided he was quite angry at Sofia and the U.S. Council. They knew Gary was as bad as a guy could get and they sent Eilana in to watch him. Now she was missing and Gavril felt like it was, at least partially, their fault.

"You have no idea. This guy is a really bad dude, Gav. He has convictions in theft, aggravated battery and everything in-between. Those are only the things he was convicted of. He was tried for attempted murder as well but the main witness recanted their story. He also has a conviction as a juvenile that is sealed, so who knows what that is for. We have to get to this guy before he hurts the kids," Darrell said, quite visibly amped up and ready to go. Gavril had seen that look before in young men going to war. They always got amped up on righteous indignation and ran into battle only to be pulled out in a body bag.

"I told you. We need to play this smart. We can't just go in guns blazing, so to speak," Marie said. Gavril smiled internally, glad that she said what he was thinking.

"She's right. We need to think this through. We know who he is and we know where he is, or at least where he is staying, right?" Gavril asked.

"Right. We need to get in there and find the kids," Darrell said.

"I think we need to get the cops involved. We should call them and say that we saw the kid from the news going into that house with a guy. They will come check it out and God willing save the kid. If they do it fast enough they can hopefully stop him from getting this other kid from your vision," Gavril said.

"You really think the boy is still okay?" Darrell asked.

"I do, or at least I need to believe he is," Gavril replied. Gavril couldn't let himself believe anything different. Gavril, and he assumed most of the other Overseers, really believed in their cause. Using a Seventh's powers to save people and protect society was what made it all worthwhile.

Living forever was in many ways a curse and could really take a toll on a person psychologically. Knowing that his personal suffering helped the world in a broader sense helped Gavril get through the tough times. Even though Gavril's job was to convince underage Sevenths from using their powers, some of those Sevenths eventually went on to do amazing things after they were old enough to use their powers. The fact that a man like Gary Franks would abuse his powers to cause harm, especially to children, was something Gavril couldn't stand for.

"I really don't know about the cops. They didn't believe me last time I called," Darrell said.

"I'll call this time and use my adult voice. I really think this is the safest bet. Marie, what do you think?" Gavril asked.

"I agree with Gavril. I mean the police really are the best equipped to handle the situation. We have done the hard work, now we can let them take care of the dirty work." Marie said.

"Okay, I guess we can go with your way and call the cops," Darrell reluctantly agreed.

Gavril was pleasantly surprised as to how little pushback the police had given him when he called. It was the complete opposite from Darrell's experience. Gavril thought his deeper voice had something to do with it, but he was pretty sure that the details sealed the deal. He hadn't dodged questions about who he was, which he knew also helped. Marie had gotten him all the info he needed to say that he was Mr. Nelson, the man who lived only a few houses away from Gary. That info, coupled with the specific details he gave about Gary and the house, and the police had no choice but to take him seriously.

The trio decided they wanted to see Gary caught, so

they made their way to his house. They found a nice hiding spot in a group of hedges one house away. Once they moved the ridiculous amounts of lights and tinsel they had an excellent view. They were a little worried that they were not going to arrive in time but were surprised to see that the police had not arrived yet.

They waited for what seemed like hours, though it was closer to fifteen minutes, before a police cruiser pulled into the driveway. You could feel the nervous energy behind the hedge as the two officers got out of the car and headed toward the front door. Officer one, who was obviously in charge, knocked on the door as he motioned the second officer to move to the side of the house. A moment later the officer gave a second knock, this time much louder. The knock was so loud that the trio could hear it despite the distance. The officer waited another moment and gave a third knock, this time with the butt of his flashlight, with still no answer. The trio watched as the officers began to peek into the windows of Gary's house. The officers obviously didn't see anything out of the ordinary in the front or side, so they headed to the back of the house. Darrell, Gavril and Marie waited in growing anticipation but were hit with stinging disappointment a moment later when the two officers came around and got back into their car. The officers were too far away for the trio to hear, but their body language told them all they needed to know: nobody was home, and they were leaving.

"Where in the hell are they going?" Darrell asked nobody in particular.

"Looks like they gave up when nobody answered," Marie said.

"Obviously, but why, when we gave them such specific info? Don't they believe us?" Darrell asked.

"I don't know if that's the case but I guess they didn't have probable cause to go in," Gavril said.

"I do." Darrell said, standing up from his hiding place.

"What does that mean?" Gavril asked, not wanting the answer he knew was coming.

"It means I'm going in myself," Darrell said, already walking toward the house.

"That is really not the best idea Darrell," Gavril said, struggling to keep up with Darrell's long stride without running. "Tell him, Marie."

"Honestly, I'm not sure I agree with you Gavril," Marie said, having no trouble keeping up.

"Wait, please!" Gavril said, reaching out and stopping both of them by the arm. "We need to discuss this before someone gets hurt."

"You're right. Someone could get hurt. Those kids could get hurt. That psycho has them in that house, doing lord knows what to them. I can't sit idly by and let something more happen to them when I could potentially stop it. I could never live with myself if I did. Are you telling me you could, Gavril?" Darrell asked.

Gavril was completely conflicted. He knew that Darrell was right. Gavril would struggle for the rest of his long life knowing that he could have potentially stopped Gary if something ended up happening to the kids. Gavril also knew that his primary responsibility was protecting Darrell and by proxy, Marie. Gavril was left with an impossible choice of whose life was more important. Gavril knew he would have to hope that the safety of one group was not mutually exclusive and if everything went right he would be able to make sure that everyone was safe.

"I get it," Gavril said. "But at the same time, I couldn't live with myself if something happened to you two."

"Then I guess you're just gonna have to come with us to make sure we are safe then," Darrell said, giving Gavril just the slightest hint of a smile.

"Fine, let's get off the street before we attract too much attention," Gavril said.

CHAPTER SIXTEEN - GAVRIL

The trio made their way to the back of the house, and began looking for a way in.

"Whoa, we don't really have to do that, do we?" Gavril said right as Darrell was about to break the window on the back door.

"He didn't exactly leave us a key, did he?" Darrell asked.

"If we break in, he will know we have been here. We need the element of surprise if they are still in there. Let me try," Gavril said.

Gavril pulled the lock pick kit out of his back pocket and knelt down to be eye level with the door handle.

"What is that? Why do you have a lock pick set?" Marie asked.

"A man has to have his secrets," Gavril replied with a sly grin.

"I'll remember that when you become a man," she said.

"Very funny. May I get to work now?"

"By all means, show us what kind of criminal mastermind you are. I would like to point out though, that you were the one against breaking into the house and yet you are the one that turns out to be best equipped to do so," Marie said.

Marie did have a point. Gavril didn't really want to show them that he could do things like pick locks, because that was bound to raise questions, but he couldn't let them go around breaking windows or they would all end up in jail. It took Gavril only a few seconds to open the door. He slowly opened it, wincing at every creak of the very old, very dilapidated door. He motioned for them to follow and put his finger to his lips, letting them know he wanted them to be quiet. He squatted and pulled up his right pant leg, revealing a large survival knife in a sheath attached to his ankle. He unsnapped the piece of leather while holding the knife in place. He pulled out the knife and stood up holding the shining eight inch blade in front of his face. He looked at Darrell who just stared back with a look of surprise, mouthing the words 'What the hell'.

He looked over at Marie and saw her pull her handheld flashlight/stun gun combo. Gavril was always impressed with that piece of technology. By all appearances and functions it was a fairly bright flashlight, but touch the butt end to someone and press the stun button and the stun gun part would activate. When she got it, Darrell agreed to be the test subject since he was the biggest person they knew. He instantly fell down and wasn't able to do anything. All of his muscles seized up and he began involuntarily shaking. Gavril began laughing so hard the he couldn't catch his breath. He felt a little bad later, but it really was funny.

Darrell threw his hands up in the air and began mouthing some more swear words as he now eyed Marie's stun gun. He backed up a step or two, perhaps still afraid of her stun gun, and showed his empty hands, palms up, as if to say he had no weapons. Marie reached into her back pocket and pulled the pocket knife she had loaned him previously. Darrell reached out, took the knife and quickly opened the blade. Gavril looked at Darrell, who was noticeably relieved, and gave him thumbs up as to ask if he was good to go now. The three slowly searched each room one by one with Gavril in the lead, until they had covered the entire floor. Gavril stopped in front of the basement door. Darrell nodded his head and got in an aggressive stance facing the basement door.

Gavril slowly twisted the door knob, and pulled the door open as quickly and quietly as possible. He had learned his lesson from the back door, and decided one quick squeak was much better than going slowly and having one really long squeak. There was nothing but blackness ahead of them as they looked down into the basement. Marie motioned to her flashlight and then motioned as if saying she should go first. Gavril wasn't keen on that idea, so he just reached over and flipped the basement light on and headed down into the basement. He caught a glimpse of Marie and Darrell having a wordless exchange, obviously not agreeing with the idea of turning the light on, but he would much rather lose the element of surprise than let Marie go into potential danger first. Besides, he thought, if the light was off, there wasn't much chance of Gary being down there. They got down into the basement and were disappointed to find nothing. It was much more of a root cellar than a true basement. The room was quite small, and only contained a few shelves full of pickled and canned vegetables.

"Nothing here," Gavril said, stating the obvious. He had hoped that somehow Gary would still be at the house, but deep down he knew that they couldn't catch a Seventh by surprise like this.

"The whole house is a bust," Darrell said. "It looks un-lived in. Almost like he moved out, trying to remove any trace he was here."

"Yeah, I know what you mean. It's almost too empty. I mean, all the furniture and stuff was left but it's like a show house with no signs of life," Marie said.

"A filthy show house," Darrell said.

"The filthiest," Marie replied.

"It's like he knew we were coming. I must have really spooked him when I ran into him yesterday," Darrell said.

"I guess, but how would he have known you were going to call the cops?" Marie asked.

"Maybe he was just overly cautious, you know?" Darrell replied.

Gavril was really not sure what to say. Part of him really wanted to tell them about Gary and how he knew they were coming, but that would mean blowing his cover. He had no idea of how Darrell would react at this point. He could be really hurt and cut Gavril out completely. He decided it wasn't worth the risk at this point, since there was no real reward for coming clean yet.

"There is no need for us to stay here any longer, especially since we are here illegally. Let's go back to HQ and regroup," Gavril said.

"We could go through the traffic cameras and see if we can find and follow him to see where he went," Marie said.

"I just hope he didn't leave town," Darrell said. Gavril silently agreed. If Gary left town, it would make catching him exponentially harder and would certainly make it less likely that they would get the kids back unharmed.

They made their way outside, no longer being careful. They were about to head around the front of the house when Marie stopped them.

"What is that?" Marie said, pointing to a metal dome about double the size of a doghouse.

"A doghouse?" Gavril said.

"No, it's too big, and who has a metal doghouse?" Marie asked.

They walked over, and once Gavril saw the door on the other side, he knew what it was. The door was about three quarters of the size of a normal door, but was obviously for a human and not an animal. It looked to be made of steel and was quite old. Time had taken its toll on the door and surrounding structure but both still looked to be in working condition.

"It's a bomb shelter," Gavril said.

"A what?" Darrell asked.

"A bomb shelter, from the Cold war," Gavril said, getting blank faces from Marie and Darrell. "Wow, your history teachers should be ashamed. After World War II there were strong tensions between America and some other nations, mostly the Soviet Union, and there was a large fear that a nuclear war was imminent. After seeing the devastation in Hiroshima, Americans became afraid that the same thing may happen here and began building bomb shelters for them to use in case the bombs came. A typical bomb shelter was buried in the ground with concrete walls at least a foot thick and stocked with non-perishable food. The idea was that you could live in there until the radiation fallout subsided."

"So in other words, the perfect place to hold kidnapped kids," Darrell said as he tried to turn the doorknob, which was locked.

"I agree, but let's be careful. He could still be in there," Gavril said as he pulled his lock pick kit back out. Again, Gavril knew Gary wouldn't be in there, but maybe he got scared because he was being chased and decided to leave the children. Hopefully unharmed.

Gavril picked the lock, stood up and began to count silently using his fingers to show he was counting to three. On three he turned the knob, and yanked the door wide open, again revealing nothing but black. He didn't see a light switch so he motioned to Marie to give him her flashlight, trading his knife, so he could go first. The walk down the stairs was a disturbing one. The stairs were very old and very creaky, giving the descent a soundtrack right out of a horror movie. The flashlight, while bright, had a very small direct beam. As he swung it around, it only gave spotlight views of everything, which added to the horror movie vibe. Gavril went through life knowing he was immortal, so he never usually feared death or things that might lead to death. He had to admit however that he was frightened by the current situation. As he reached the bottom of the stairs and began to swing the flashlight around he was blinded by a sudden influx of light.

Someone had turned on the lights. As he frantically turned, simultaneously looking for who turned the lights on and trying to get his eyes to adjust, he saw Darrell standing by the light switch. He also noticed Marie giving Darrell a look that could kill. Apparently, she had been as surprised as Gavril.

"Sorry guys. I thought the overhead light would help," Darrell said, suddenly getting a strange look on his face. He was looking past Gavril and obviously staring at something or someone.

"What is it?" Gavril said, not wanting to turn around.

"This is the place, or at least was the place," Darrell said.

Gavril turned around and immediately saw what Darrell was talking about. Right in the middle of the shelter stood two cages. The sides of the cages were made of steel bars going vertically, giving the appearance of small jail cells. The cages seemed to be too large for keeping animals but too small for keeping most adults comfortably. Gavril wondered briefly if the cages were homemade and how long Gary had been planning the kidnappings. Gavril walked over to the now empty cages, meeting up with Darrell who had wasted no time checking them out.

"They were here," Darrell said, gripping one of the bars so hard his knuckles turned white.

"You're sure?" Marie asked, still near the stairs, obviously not wanting to get any nearer to the cages.

"This hat is the one the little girl was wearing in my second vision," Darrell said. "And the jacket was the little boy's. So that means my vision was not of the future. We're too late. We're too late for either of them."

"I'm not so sure about that," Marie said.

144

"What do you mean?" Gavril asked.

"I don't think we are too late to save them. Look at this place. I mean look around. This place is a lot like the house, in that it has been cleaned of all traces of being inhabited. Everything has been cleared except those two items and the two cages. It's like he wanted someone to find them. He wanted the police to know he had kidnapped them. It's like he is issuing a challenge. He is saying "You know who I am, and you still can't catch me.""

"That's a great point. I doubt he would do that if the kids were already dead. It's like he wants to play a game," Gavril said. Gavril wondered if Gary knew about Darrell's powers and if that is why he was issuing the challenge. He must know. A Seventh would know that the police would offer no challenge to him if was playing some sort of sick game. Gavril grew more worried the more he thought about it. Catching a deranged Seventh playing a sick game was not going to be easy and what if Gary knew about Darrell being his son?

"He is going to be sorry he played with me," Darrell said. He looked angrier than Gavril had ever seen him. Despite knowing how much of a softy Darrell was, that look combined with his size made Darrell a very intimidating figure.

"We need to get the police involved," Marie said.

"We already tried that once and how did that go?" Darrell asked.

"This time it will be different. Police have specific structure and laws they need to follow. This time I will tell them that I found the bomb shelter, and the kids' stuff. With me already having opened the shelter and finding the stuff, I think they will have the rights to search it," Marie said.

"But what will they do to you?" Darrell asked.

"I'm pretty sure they won't do anything. At worst I was trespassing. I'm pretty sure they would need the owner to press charges and I don't see him around anywhere. In the end, with what I found, I don't think they will do anything to me," Marie said.

"That's a pretty big risk," Gavril said.

"And one I'm willing to take. The police may be able to find some forensics in here that will help find those kids. That trumps any minor trouble I may get into," Marie said. Gavril could tell that she would not be swayed, and despite his better judgment, he thought she was right.

"I'll stay too," Darrell said.

"No. You two go back to HQ and check the traffic cams."

"You sure? Do you think you'll be okay here by yourself?" Darrell asked.

"I'll be fine," Marie said, holding up her flashlight/stun gun. "Besides, I don't see him coming back here. Do you remember how to get to the traffic cameras?" Marie asked.

"Yeah, I wrote down the instructions when you showed me before," Darrell said.

"Good, now you two get out of here. I have a call to make," Marie said, as she pulled out her phone and began calling 911.

CHAPTER SEVENTEEN - DARRELL

Darrell had been looking through the cameras for the past ten hours with no luck. Gavril had helped for the first five hours or so, but said he had something else he needed to do. Darrell couldn't think of anything more important than finding the kids but he tried not to be judgmental. Maybe Gavril had an idea that he didn't want to share with Darrell just yet. He could understand not wanting to continue watching the camera footage though. Not only was it mind numbingly boring, it had become painful. Darrell had been staring at those screens with such intense concentration for so long, that his eyes were about to revolt. He had only taken two breaks since he began. The first break was to shovel down some leftover pizza and a couple of cans of highly caffeinated soda, and the second one was to watch Marie on the five o'clock news. Apparently she had been right. The police were so happy to get the clues and find out who the kidnapper was that they didn't care about how she found them. She had told Gavril she overheard the police talking, and apparently they were getting a lot of pressure from the community to find the missing kids. She also said the police seemed very hopeful after the bomb shelter discovery.

She said that the news vans showed up right after the cops did, and the Channel Eight News reporter was interviewing her before she even knew what was going on. Darrell was impressed and a little concerned at how good of a liar she was as he watched her on the news. She must have really worked on her story while she waited for the police to arrive because she had it down pat. She almost had him believing that it went down like she said. He was surprised at how long her interview was, but Darrell figured the news stations were under pressure to fill time with the kidnappings. The missing children were by far the biggest local news story and the police weren't talking to the press at all. They kept replaying Marie's interview to fill time.

Darrell stood up, placed his hands on his hips and leaned back, stretching and cracking his back. He was never sure why he did that since it only felt good for a split second before it hurt worse than it had before. He rubbed his eyes, trying hopelessly to make them feel less strained. He decided that he needed to really take a break. At this point he was so fatigued that he was more likely to miss Gary's car. He went into the main room of their HQ and laid down on the couch. It was not only the longest couch Darrell had ever seen, it was the only one he had ever come across that his massive body could lay down on and not have his feet hanging over the end. He stretched one final time before turning on his side and closing his eyes.

His vision seemed to start almost immediately after falling asleep, and this vision felt different right from the start. Darrell could tell immediately that he was having a vision. Most of his previous ones had a mostly dream-like feel. Only after he woke up could he feel it was a vision, both physically and mentally. The last one was a little different since he could tell somewhat that it was a vision, but this one was something else entirely. Darrell felt the humming in his brain that told him this was a vision and felt a little bit like he was in the vision. Most of the previous visions felt like they had a distant point of view, like he was just observing from afar. There had been a few where he could control that point of view and the one that had the point of view from the eyes of Gary, but this one felt like he was completely in the vision and in total control of his movements. He wondered if this meant he was getting stronger or if this vision was special somehow.

Darrell was in a kitchen that he didn't recognize. He looked around for a few moments, trying to figure out where he was and trying his best to make note of anything that may be important in case this was about Gary. Suddenly, he heard a sound coming from another room so he walked out of the kitchen, and seemed to be in the back of a living room. There was a man on a couch watching TV. He changed the channel until he got to Marie giving her interview on the news.

"She really is a pretty little thing, don't you think? Perhaps she should join the game," the man said as he turned around, and now Darrell could see it was Gary.

"I'll kill you!" Darrell yelled as he started running at him.

"Not just yet," Gary said, raising his hand palm out as if to say stop.

Darrell couldn't move. He tried his hardest to make his way to Gary but his feet were stuck to the ground. He looked down at his feet and nothing was there, he just couldn't move them. He looked back up to Gary, confused and violently angry.

"You have a lot to learn Darrell," Gary said.

The next thing he knew, Darrell was awake. He laid on the couch for a few moments trying to figure out what just happened. He had been in more control than in any other vision he had previously, then he lost all control. It seemed like Gary had taken control. How did Gary know his name? Was his mind simply playing tricks because he was so tired? In nearly all of his previous visions the subjects of the visions were passive participants. The lone exception was the end of his previous vision where Gary winked at him. Now, Gary had talked to him and addressed him by name. What on earth did this mean? Darrell really didn't like having more questions than answers.

He went back through the vision and couldn't see anything that would tell him what house he was in. He thought more about what Gary had said about Marie. What did he mean by her joining the game? Darrell got a pit in his stomach, what if Marie wasn't safe?

He grabbed his phone and franticly dialed her number. It rang four times and then went to voicemail. He quickly redialed her number with the same result. Maybe she is somewhere she can't talk, he thought, and sent her a text message. He waited impatiently for a response that he somehow knew would never come. He called Gavril, hoping he had heard from her recently.

"Hey," Gavril said, picking up on the second ring.

"Gav, have you heard from Marie?"

"Not in a few hours. I talked to her after the TV interviews, and she said she was going home because the reporters were following her and she didn't want to lead them back to HQ. Why?"

"I had another vision, and I think Gary might be targeting her?"

"What happened in the vision?"

"Gary was watching her interview on the news. He said she was pretty and she should join the game. I don't know what it means but it doesn't seem good. She is not answering my calls or texts. We need to find her and make sure she is safe."

"I am closer to her house than you. How about I swing by, pick her up and we head to HQ?" Gavril asked.

"That sounds good. Please hurry," Darrell said.

"I'll call you as soon as I find her," Gavril said just before hanging up.

Darrell sat on the couch feeling helpless. He cared for her so much, he couldn't lose her. He was still healing from the death of his mother and this was just too much for him to take. He was questioning his decision to not tell Gavril about how weird his vision was, and how Gary had addressed him by name in it. He decided that it was best to not muddy the waters and distract Gavril for now. He knew it was weird, but didn't see any value in telling Gavril or Marie just yet.

CHAPTER EIGHTEEN - GAVRIL

Gavril hung up the phone and collapsed into his chair. He got the feeling that Darrell was hiding something from him, but Gavril knew it would do no good to confront him right now, besides he would feel really hypocritical asking Darrell to share his secrets while Gavril had so many big ones of his own.

Did Gary really have Marie? Gavril didn't know what to think. He had grown to really care about Marie, and his emotions were about to get the best of him. He sat there for a moment, trying to pull his emotions back and focus. He knew that if Darrell lost Marie so close to losing his mother, it would be too much. The early development of a Seventh's powers was almost always driven by a major emotional moment like Darrell's mother passing. Another tragic event so close would wreak havoc on his node. Since the node was still developing, that could potentially lead to Darrell becoming mentally unstable or even dying.

Gavril finally gathered himself. He knew he had a job to do, but the situation was now far more personal and emotional than simply a job. He jumped on his bike and pedaled faster than he even knew he could. He made it to Marie's house in a matter of minutes.

He knew that Marie's father hated Christmas, but seeing how bare Marie's house looked because of the lack of decoration compared to the others in the neighborhood struck Gavril as sad. He jumped off his bike and ran to the front door, ignoring the pain burning in his thighs. Marie's father answered on the second knock to see Gavril doubled over, trying to catch his breath. He was silently cursing his laziness. Gavril forced himself to stand and face Marie's father.

"Mr. Clarkson, can I talk to Marie?"

"She's not here. I thought she was with you?" Mr. Clarkson said.

"Oh she was, but we got separated," Gavril said quickly, trying to cover his tracks. "I figured she would come back home. You haven't heard from her?"

"No, I haven't seen her in a few hours. I saw her on the news and kind of freaked out on her for not telling me what happened. I shouldn't have to hear about something like that from the news. She should have told me. I was also really mad that she would put herself in a dangerous situation like that, and to put herself on the news talking about it could also be dangerous. She got really defensive and took off. She said she was going to meet up with you and Darrell. She never met up with you guys, did she?"

"Well actually, I was somewhere else so I'm sure she is with Darrell then," Gavril said, not wanting to scare

Marie's father.

"She isn't answering my phone calls. You tell her she better call me soon or she is going to be in even more trouble."

"I will Mr. Clarkson. Sorry to bother you. I'll let you get back to the game," Gavril said, picking up his bike.

"Seriously son, you tell her to call me. I'm worried, and if I don't hear from her soon I'm going to call the police."

"I'm sure there is nothing to worry about."

"That kidnapper knows what she looks like and knows she is the one that led them to his identity. There is plenty to worry about. You tell her to call me soon or I will have the police find her and bring her back home," Mr. Clarkson said.

"Yes sir," Gavril said.

Gavril got on his bike and started pedaling hard. He was not sure where his body was getting the strength, but he knew he needed to get to HQ quickly, and figure out where in the hell Marie was. Would Gary really have taken her? Mr. Clarkson did have a good point about the news showing Gary who was responsible for his name now being broadcast over every media outlet in the city. Not to mention his car and license plate being plastered all over the city on the AMBER alert bulletin boards. Gary could see the future, but not always the entire future. There was certainly the possibility that Gary hadn't foreseen this outcome and was upset about it. The more Gavril thought about it, the more he knew it was not only possible, it was probable. He was angry at himself for not realizing that major flaw in their plan. Gary was by all accounts an angry psychopath and he would certainly want to seek revenge.

There were so many questions. Would he kill her or hold her like some sort of pawn? Was Marie part of the plan from the beginning? Did Gary see how that would play out from the beginning? Gary might be getting flustered and knocked off his game and maybe that could be working in their favor.

In the end though, Gavril didn't know what to think. Were the other kids still alive? There had been no blood or other signs of him hurting the children in the bomb shelter, which had to be good news. Gavril thought that if Gary was playing some sort of a twisted game, he would want people to think the kids were still alive so the police and parents would remain vigilant in their pursuit. For all they knew, Gary had killed the kids right away, and staged the bomb shelter to look like they had been kept there.

Gavril couldn't let himself think about that. He had to believe that if Gary had kidnapped Marie he would want to keep her alive. He pedaled even harder now, lost in the thought of finding Gary. With the entire police force, and a fair amount of FBI agents, concentrating on finding this man, could he and Darrell really find him first? They did have an ace up their sleeves with Darrell and his ability to potentially see the future, but unfortunately he was so untrained that asking him to have visions on demand was going to be a large undertaking. Gavril wasn't sure he would even have the time to teach him, and even if he could do it would his visions be reliable, or just send them on a wild goose chase? Not to mention that to teach him Gavril would have to come clean and he really didn't want to do that.

Gavril pulled up to the office building and jumped off

his bike. He ran through the back door, and into their living room. He was hoping, despite his gut knowing it was false hope, to see Marie's bright smiling face there to greet him. Instead he was greeted only by Darrell who had apparently been crying recently. Darrell obviously had the same hope of seeing Marie when he had heard Gavril come in.

"She wasn't there?" Darrell asked weakly.

All Gavril could do was shake his head and sit next to Darrell. Fighting back his own tears, he put his arm around Darrell's massive shoulders and squeezed. Darrell returned the gesture. They sat there for a moment, neither speaking nor feeling awkward. Both of them seemed to know that the other was on the brink of losing their composure. Gavril finally cleared the lump in his throat and spoke.

"We'll find her," Gavril said. Gavril hoped he sounded reassuring and convincing, but he wasn't entirely sure he pulled it off.

Darrell just sat there, the tears running down his cheeks and falling onto his lap. Gavril soon followed suit and for the first time in a very long time, he allowed himself to cry.

CHAPTER NINETEEN - DARRELL

Gavril and Darrell sat silently, both trying their best to compose themselves. Darrell was the first to speak.

"Wait! When I called her, her phone rang four times before it went to voicemail," He yelled as he stood up. He was annoyed that it had taken him so long to realize.

"I'm lost, is that supposed to mean something?" Gavril asked wiping his cheeks and standing up as well.

"That means her phone is still on. If her phone was turned off it would go straight to voicemail instead of ringing."

"So her phone is still on, but she obviously can't answer it."

"I can use the 'Find Me' application on the computer," Darrell said. "If her phone is on that means that her GPS might still be on and we can track it!" Darrell said as he ran into the conference room.

"Do you know how to do that?" Gavril asked as he

followed.

"Maybe. If her GPS is still on it should be as simple as pulling up the website and finding her phone."

Darrell quickly opened one of the laptops and typed the URL for 'Find Me'. He stared at the login screen for a moment, not knowing what to type in. Darrell didn't know Marie's login and wasn't exactly sure what it would be. The username was easy enough since it was just an email address. Marie had used the same one for years. Darrell typed Marie@MarieClarkson.com in the username and stared at the password screen for what seemed like ages before it came to him. Darrell typed Ogreis2cute in the password field and hit enter. He remembered her making that password when doing a school project years before. He was partly surprised and partly elated when he saw the screen with a big "Find Me" button. He laughed to himself that someone that was so good at hacking would have such an easy password.

"Nice," Gavril said, looking over Darrell's shoulder.

"Let's just hope it works," Darrell said as he hit the button.

The screen showed a big swirling comet as it searched for Marie's phone. A moment later it showed a map of the city. There was a giant push pin marking the location of her phone.

"Hell yeah!" Darrell yelled as he hit the "Send to phone" button on the browser, signed in to Marie's account on his phone, and made sure it pushed the tracking to it.

"So that is where her phone is?" Gavril asked.

"Yes, and now with it on my phone we can keep track

and see if her phone moves while we are heading to it," Darrell said, already gathering his things and heading toward the door when it hit him.

Darrell's visions had to this point only manifested while he was sleeping, making him completely unprepared for one hitting him mid-stride. Darrell fell face first, his shoulder hit the table during the fall, making his body turn as he fell on his side.

Darrell could tell this vision was different right away, it was completely disjointed. First he saw a vision of Gary hiding in the bushes in front of Marie's house. Next he saw a quick vision of Gary injecting something in Marie's neck. That quickly changed to Marie lying unconscious on the floor of a cell. The cell looked just like the ones they found in the bomb shelter. Finally it changed to a quick glimpse of Gary staring at him, curling his pointer finger over and over as if to say come here.

Darrell awoke to Gavril leaning over him, gently shaking him and saying his name over and over.

"I'm okay," Darrell said, sitting up quickly. He grabbed the crown of his head which was throbbing in pain.

"You had another vision?" Gavril asked.

"Yeah, that psycho has her for sure," Darrell said, pulling on the table to pull himself to his feet. "We need to go before he hurts her."

"You need to sit for a moment and get your bearings."

"There is no time," Darrell said.

"Please sit down Darrell. I really need to tell you something. It might help us find her," Gavril said, reaching out to stop him.

Darrell looked down at Gavril and could immediately

tell he was serious and what he needed to say was very important to him. Darrell pulled out a chair and sat down. He forced himself to sit and pay attention to Gavril despite his body screaming at him to run out that door and find Marie. Something about the look on Gavril's face wouldn't let him though. Darrell knew he had to listen.

"I know why you have visions Darrell," Gavril said, sitting in the chair facing Darrell.

"What do you mean, you know why?"

"My name is really Gavril but I am not really sixteen years old. I am actually over two-thousand years old and belong to a group of people called Overseers. Our job is to look after people with the sight like yourself, help you understand how to use your powers, and to convince you to use them for good."

"What are you talking about? This is not the time for jokes," Darrell said despite some part of him deep inside believing every word Gavril was saying.

"I know it is a lot to take in but I need you to believe me if we are going to move forward. Hold on a sec," Gavril said. He walked out of the room and returned a moment later with a large first aid kit. "Don't be frightened," he said as he quickly pulled out his survival knife and shoved it right through his heart, burying the knife to the hilt. "See, I am immortal," he said through gritted teeth, obviously in pain.

"Jesus Christ!" Darrell screamed.

Gavril grimaced as he slowly pulled the knife out of his chest and grabbed a handful of gauze to cover up the new wound. The large gash was bleeding but quite slowly, certainly not what you would expect from a stab to the heart.

"Don't be afraid, I am not hurt, or at least not mortally hurt," Gavril said as held the gauze in place and began trying to thread a needle with his free hand.

"You stabbed yourself in the freaking heart!"

"I know."

"And you are acting like it is no big deal."

"Oh, it is kind of a big deal. I will not die from it, but it still hurts very much. Obviously not nearly as much as a normal person getting stabbed in the chest, but it hurts," Gavril replied. "Can you help me with this?" he asked as he handed Darrell the thread and needle.

"What is this for?"

"I need to stitch the wound up. I may be immortal but I still need to heal," Gavril replied as he took off his shirt.

"Why on earth would you do that?"

"I needed to prove that I was telling the truth and we are short on time."

"Couldn't you have just, I don't know, drunk some poison or something? At least then you wouldn't have a giant hole in your chest," Darrell asked as he handed back the now threaded needle.

"I hadn't thought of that, but besides the grander the gesture, the more likely you are to believe quickly," Gavril replied as he removed the gauze and began stitching up his wound.

"Wait, does this mean I am immortal too?" Darrell asked.

"Far from it, I'm afraid. I am an Overseer and my job is to oversee Sevenths such as you. I am immortal because it truly takes most people decades to study enough to be able to help the Sevenths," Gavril said through gritted teeth as he continued stitching.

"You keep calling me a Seventh, what does that mean?" Darrell asked. Darrell was struggling with what Gavril was telling him. He knew that it couldn't be true. People can't be immortal, but how could Gavril fake something like stabbing himself in the chest? Darrell's brain was telling him Gavril was making it up, but his heart was telling him otherwise. After all, he could see the future and only a few months ago he would say that seeing the future was impossible. If he could see the future, why couldn't Gavril be immortal?

"That means you are a seventh son. To be more specific, you are the seventh son of another seventh son. That is what gives you the power to see the future," Gavril said, finishing his stitching and cutting off the extra thread.

"Isn't that the name of some old heavy metal song?"

"Yeah, it is," Gavril said laughing. "That song is based on hundreds of years of folk lore that was started by some angry Overseers."

"So if a guy has seven sons, the seventh one gets visions like me?"

"Not exactly, that father would have to be a seventh son himself. Man, I should have thought this through more. I ruined my favorite shirt," Gavril said as he held up his shirt to examine the hole in the center.

"You should have thought through stabbing yourself in the chest more? That might be the dumbest sentence ever said. Ever. Besides that shirt was too small."

"You may have a point. About the sentence, not the shirt."

"What about the mother? Do all of the sons have to have the same mother?" Darrell asked.

"No the mother doesn't matter. The more generations it goes back though, the more powerful the man can be. Your particular line goes back very, very far. Usually however, the powers don't develop until the man is around thirty-five. You developed very young, which is why you got me. Most overseers are stuck looking like grownups. It helps them better interact with their assigned Seventh. I became immortal when I was thirteen, which is why I look like a teenager and got assigned to you."

"Thirteen? You look older than thirteen," Darrell replied.

"We do age. We just age very slowly. I would say I have aged about four years over the last two-thousand. I know this is a lot to take in."

CHAPTER TWENTY - GAVRIL

Gavril sat, watching Darrell in silence, and he was growing more and more concerned. His job was always to convince his Sevenths to not use their powers. He had only come clean and told his Sevenths who he really was three times prior. If those were anything to go on, Darrell was an anomaly. The Sevenths he told before had all been instantly angry at being deceived. Darrell was giving no reaction, which Gavril feared was going to lead to an even angrier response.

"He must be one too, that is how he knew my name," Darrell said.

"Who must be one and, what do you mean? Who knew your name?" Gavril asked.

"In the last few visions he has turned to me. You know, my point of view, like he was looking directly at me. He spoke to me, using my name."

"Oh, wow. That is not good. You are right though.

Gary is a Seventh too," Gavril said, not liking where this was going.

"How long have you known?"

"I just found out yesterday, from my boss. Gary developed powers last year and had an Overseer assigned to him. Recently he began using his visions to commit crimes. The council fears that he has killed his Overseer."

"Wait a minute! You knew who he was before we did? You could have stopped this whole thing and prevented the kids and Marie from being kidnapped!" Darrell yelled as he came to the realization. He stood up and looked down on Gavril. "You could have stopped this!"

"I only found out who he was minutes before you did. Literally minutes before. I was on my way to tell you but when I got in, Marie had already figured out who he was."

"But others knew. He was assigned a, what did you call it, an Overseer? They knew he was bad news, you said it yourself. Nobody did anything. They just let him kidnap kids and my best friend!"

"Please Darrell, let's not waste time laying blame, it will only hinder us."

"Of course you don't want me to lay blame because it all falls on you," Darrell said. His face was flush with anger.

"Darrell, please. I was under strict orders to not reveal myself."

"Don't you dare hide behind orders with me! You were supposed to be our friend and you were nothing but a liar."

"My feelings toward you and Marie were not a lie. I really do consider you two to be great friends."

Darrell got up and began to pace back and forth. Gavril

could tell that he was incredibly angry, but then to Gavril's relief, Darrell took a deep breath, let it out slowly and sat back down calmer.

"So if Gary is able to have visions too, is that why he was gone? Did he know we were coming?"

"I can only assume so. It makes sense."

"So how are we supposed to catch a man that sees us coming?"

"Now that I know that he addressed you in your visions, I am pretty sure he wants us, or at least you, to find him," Gavril said.

"What makes you think that?"

"He seems to be pushing your visions on you, instead of you having the visions naturally. That is how he is addressing you. He is building the vision in his mind and pushing it to yours so he can make it be whatever he wants."

"That doesn't sound good. How can I even trust a vision if he can make them whatever he wants? This is also something that would have been useful to know before," Darrell said. His demeanor was calmer, but he was obviously still angry.

"I had no way of knowing he was doing that. He isn't supposed to even know how. This technique, known as Inductum, is an old and sacred one. It is not supposed to be taught. In fact, I have never met an Overseer that even has the text to teach it. I didn't even remember it existed until I came across it while researching your headaches. I really don't know how he could have learned it but based on your visions there is no other explanation," Gavril said.

"You think that is why I have the headaches now?"

"It seems quite likely, but I can't be sure. Like I said, the technique is really rare. Most Sevenths wouldn't even think about doing something like that because it generally has no real moral use. This man is psychotic so it makes sense he would try to figure out bad ways to use his gifts."

"We don't even know if my visions are true. He could be sending me the wrong info. There is nothing we can do," Darrell said slightly defeated.

"Not exactly. I don't know much about Inductum, but like I said, I did read a few things about it the other night. The main thing people say is that the receiver of the pushed vision can tell the difference physically."

"What do you mean?"

"You have obviously already recognized the way your body reacts when you have visions. Visions you get from Inductum will feel different."

"Like me getting nauseous when I wake up? That just began recently."

"Partly. The nausea and the headache seem to be a side effect of interacting with another Seventh, or being very close to one," Gavril replied.

"Like the headache when I ran into him?"

"Right. So those feelings wouldn't necessarily mean that he was pushing the vision, because theoretically having a vision of him normally would have those effects. Like your first vision of the kidnapped boy."

"Theoretically? That doesn't sound promising."

"Well, there is not a lot of precedent of Sevenths having visions of other Sevenths, at least not that I could find. Anyway, apparently you can feel the difference in your node when the vision is pushed."

"My node?" Darrell asked.

"That is a small part of your brain where your powers come from. It is located right at the crown of your head," Gavril replied.

"That makes sense. I can feel it vibrating sometimes, for lack of a better description. So it is supposed to feel different when he sends me visions?"

"Not exactly. Reportedly it feels different when you get pushed lies. Your power is a divine power and the node in your brain is designed to see what your body can't see. Your visions may not always come true but they are always the truth, if you know what I mean. When your node processes a lie it doesn't like it, and your body will react differently. So you can't necessarily feel when he is pushing you a vision but you can tell when he is pushing you a lie. Unfortunately since the power of Inductum is used so rarely, there is very little research on it. None of the accounts I have read describe the feeling more than it being different, so hopefully you can tell the difference."

"You said my powers are divine. Does that mean they come from God? Does that mean God is real?" Darrell asked. Gavril knew this question was coming. It was nearly always one of the first questions a new Seventh asked.

"It means they come from a power higher than us. Some would call that power God. Over the course of my long lifetime I have seen the power called many things, but it's always the same power. I wish I had a more definitive answer for you, but as you will learn, the answers about God and Heaven still aren't as clear as we want them to be. What I can tell you is that there is something higher than us and it gives you your powers to help humanity."

"I've never been religious. I'm not really sure what to make of this," Darrell said.

"Religion isn't important right now. We can reflect more on that later, so please don't get bogged down on the God aspect."

"Right, so if I can tell when he is lying we can avoid his traps. Is that your point?" Darrell asked.

"Yes. But we also need to remember that while he can't send you lies without you knowing, it doesn't mean he has to send you the entire truth. I am not certain since I don't have firsthand experience in the matter but I don't think a lie of omission would register as a lie. We have to be very careful of anything he sends you," Gavril replied.

"So if he is making up my visions, how are we supposed to know what to do? How are we supposed to find Marie?"

"Like I said, I'm certain he wants us to find Marie. I am pretty sure that it is you that he wants. He is just using Marie as a way to get to you," Gavril said.

"Why would he want me?" Darrell asked.

"I guess just because you are the only other Seventh he knows about. Sevenths are actually very rare and we take special care to keep them apart," Gavril said, deciding against letting Darrell know Gary was his father. He really wanted to tell him the truth, but the waters were muddied enough already. Adding that extra emotion to the mix, could be disastrous. Darrell was going to hate him when he found out and that would hurt Gavril for a very long time, but if it saved Marie it would be worth it.

"Why would you keep them, I mean us, apart?"

"You know that headache you got when you ran into him? That's because you interacted with another Seventh.

Imagine if there were several in the city and that headache could happen at any time. That would be very uncomfortable for the Sevenths. The main reason we keep you apart though is to help as many people as possible. Overseers have been studying Sevenths for pretty much as long as there have been people on this planet. We still don't know everything, but we have a good understanding of how things work. Sevenths seem to be on earth for the sole purpose of helping those in need. I have always thought of it as the higher power's way to balance out all of the terrible things his creations do. We found out early on that Sevenths generally only have visions of people and places that they can actually get to and affect. So the more we spread out the Sevenths, the more good can be done in the world."

"What about father and son? I was adopted but others live with their children so they are near them all the time, right?"

"Yes, but the side effects don't start until the children develop powers. By that time we have usually convinced one of them to move. Remember that for most people this means the child is around thirty-five, so they are not likely still living at home."

"That makes sense. If Gary wants us to find him, and purposely showed me that he has Marie, do you think her phone is a trap?" Darrell asked.

"I'm pretty sure the entire thing is a trap but I don't see any other options. We are at his mercy for now, so we play into his hand. We will figure out how to beat him and get Marie back safely, I promise," Gavril said.

"No offense, but I don't want to hear promises from a

guy that has been lying to me for the past year. I'll work with you for now because I need you to help me get Marie back. After this is over we are done," Darrell said.

"I really am sorry Darrell," Gavril said.

"Keep your sorry. Let's go," Darrell said, getting up and gathering all his things. "Her phone is still in the same place, let's go find out what kind of trap this psycho has set for us."

Gavril followed Darrell outside and grabbed his bike, but Darrell stopped him.

"Bikes aren't going to be fast enough, let's take that instead," Darrell said.

"Your dad's Mustang? Your dad is going to kill you," Gavril said "Your dad doesn't even let you touch it. Last week he refused to even let you wash it."

"That was more about the twenty bucks I was asking him for washing it than the actual washing. Besides, he is passed out so he will never know. If he finds out, I'll deal with that later. For now, let's go find Marie. You drive," Darrell said tossing the keys to Gavril. "I figure if you're two-thousand years old you are bound to be a better driver than me, right?"

"You better believe it," Gavril said, catching the keys.

CHAPTER TWENTY-ONE - MARIE

Marie breathed a huge sigh of relief when Gary finally went back upstairs and left her alone. She had thought he would never take his eyes off of her. She looked at the lock holding her cage shut, and knew she would never be able to get past it. Not only did she not possess Gavril's lock picking tools, she wouldn't know how to use them if she did. She made a mental note to order a set as soon as this ordeal was over. She did however know how to take care of herself, and had gotten the best of many bigger men in her Muay Thai and Brazilian jujitsu classes. She just needed to put herself in position to take advantage of the situation when the opportunity presented itself.

Marie scanned the basement, looking for anything that might help her out of her current predicament. As she looked around, she had to admit that in different circumstances, the basement might be quite nice. It had a very pretty exposed beam celling with cute navy blue walls.

Unfortunately for Marie the basement was built for leisure, and not for work, because she couldn't find anything that would help her out of her cage. Finally, she remembered she still had a pen knife stuck in her sock. She had put it there as a backup when they were going to Gary's house and had forgotten all about it. Having her hands bound behind her back didn't make it easy but she got to her knees with her legs folded under her. This allowed her to reach her sock. It took her a couple of minutes to finally pull her sock down and reveal the knife. She made another mental note, this time to not wear knee-high socks the next time she was going to stash stuff in there.

With her knife out and open she began to saw through the ropes that were binding her wrists. She was very disappointed in the speed at which she was able to cut the ropes. The movies always made it seem so easy, but she was now several minutes into cutting and she was only about three quarters through. She knew Gary would be back at any moment, and she needed to get free. Finally, she felt the rope give way. She immediately pulled her hands in front of her and began rubbing her wrists in an effort to ease the pain. She looked around trying to figure out her next move. She was no longer bound but she was still very much incarcerated with no easy way out. Knowing time was short, she decided her best option was to pretend to still be bound. She would wait for him to open the cage, then she would attack.

Hearing Gary opening the door to the basement, she sat back and put her hands behind her, pretending to still be tied up. Gary was walking down the stairs when she noticed her knife sitting beside her. She quickly reached out and grabbed the knife and put her hands back behind her back. She decided that would be her main attack. She gripped the knife, ready to lash out and stab him with it when the time came.

"You look a little flush. Is that sweat on your forehead? What on earth could you be doing in your little cage to be so sweaty?" Gary asked.

"It's hot, moron. People sweat when it's hot. Would it kill you to turn down the heat?" Marie said.

"Alas, I'm afraid I can't. You see, because of you and your incredibly nosey friends, I had to leave my house and take up residence in this one. I was in a bit of a hurry, and had other things to worry about," Gary said, as he pulled a big tarp off of two other cages and motioned to the other two kids lying motionless in the cages.

"You killed them?" Marie asked.

"Did I kill them? No I didn't kill them. They are not dead, just unconscious. I'm afraid they were quite difficult to move, so I had to drug them to keep them quiet. They should be awake in a few hours," Gary answered. Marie felt a wave of relief. She and the kids were still in a lot of danger, but at least they stood a chance. If he really wanted to kill the kids, she supposed he would have done it by now.

"As I was saying before you rudely interrupted, I had to find a new house. Unfortunately I chose this house, with two old people. They were easy enough to dispose of, but apparently they had wanted to keep it as hot as Florida and without air conditioning, it will take a while to cool down. Besides, if it makes you uncomfortable I am all for it."

"What about the home owners? Did you kill them?"

"No, I sent them on a Caribbean vacation. Of course I killed them! I thought you were supposed to be bright. They weren't exactly going to let me and my three playmates take up residence in their home, so I negotiated with them. They said no. Actually it was more like 'please no'," he said in a high-pitched mocking tone. "I said 'yes'. They said 'please no' again, so I stabbed them in the throat so they couldn't say it again." Marie saw something flash in his eyes as he said that. She could tell that he had enjoyed killing them. He hadn't really killed the couple out of necessity, he killed them because he wanted to. She knew he was a bad man from his rap sheet alone, but words on a screen didn't properly convey how disturbed he was.

"You really are a sick man."

"I prefer to think of myself as liberated. I'm liberated from the shackles of morals. Morals do nothing but keep people from doing the things they really want to do. I have moved beyond them and can now do whatever my heart desires."

"Why did you take them? Why did you take me? Are you some kind of pervert that gets his kicks on kids?" Marie asked.

"Oh, I'm afraid you have me pegged all wrong. I mean these children no harm. At least not in that way. The harm, you see, is meant for their parents. Let's just say their parents have done some wrong that I feel they need to be punished for. Taking their loved ones from them is the best way to make them feel that pain. You on the other hand, you are here because of your friend Darrell. You and he just couldn't stay out of my way, so now he has to play the game too. You and these two little ones are only innocent pawns in my game."

"What game are you talking about?"

"The game of getting you back. You see, those kids' parents are just ordinary bad people. The plan was to play with them by making them suffer. I would let them think that they were getting close to finding their kids and then pull the rug out, so to speak. It was going to be fun for a while and then I figured I'd kill them all and move on. Darrell, however, is special and he is going to take the game to the next level. I really am excited about this new turn of events."

"What about those kids? If you are worried about me and Darrell, then you can let them go."

"Yes, I suppose I could. They are innocent, but I think their parents should still suffer some more. Just because I have moved on to another game doesn't mean it should be over for them."

"Darrell is a genius you know. He is going to find me," Marie said.

"Oh, I know he is a genius. Like I said, he is special. He comes from great genes."

"Darrell's adopted, that's not his real father, you idiot."

"Oh yes, of course. Well anyway, he is certainly a worthy opponent," Gary said with a sly smile.

Marie just glared at him hoping he would open her cage soon so this could all be over.

"I brought you some food, and I thought you might like to stand up and stretch. I am sorry about the size of the cage but I'm afraid it was originally meant for someone else," Gary said.

Marie couldn't help but shudder. If her cage was meant

for someone else and it was small, he must have been planning to kidnap another child. How many did he plan to kidnap, and since he seemed to have strayed from his plan to kidnap Marie, would he now abandon those plans?

Gary placed the tray of food on the top of the cage, and knelt down to open the lock. It took him a moment to find the right key, and Marie used that time to her advantage. She maneuvered herself to the right position. She was still on one knee, but had the other leg planted underneath her. Marie's plan was to lunge at him with the knife as soon as he opened the cage. He was in a very relaxed mood since he knew he had the upper hand, and wouldn't be expecting it.

Gary finally found the right key and opened the lock. He looked up and smiled at Marie as he swung the cage door open. Marie didn't hesitate and lunged straight for him. Her arm was outstretched with her knife aimed right for Gary's throat. It seemed like slow motion to her. She saw her knife heading right for his throat. At the last moment, Gary turned slightly so that her knife would barely miss him and in the same movement raised his fist so that Marie's lunge propelled her face right into it. Marie felt her nose crush under his fist and she knew instantly it was broken. She felt the blood gushing. It was not only rushing down her face but she could feel it sliding down the back of her throat and taste it in her mouth. The pain was blinding as she fell to the floor, dropping her knife, and grabbing her face with both hands. Marie was not sure she had ever felt something so severe. Her mind kept telling her to get up and attack Gary but her body was rebelling. No matter how much she tried to force herself to get up, her body refused. She felt Gary pick her up and hold her up by her collar. He must have been face to face with her, because she could feel his hot breath on her hands. She willed herself to put her hands down so she could see his face through tear-filled eyes. As if waiting for her to look at him he took the cue and began to speak.

"Now you listen to me you stupid girl," Gary growled. His voice was much different than before. Marie thought it might have been the most frightening thing she had ever heard. Before he had an air of nonchalance, now he had a feral quality in his voice that made Marie's heart stop. "I let you off easy this time with a broken nose. You may never be pretty again but you will live. If you try anything stupid again, I'll know. Next time it won't be a broken nose. I will skin you alive from head to toe. I wonder how much skin I will get off before you pass out and die."

Marie knew instantly that he wasn't being hyperbolic. There was something in his voice that told Marie he meant what he was saying. Still holding her collar, Gary lowered her and shoved her backwards into the cage very hard. Her head hit the bars in the back, adding a pounding headache to her broken nose.

"Darrell will find you," Marie said, although it wasn't the most clear due to her new injuries.

"You really think that don't you?" he asked, apparently understanding Marie's mumbling. His voice had changed back into his airy carefree tone. "You know, he isn't the only special one around."

That statement stuck out to Marie. Gary kept using the word special to describe Darrell and now alluded that he was special himself. Could Gary have the ability to have visions too? It would explain a lot, like how he always seemed to be two steps ahead of them and the police. If he had visions of when people were coming looking for him, it would make it easy to leave ahead of time. It would explain how he was able to clean out his house and bomb shelter. He knew they were coming. Marie was surprised by Darrell's visions, and if she hadn't seen such proof of their validity, she would never have believed it. Now, was she to truly believe that two people in her life could see the future? It would also explain how he so slyly dodged her attack and punched her. If he knew how and when the attack was coming it would have been easy for him to do. Marie remembered what Gary had said about good genes. Did Gary know Darrell's birth family? Or even worse, was Gary somehow related to Darrell? The thought made her skin crawl, but maybe that would explain how they both could see the future. Maybe the power was genetic somehow. She began to worry for Darrell. Was Gary being crazy a by-product of the visions? Did having the ability to see the future and seeing so many potentially horrible things drive Gary crazy, and would the same thing happen to Darrell?

"Starting to sink in yet?" Gary asked.

"You have them too?" Marie asked, her words still sounding like a garbled mess.

"The visions? Oh yes, I have the visions too. I wasn't sure if Darrell had shared his secret with you, but I guess he trusts you. I on the other hand didn't tell anyone for quite some time because I thought I was crazy. So, you see, his special powers are not going to help him. Not only can I see him coming, I have had my powers for longer and can do far more with them than he has even dreamed. That's what makes this game so interesting. What I can't figure out just yet is how his Overseer plays into it."

"Overseer?" Marie asked, confused.

"You don't know about his Overseer? Well you guys must have all sorts of secrets. Since he has powers, he would have been assigned an Overseer. They look like normal people but are immortal and usually hundreds of years old. Their job is to make sure the Seventh, oh you must not know what a Seventh is. We, which is to say, the Seventh's, are-" Gary said.

Gary kept explaining how Darrell's powers worked and although Marie was getting it all, she was only half listening. Gavril had to have been the Overseer he was referring to. Was he really hundreds of years old? That would explain so much.

"Are you even listening to me?" Gary asked.

"Yes, I'm listening," Marie said shaking her thoughts of Gavril out.

"Anyway, the Overseer's job is to make sure we don't do bad things, not that mine was much help in that department," Gary said with a grin.

"Obviously. Regardless, Darrell will find a way. He doesn't need his powers to beat you," Marie said.

"Okay, that last part was a little hard to decipher. I'm not sure but I think something is wrong with your nose. It seems to be giving you a bit of a speech impediment. Anyway, I think you said he didn't need his powers to get me. I certainly hope you aren't talking about using technology. That cellphone you so cleverly hid in the trunk of my car, I assume it has GPS and you thought it would lead them right to us, huh? I hate to break it to you sweetheart but that phone is only leading Darrell to my trap. It will lead him to a basement all right, just not this one. It will lead him to the basement right across the street. If you can be a good little girl I might even let you watch through the window," Gary said.

"He won't fall for it," Marie said.

"Really, I think you may be giving your friend a little bit too much credit. You see, one of the drawbacks to our powers is that visions of other people with powers are not always as clear as we like them to be. That just makes it more exciting, doesn't it? Neither of us can see the other clearly. Will he know it is a trap? Do I really know how this will turn out? I guess we will both have to watch and see," Gary said.

CHAPTER TWENTY-TWO - DARRELL

"It's that house," Darrell said, pointing to a house across the street.

Gavril pulled the car over and put it in park. Just as Darrell put his hand on the door handle, it happened again. This vision was much clearer than the previous one and once again he felt in control. Marie was sitting in the bottom of a cage, like the ones they found in the bomb shelter. She was looking at something in the distance, perhaps just lost in thought. Her nose was very broken. Her shirt was covered in blood, which Darrell assumed happened when she broke her nose, but her face had been cleaned up. Darrell looked around and noticed the other two kids in their own cages. They appeared to be unconscious or sleeping but seemed to be alive, because he could see their chests rising and falling. Darrell looked around some more and could tell they were being held in a basement. Just as he was about to look around for any other clues, the sound of an airplane shook the house and was deafening. Darrell woke from his vision and realized Gavril was staring at him.

"Another one?" Gavril asked him.

"Yeah, I saw Marie and the two other kids. Marie had a broken nose but other than that they all seemed okay." Darrell said.

"Any other important things?" Gavril asked.

Just as Darrell was about to answer, a large airplane flew overhead. It was very low and making it's descent to land at the nearby airport. The plane shook the car that they were in so much that their instinct was to hold on.

"That!" Darrell said as he jumped out of the car and began running toward the house.

"What? The plane?" Gavril asked as he got out and ran next to Darrell.

"I heard the plane in my vision. They are in this basement," Darrell said, now slowing down as he reached the outside basement entrance.

"Wait!" Gavril said as he put himself in-between Darrell and the basement door.

"What are you doing? Get out of the way! They are in there," Darrell yelled.

"Think about it, it may be a trap. I have a very bad feeling about this. I think Gary has set us up," Gavril said.

"We have no reason to think that. The vision I just had felt like the old ones. Gary didn't send it to me, there was no trap. Now get out of my way before I move you myself," Darrell said.

"Please humor me for a moment. I know I don't get visions but I do have a certain intuition, and this seems off.

I want you to try to force a vision and see what is behind the door."

"What do you mean force a vision?"

"Sevenths have the ability to sometimes force visions if something of significance is going to happen. I think if you touch the handle and focus you will be able to see if there is a trap in there," Gavril said.

"Gav, we don't have time for this."

"In your vision were they in immediate danger?"

"No."

"Then we have time to make sure that the door is not rigged to explode or something, all right?"

"You really think he'd do something like that?"

"This guy is a complete psychopath. I wouldn't put anything past him. Now please just hold the handle and concentrate," Gavril said.

"Fine, if it will get you out of my way," Darrell said as he put his hand on the handle. "I don't see anything."

"You need to really concentrate. I want you to mentally focus on the very crown of your brain. Like I said, that is where your visions come from," Gavril said.

"I'm trying, but I don't see anything. We are wasting time; I'm going in," Darrell said as he grabbed the handle and pulled it open.

"See, no trap," Darrell whispered this time. "Let's go."

Darrell and Gavril each pulled out a weapon to be ready. Darrell felt much better this time since he came prepared.

"I still have a bad feeling about this," Gavril whispered, as he followed Darrell down the basement stairs.

They got to the bottom of the stairs, and were both

shocked at what they saw. The basement was completely bare except for one small object in the middle of the floor. Darrell hurriedly walked over and picked it up.

"This is Marie's phone, but where in the hell is she?" Darrell said.

"Gary must have known we were coming," Gavril said.

Suddenly, Marie's phone began vibrating and the screen indicated there was one new text message. Darrell swiped the screen to read the text, and was taken aback to see the message was a picture of Marie. It was apparently taken after she broke her nose, but before she cleaned up her face. The photo was quite disturbing, as Marie's nose had apparently bled a lot. Her face was completely covered in blood. Darrell thought it looked like something out of a horror movie. If he hadn't had the vision letting him know that all the blood made it look much worse than it was, though her nose was broken quite badly, he would be really freaking out. Out of the corner of his eye, he noticed Gavril, who wasn't privy to the vision, covering his mouth.

"It's not as bad as it looks," Darrell said.

"What do you mean? Look at her!"

"I saw her in my vision. Her nose is broken pretty badly but it just looks worse here with all the blood. He is trying to freak us out," Darrell said.

"It's working," Gavril said.

Another text came through, this time it was just the words "Strike 1".

"What does that mean?" Darrell asked.

"I think he is referring to baseball, in which a batter has only three strikes before he is out. He is definitely playing a game."

"What is it with all of the baseball references lately?" Darrell asked.

Darrell hit the phone icon next to the text message to call the sender.

"What are you doing?" Gavril asked.

"I'm calling him back. But it's no good, it goes straight to voicemail. He must have turned it off right after he sent the text. I don't get it. I had the vision that showed them here," Darrell said.

"Are you sure they were here? Look around, was it certainly this basement?" Gavril asks.

Darrell looked around and was disheartened even more when he realized that it was the wrong basement. Not only was it missing the obvious, the cages and the kids, the ceiling was different. This basement had a popcorn ceiling and the one in the vision had an exposed beam ceiling.

"It's not the same. This doesn't make sense. What about the plane?"

"Maybe he planted it to make you believe it was this house," Gavril said.

"I don't think it was planted. It felt much more like one of my previous visions. The ones he planted felt a little different like you were saying before."

"Maybe they are in a different house but still close to the airport," Gavril said.

"That must be it, but how do we find them? You want to just start on the end, down there?" Darrell said.

"Darrell, we can't just go door to door breaking into people's basements. We will be arrested or shot in no time. We need to go back to HQ, regroup, and figure out plan B," Gavril said.

"Plan B? We need to find her now. We don't have time for more planning," Darrell said.

"This guy has been one step ahead of us the entire time. You need to remember that this guy has visions, and he can easily see us coming. Like I was telling you earlier, you can sometimes force visions, when something important is going to happen. Us finding him would certainly qualify as something important. We need to come up with a plan to overcome his advantage. I have an idea but we need to get back to HQ and work on it," Gavril said.

"I can't give up. We are so close," Darrell said. He knew Gavril was right, but he didn't want to admit it. How could he be so close to saving Marie, and give up?

"I know this is hard, but we need to do what gives us the best chance to get Marie back safe, and right now that means regrouping and coming up with another plan. Besides, we may not even be that close. Unless your vision showed you the address, there is nothing more we can do here," Gavril said.

"I guess you're right," Darrell said defeated. He turned to walk toward the basement entrance.

CHAPTER TWENTY-THREE - DARRELL

"You really think she is going to be all alright?" Darrell asked as they got into the car.

"I really do. I have been doing this a long time and I have never had a Seventh as smart and resourceful as you. Gary really doesn't know what he is getting himself into," Gavril said. Darrell hated getting complements in times of stress. He always felt like they were a hollow way to try to reassure him, especially when the compliments were about his intelligence. It always seemed like others had far more confidence in his intelligence than he did.

"But, have you ever seen someone as nuts as Gary?" Darrell asked.

"I'm sad to say that I have. Unfortunately, some people can't handle the visions and it drives them mad. Gary is not quite like those others though. He was generally a terrible person and lacked morals before he ever had a vision. The visions just compounded his issues."

Darrell's phone began ringing. When he pulled it out of his pocket and looked at the screen, his heart skipped a beat. "Marie Calling" flashed at the top of his screen. He quickly pressed the green button to answer.

"Marie!" Darrell said as he put the phone to his ear.

"No, this is Marie's dad. I take it from your greeting, that you haven't heard from her either?" Mr. Clarkson asked. Darrell now realized that the call was from Marie's home phone. He silently cursed himself for being so stupid. After all he had Marie's cellphone in his back pocket, how would she be calling him. He felt like a moron, and Gavril would have him believe that his superior intellect would help find Marie. Darrell could hear the concern in her dad's voice. He couldn't ever recall hearing the man sound worried about anything.

"No sir, I haven't," Darrell said. He figured the truth was the best thing at this point.

"I'm really starting to worry. I know we haven't been getting along very well lately, but I don't think she would run away. If she did, she would be with you. I'm sure of that. Are you being honest with me? You really haven't seen her?"

"I really haven't, Mr. Clarkson, and I'm beginning to get worried too," Darrell replied. He knew he couldn't tell him that she was kidnapped, but Darrell figured he would come to that conclusion on his own.

"I think I'm going to have to call the police, Darrell. I don't know what else to do."

"I think that would be smart Mr. Clarkson," Darrell said. Darrell needed to get Marie back safely, and if that meant bringing in the police, then he was okay with it.

Even if it meant that he was arrested for the crimes he already committed trying to catch Gary himself. He didn't know if the police could really help, but maybe their presence could get Gary off his game and swing things in their favor.

"Okay son, I guess that is what I am going to do. Please call me immediately if you hear from her."

"I will, and you do the same," Darrell said.

"I will son," Mr. Clarkson said as he hung up.

"Her dad is worried?" Gavril asked.

"Yeah, he said he was going to call the police. I told him to go ahead. I supposed any extra people looking for her can't be a bad thing, right?" Darrell asked.

"It certainly couldn't hurt, although I don't think they will have any success against a man like Gary."

"I suppose you're right," Darrell said. He was growing more depressed by the minute. This had all been his fault. If he hadn't gotten Marie involved in his half-baked scheme to find the boy, Marie would still be okay.

"Listen Darrell, I'm gonna drop you off at your house. You need to get some rest," Gavril said.

"Are you kidding? How could I possibly rest at a time like this? Besides, we need to work on the plan. You said you have an idea."

"I do, but it doesn't exactly involve you."

"What in the hell do you mean it doesn't involve me?" Darrell asked indignantly.

"You know how you and Gary seem to have a bond of some sort, where you get the funny feelings, and he can send you visions?"

"Yeah, so?"

"As Overseers, we have kind of the opposite effect. I guess you haven't noticed that I am not in any of your visions?" Gavril asked.

"Now that you mention it, you aren't. Why aren't you?" Darrell couldn't believe he never noticed it before, although in hindsight it did make some things make more sense, like the paint on the bus.

"Part of the, for lack of a better term, magic that makes us immortal also seems to hide us from visions. No Seventh can see an Overseer in a vision, no matter how hard they try," Gavril said.

"So I can't see you, but that means Gary can't see you either?" Darrell asked.

"Exactly. I can be a complete surprise to him. The main caveat though, is you can't know about any plans I make or he may be able to see them or at least part of them. He wouldn't be able to see me but he may be able to make out that you were expecting someone to do whatever the plan is. At least in theory. We seem to be in a bit of uncharted territory," Gavril said.

"Won't he be expecting something? I mean he knows I have an Overseer, right, since everyone does?"

"Perhaps, but he may not be thinking about it since the fact we can't be seen in visions is not something we advertise, though many have figured it out and he could very well have. Anyway, couple that with the fact that most underage Overseers wouldn't even think about helping a young man do stuff that is so dangerous. So far he has not done anything that makes us believe that he knows I am helping you. I think we will still have the element of surprise," Gavril said.

"So you want to go back to HQ and work on a plan but I can't see it or he might know?" Darrell asked.

"Pretty much," Gavril answered.

"All right, I guess I'll trust you. You can't take me home though, my dad's gonna go crazy about his car. I'd rather postpone that until we save Marie. What about your place, can I stay there?"

"I guess that will work. Andrea is out of town, so you would have the place to yourself," Gavril said.

"Andrea? Holy cow, I just realized she isn't your mother is she?" Darrell asked.

"Nope. She is actually my boss."

"So she is immortal and an Overseer too?"

"Yes, and kind of. She is immortal, although only a few hundred years old. She is not an Overseer exactly as she has never been over a Seventh of her own. But she is a member of the Overseer family. All members are chosen by the council based on skill sets that the council feel would be helpful to the cause. She was previously a queen that had a natural ability to solve problems and get people to follow her."

"So the council, what, comes up to you and asks you if you want to be immortal?"

"Not exactly. They actually revive you after you die and lay out the cards on the table. They let you choose if you want this life. Most people say yes, although I am certain many of those think it is some kind of joke."

"You said being a Seventh was a divine power, is being an Overseer the same sort of thing?"

"In a way. The power that made me immortal was certainly divine but a Seventh doesn't get chosen, they just are. Overseers are chosen by the council and a ritual is performed to ask for the power to be bestowed on the chosen person. Andrea was brought into the family to be a leader. She currently has four Overseers that she handles in this part of the United States. There is me down here, a man in Charlotte, one in Boston and a woman in Chicago, which is where she is now. Apparently something big is going on up there."

"That's why she travels so much?" Darrell asked.

"She spends time with each of us, although a little more with me since it would drive suspicion to have a teenager by himself all the time. With the crisis in Chicago, she has been gone a little more recently."

"We are kind of having a crisis right here."

"I know. I told her we had it all under control. This would all be much harder with her here," Gavril said.

"Park here," Darrell said as he motioned to the side of the road.

"Why? We are two blocks away from my house."

"Exactly. You can hear my dad's car from a block away. The last thing we need right now is him hearing us coming down the street and catching us with his car."

"Good point."

They arrived at Gavril's house a few minutes later, and Gavril showed him around the house so he knew where everything was.

"How is it we have been friends for nearly a year and I haven't been over to your house?" Darrell asked.

"As you can see, it is not exactly ready for guests. It would have taken all of three seconds for you to notice all of the so called occult imagery and books. You probably would have thought we were some weird devil worshipers."

"That's a good point. What is all this stuff anyway?" Darrell asked looking around. Gavril was right, the house was practically overrunning with crazy looking books that screamed devil worshiper.

"It's all just Overseer stuff. We have our own ancient language which consists of symbols instead of letters."

"Like hieroglyphics?"

"In a way, but even older than that. Over the years, people have seen some of our symbols in one form or another and used some of the symbols for whatever occult crap they were making up. This symbol for example," Gavril said, pointing to a pentagram. "Is supposed to be this big evil symbol, yet it actually just means home in our language."

"Weird, how do you say it?" Darrell asked.

"The verbal form of our language is not widely known. They teach us the written form but only the oldest on the council still know how to speak it. Well, I should say the oldest that care. I am one of the oldest alive, but I stopped speaking it thousands of years ago. I felt weird, like a teenage girl with a secret code language. It's actually pretty annoying when they start conversing in it during a council meeting. I always feel like they are talking about me," Gavril said.

"I know what you mean. I used to feel that way when my mom took me to the nail salon where everyone spoke Vietnamese," Darrell said.

"Anyway, here are a few books written in English. They tell more in-depth stories about the history of Sevenths and have some good chapters about using your powers. They are basically the training manuals that we give to new Sevenths," Gavril said.

"I wasn't going to get one, was I?"

"No, the plan was to convince you to not use your powers, at least until your thirties. Gary threw a big wrench in that whole plan. Anyway, they should keep your mind occupied while I am working on my plan. I'll be back soon, I have a feeling that Gary will be sending you a vision by morning to let you know the next phase of his sick game. Help yourself to anything in the kitchen, except the birch root beer. That's mine," Gavril said with a smile.

"Got it, stay away from everything except the birch root beer," Darrell said smirking.

"Very funny. Call me with any new visions," Gavril said as he walked out the door.

Darrell opened the first book and began thumbing through. He stopped when he came across medical pictures that explained what part of the brain his visions came from. He was surprised the book didn't just have drawings. It had complete autopsy photos showing the extra little node in the crown of the brain. Darrell was simultaneously fascinated and disgusted. The normal photos had been okay enough but the photos showing nodes that had problems really got to him. One in particular showed the brain of a twenty-one year old whose node was inflamed and partially turned black. The text had explained that the boy had developed his powers at the age of twelve. Due to a clerical error he was allowed to use his powers without an Overseer for eight years. By the time it was figured out the damage was far too extensive and the young man was institutionalized. He took his own life shortly after.

"How did my life get so crazy?" Darrell asked himself.

CHAPTER TWENTY-FOUR - MARIE

The sound of the air horn surprised the sleeping Marie so much that she jumped up, hitting her head on the top of the cage. She looked around, rubbing her head, and saw Gary standing over the cage with a giant grin on his face. She slumped back down. She was disappointed that it wasn't all a horrible nightmare. She looked around and noticed the other two cages were empty. Her heart skipped a beat. She didn't want to ask the question but she knew she needed to.

"Where are they?" Marie asked, fearful of the coming answer.

"Oh them? I decided you were right. I didn't need them anymore. The game with Darrell is far more interesting than the game with those brats' parents and the police," Gary said, with a persistent smile.

"What did you do with them?" Marie asked.

"Oh, don't worry dear. I didn't hurt them. I left them in

front of the fire station. I have always heard that's what you do with unwanted children," Gary said.

"I don't believe you. That doesn't sound like you," Marie said.

"Honestly, whether you believe me or not is unimportant. They were unharmed. I decided that if I left them unharmed when they were returned to their parents the pressure from the police would be reduced. They would decide I wasn't worth all the extra effort, and I'm sure considerable expense, if the kids were safe," Gary said.

"You're afraid of the police?" Marie asked.

"Oh, not even in the slightest. I can always see them coming. They can, however, force me to change my plans. If I see them coming I might have to move again or not do what I was planning. At this point in the game, the less interference the better."

"But can't you see where they would be in advance and just not go there so they don't make you move?" Marie asked.

"You have a lot to learn about our powers. Yes I can see the future, but not always the entire future. Also the funny thing about the future is that it is always changing. What we see mostly comes true, but not always. You see that people have free will-"

"You know I really don't give a crap," Marie cut him off. "At least not from you. What time is it, and why did you wake me up?" Marie asked.

"Aren't you feisty in the morning? Are you always this rude?"

"Only to psycho morons."

"I'm gonna pretend that you didn't say that because I

don't want you too banged up when Darrell sees you. Anyway, it's about four thirty in the morning, and I decided it was time to ramp up the game," Gary said.

"What do you mean ramp it up?" Marie asked.

"That is for me to know and you to find out my dear. Rest assured though, it is going to be really cool. For this round we need to move to another location. That means I need you to get out of that cage. No funny business by the way. Remember what happened last time you thought you could be a hero? I can always see it coming and I really don't want to mess up that pretty face any more than I have to. Well, it was a pretty face. Maybe once this is over, you can get a plastic surgeon to fix that up," Gary said.

"I don't need to be the hero. My friends will do that for me," Marie said, realizing he already knew her new plan to escape. Was her nose really that bad? She had tried to look at it in the reflection on the cage bars, but couldn't really tell. Marie had never put a lot of thought into her looks, but she knew deep down that was only because she knew she was naturally pretty. Even with her lack of vanity could she really handle going around with a sideways nose?

"I hate to burst your bubble little one but your friends list is not as long as you think. Darrell is the only one even trying to help. I have seen what he attempts and trust me when I say he may be a genius but he doesn't do his best thinking when you are involved. His emotions seem to get the better of him. I think he may have a little crush on you. Do you think he will feel the same when he sees your new nose?" Gary asked with a high pitched laugh, that Marie thought sounded like it should be coming from an old witch, not a man. Maybe the laugh wasn't real. Marie had read somewhere that psychopaths didn't feel regular emotions. Maybe Gary thought it was supposed to be funny and chose to laugh, but he didn't really know how. Then again, Marie thought, maybe she was over-analyzing Gary. Maybe he was just a crazy person with a stupid laugh.

Marie wasn't sure what to make of Gary's comments. Why had he said that only Darrell was trying to save her? Had something happened to Gavril? He was certainly helping before Marie got captured, why would he stop after? Suddenly Marie had a thought. Since Gavril had been helping before, Gary would have certainly had visions that included him while they were searching for the kids. Why would he act like he didn't exist, unless of course he couldn't see Gavril for some reason? Marie still wasn't sure how or why Gary and Darrell got the visions. Gary could have been making then entire thing up. Even if he had been telling the truth, she still didn't really know how they worked, but she thought this made sense. Were some people shielded from the visions somehow? If Darrell and Gavril knew this maybe they really did have a chance to beat Gary. She suddenly had a bit more confidence, but she had to admit that Gary was really scaring her. Whatever his next sadistic plan was, she knew it wouldn't be good for any of them.

"Lost in thought?" Gary asked.

"Just thinking of how much I am really going to love watching Darrell beat the living hell out of you," Marie said.

"Oh, that's so cute, but we both know that despite being built like a giant, he is just a big teddy bear," Gary said.

"You keep telling yourself that. I have seen him lose his temper and it was bad news. That was just because someone pushed me down the stairs. That guy ended up in the hospital: imagine what he is going to do to the guy that kidnapped me and broke my nose," Marie said, exaggerating the story a little bit. Darrell did really lose his temper and it was scary. Marie had never seen him like that and she really thought he was going to kill the boy that pushed her down the stairs. As it turned out, apparently the boy thought so too and when he saw Darrell coming toward him with that look, the boy turned and ran away. The boy didn't look where he was going and ran right in front of a car. Luckily it was a school zone so the car wasn't going very fast. The boy ended up in the hospital with a concussion and broken ribs, and never messed with Marie again.

"You really don't get it, do you? This game has already played out in my visions. I know what happens, and your hero doesn't win," Gary said.

"If you already saw it, then you already got your enjoyment, right? Why play the game if you know the result?" Marie asked.

"Oh sure, there is a little pleasure in seeing the vision, but nothing can compare to actually having the blood on your hands and feel it dripping from your fingers. That is why we need to play the game," Gary said, his sadistic smile coming back.

Those last words hit Marie like another punch in the face. Gary kept calling this a game but he had truly sinister motives, and this scared her even more. She didn't know whose blood he was talking about, but it certainly didn't sound good.

"No witty retort? Well, I guess that means it's time to go. I am going to open your cage and I want you to slowly walk out and turn around so I can handcuff you," Gary said. "I can just drug you, but I really don't want to have to carry you, so please be good."

Marie did as she was told and slowly walked out of the cage, but she had to fight the desire to attack him again. Her fight or flight response had always been stuck in the fight position. All the years of martial arts training had done nothing but make her natural response to fight even worse. Every inch of her small frame wanted to turn around with a spinning back-fist and knock him out, but her brain knew it was a mistake. Her nose still hurt worse than just about anything she could remember and served as a reminder that fighting someone that could see the future was not a good idea. Marie wondered what a fight would be like with two people that could see the future.

She put her hands behind her back and Gary put the handcuffs on her. He grabbed her arm and led her up the stairs, out the door, and put her in the back of a panel van.

"A little obvious with the pedophile van, aren't we?" Marie asked.

"You really can't turn off the charming wit, can you? The van was a necessity. Not only did I have to ditch my car since you tipped off the cops, I needed it to transport our toys for the next game."

She was trying to find a comfortable position since there weren't seats, only an open cargo area, and as her eyes adjusted to the dark she noticed a big lump under a tarp. The more she looked at it, the more it looked like a body.

Despite her brain telling her not to, she reached out a foot and lifted up the tarp, revealing a face. The man was obviously dead and his dead stare was boring right through her.

"Jesus, you have a dead guy back here!" Marie yelled.

"Oh yeah, I picked him up earlier. He is for the third phase though, so don't worry about him right now," Gary said.

"There won't be a third phase. Darrell will stop you today," Marie said.

"You really place a lot of faith in him. Are you really that amazed by his visions?" Gary asked.

"Why do you think they won't help him?" Marie asked.

"As I said before, he and I are Sevenths. This gives us our powers. However, powers aren't supposed to manifest until the mid-thirties, this gives the brain time to fully form so that the Seventh can use the full potential of the brain. Darrell got his powers very young and his brain isn't fully equipped to use them. That combined with the fact that I have had my powers for longer and have practiced all facets of the powers, you can see he is no threat to me. I'm afraid your mighty hero is simply out matched," Gary said.

"David was outmatched when he fought Goliath and look how that turned out," Marie said.

"I have it on good authority that David versus Goliath didn't go down exactly like you may have heard. Regardless, I have prepared for every situation. Today is going to be glorious. Well, for me at least," Gary said.

Gary was exceptionally confident and cocky. Marie was hoping his over confidence would lead to a mistake. He pulled the van into a parking space right in front of a huge warehouse. He opened the back doors and pulled Marie out. He led her inside the warehouse and closed the door behind them. Marie saw a large raised platform with a ten-foot tower sitting on the back of it. She wasn't sure what to make of it.

"What in the hell is that?" Marie asked.

"That my dear, is the masterpiece that is phase two," Gary said.

"How in the world did you have time to build this?"

"Oh, I began building this weeks ago. This was originally meant for the father of the boy to play, but plans have changed. I must say that I am much more excited at the idea of Darrell playing than the other guy. I'm sure he will be much better at it, so this will be much more fun."

Gary grabbed her arm and had her climb on top of the platform and suddenly she knew what it was, but it still didn't make any more sense. They began walking across the giant circular platform and over to the tower. When they got to the ladder, it was obvious that she couldn't climb up with her hands cuffed.

"I'm going to un-cuff you, but remember, no funny business. If you're good, I'll keep you un-cuffed for the remainder of the phase. Do you agree?" Gary said.

"Fine," Marie said.

Gary removed her cuffs and she climbed up to the top. He picked up a contraption and put it over her head and locked it around her neck. It seemed like a torture device right out of a horror movie. She was really confused and growing more worried. Gary was so unpredictable, she couldn't figure out his plan and she was beginning to think the anxiety of not knowing was becoming worse with each passing minute.

"Wait here," Gary said.

"What is all of this? What is going on?" Marie asked.

"All will be revealed in due time, your place will be down there. Don't worry, it won't hurt much. For the time being, though, we will wait up here for our guests to arrive," Gary said.

CHAPTER TWENTY-FIVE - DARRELL

It took Darrell a few moments to gather his bearings and realize where he was when he awoke from his vision. He pulled himself out of the recliner. Despite getting some much needed sleep he was still very tired. Going on such little sleep was certainly taking its toll on him. He had not planned on sleeping at all when Gavril dropped him off, but he passed out within minutes of sitting down to read the books. He grabbed his phone to call Gavril, then had the thought that maybe Gavril was already home.

Darrell was surprised to realize that Gavril's house was laid out exactly like his own. He always knew that the outside seemed similar but the insides were exact, well the set-up, not the stuff inside. Andrea and Gavril had all kinds of crazy stuff around. Gavril was certainly right when he said a normal person would take less than two minutes to label them as devil worshipers. Gavril's room was more of the same. Very old occult looking books piled several feet high in nearly every part of the room except one corner that had a very old looking record player and tons of vinyl records. Gavril was sound asleep, much like Darrell had been, with books piled around him. Darrell shook Gavril awake and deftly dodged the punch that Gavril shot out.

"Whoa, dude. What's that about?" Darrell asked.

"Sorry man, I don't wake up so friendly. Thousands of years of not fearing death have led to me making more than a few enemies," Gavril said, rubbing his chest. "Man, this thing needs to stop hurting"

"You're immortal, but do you have super healing like that comic book guy Wolverine?"

"I heal quickly, but not that quickly. This should be better in a couple of weeks. A broken leg would only take a couple of days. The healing is not the problem; normally, it's the pain. We still feel pain and it sucks."

"I bet, but it kind of serves you right for being an idiot and stabbing yourself in the chest. Anyway, I had another vision. I know where they are, or at least going to be," Darrell said.

"What time is it?" Gavril asked as he swung his legs over the edge of the bed.

"About five in the morning," Darrell said.

"Figures. He is purposely trying to put us at a disadvantage when it comes to sleep. What kind of vision was it?" Gavril asked.

"What do you mean?" Darrell asked.

"Was it natural, or did he feed it to you? Could you tell if it was truthful?"

"Oh, I'm pretty sure it was fed, since it felt kind of like

the others. As far as it being truthful, I would say that the majority of it was truthful. There was a part where he showed me the two kidnapped kids and that felt weird so I'm not sure what that means. If I had more experience, I would be able to tell more definitively," Darrell said. He was surprised how quickly he was beginning to accept all of this Seventh and Overseer stuff, but there really wasn't a better explanation.

"Don't be too hard on yourself, you are doing very well for someone that hasn't had their powers very long. As for the kids, I saw on the news late last night that the kids were dropped off in front of a fire station, unharmed. So that part was most likely a lie. He wanted you to believe he still had them. So if it is fed and he lied, we can assume it is a trap. Tell me about it," Gavril said.

"I'm not really sure how to explain it. It was very disjointed, like the other one. First I got a glimpse of a clock. It showed 5:20, so we can assume that is the time he wants us there. Next, I saw a few different signs that showed me the name of the place and a few streets. We should be able to do an internet search and figure out the address. Then I saw a big warehouse, so I can recognize it, I guess. Next I saw the two kids in their cages. That is the part that felt strange. The last thing was really strange. I'm not sure what to make of it," Darrell said.

"What was it?" Gavril asked.

"It was an old video game. You know like the really old ones that were at an arcade," Darrell said.

"You realize that wasn't that long ago right?"

"Sure. Anything you say. Anyway it had a big gorilla on it."

"Donkey Kong?"

"Maybe. I'm not really up on old games. It was very weird though."

"That is quite odd. I'm not sure what it means either but I'm sure Gary will let us know soon. I wonder why the visions are disjointed now. Maybe he is just being careful not to show you too much."

"Maybe. We need to figure out where this place is so we can get going," Darrell said.

"Fire up my computer over there," Gavril said.

"Where?" Darrell asked.

"Over there. The tower is under the desk," Gavril said pointing to what Darrell was sure was the oldest computer he had ever seen, even on the internet.

"Dude. That is not a computer. What does that thing run on, vacuum tubes?"

"Very funny. When you live as long as Overseers do, you tend to not throw things out so quickly like you kids seem to do now days. It may be old, but it will still do the trick."

Darrell went over to the computer and pushed the power button. The ancient computer slowly booted up and showed an operating system Darrell didn't recognize.

"How are you supposed to get on the internet?"

"Just click here." Gavril said taking over the mouse and double clicking on an icon.

A moment later the computer started making really loud sounds. Darrell thought something was broken.

"What is wrong with your computer man?"

"Nothing. That is the sound it makes when it is dialing to connect to the internet," Gavril replied.

"Dial up!" Darrell yelled. "You have to be kidding me with this. How can you stand it being so slow?"

"We also tend to be more patient."

"Unbelievable. I'm just going to use my phone, it will be much faster." Darrell pulled out his phone and within seconds he was on the map search engine and typing in what he assumed was the name of the warehouse. He wasn't surprised that the result came up almost instantly. Darrell knew Gary wouldn't leave him finding the warehouse up to chance, despite the chaotic nature of the vision.

"Looks like the warehouse is about fifteen minutes away. We should probably get going," Darrell said.

"Okay, just let me get my stuff," Gavril said.

Darrell watched as Gavril went into his closet, knocked on a couple of panels in the back, pulled one of the hangers down and revealed a large hidden compartment in the back of the closet. Gavril reached in and pulled out a very large black case. To Darrell it looked like a suitcase on steroids. It was a little larger than a normal full-size suitcase but looked far more durable. The outer shell looked like it was made of carbon fiber and on the side it had one of the craziest locking mechanisms Darrell had ever seen.

"Is that an eyeball scanner on the lock?" Darrell asked in amazement.

"Pretty cool, huh?" Gavril asked.

"Um, yeah, it's awesome but what is in the case?" Darrell asked.

"That is not for you to know," Gavril said.

"What do you mean?" Darrell asked.

"It's my plan. You know I can't let you in on my plan

without risking Gary learning about it. Surprise is our best weapon right now and we need to keep the plan a surprise. We have to remember that we are on his turf, and we need every advantage we can get," Gavril said.

"Understood. The curiosity is killing me though. We should get going. You still have my dad's car?" Darrell asked.

"I pushed it into the garage just in case he was going around looking for it, or you," Gavril said.

Darrell headed for the back door and Gavril picked up his huge case easily and followed him. Looking at Gavril, Darrell wondered if the case was much lighter than he imagined or was Gavril just really strong. Did he have some kind of super strength to go along with being immortal? Would Darrell develop powers other than his visions? Now was not the time, but he would have to remember to ask Gavril when this was all over. Gavril pushed the buttons on the keychain remote, unlocking the doors and popping the trunk open. Gavril headed toward the trunk with his case and Darrell walked around getting in the passenger seat. Knowing how bad of a driver he was, Darrell decided it was best for Gavril to drive again. He knew his dad was really going to lose his cool when he confronted Darrell about taking his Mustang, but if he put a dent or scratch in it Darrell would certainly get a physical punishment, not just grounded.

Gavril climbed in the driver's seat, and placed the keys in the ignition.

"You want me to drive again?" Gavril asked.

"Yeah, I am a really bad driver," Darrell said.

"I thought you took driver's education last year."

"I did, but I didn't do very well. I had a major problem with concentration."

"Why is that?"

"Ms. Lopez taught that class and had her top unbuttoned so her cleavage showed every day. I found it really hard to concentrate on anything else. Hey, you're really old, does that ever go away?" Darrell asked.

"Nope, not even a little bit. I have Ms. Lopez for Spanish and if I wasn't already fluent in Spanish, I would not be passing," Gavril said.

"That's funny. Holy cow! I get it now. I get how you know every freaking thing in the world. You lived it! Marie and I would always try to figure it out. She thought you had a photographic memory. I said that you always tried to look cool at school but went home and studied as hard as you could. I guess neither of us was right," Darrell said.

"Actually you are both right, at least kind of. I wouldn't say I have a photographic memory per se but I do have a very good memory. I also do spend a fair amount of time studying, just not necessarily the stuff they are teaching in school," Gavril said with a laugh. "I supposed we better push the car down the street before I start it up."

"That's a great idea," Darrell agreed.

The two of them pushed the car out of the garage and down the street. Darrell was again surprised at Gavril's strength. They got in and Gavril started up the car. Darrell booted up the car's GPS system and entered the address of the warehouse. He began to try to psych himself up for the coming confrontation. Darrell hated confrontation and he wouldn't admit it but he was scared to death.

CHAPTER TWENTY-SIX - DARRELL

They pulled into the parking lot right at 5:20. Gavril drove around the warehouse a few times, despite Darrell's protests, before finally parking in the front parking lot. Darrell began to get out of the car, but Gavril grabbed his arm and stopped him.

"What are you doing?" Darrell asked.

"Wait."

"Wait for what?" Darrell was growing impatient.

"Two things. One, we need to make sure that we don't see any traps, but most importantly we need to make him sweat a little bit. Show him he isn't in complete control."

"But he is in control."

"Exactly. If we can take that from him, it could make him make a mistake. Let's just wait five minutes. Trust me. I have seen a lot of people like him over the centuries and they always hate it when they aren't in control. Don't worry. He won't dare hurt Marie because he needs her to get to you and that is what he really wants. We will go in at first light."

"Fine," Darrell reluctantly agreed.

It was the longest five minutes of Darrell's life. He wanted to ignore Gavril and go anyway, but Darrell needed to trust him. Gavril did have more experience and Darrell knew Gavril wouldn't let Marie get hurt. Darrell just sat there staring at the horizon waiting for the sun to peak its head out.

"There it is. That's first light, let's go," Darrell said as he grabbed the handle and got out of the car. He didn't give Gavril any time to object. Gavril got out and pulled his giant case out of the trunk.

"Don't suppose you have changed your mind about telling me what you are doing?" Darrell asked.

"You really have a problem, you know," Gavril said.

"I get that a lot. I suppose you want me to go in first so I don't know where you go?"

"That would be best," Gavril replied.

"Okay. I'm really worried about not really knowing what I'm walking into," Darrell said.

"That's understandable, but I need you to know, I mean truly believe, that I have your and Marie's back. This may get a little sketchy but I don't need to see the future to know that we will take this guy down."

"Thanks Gav," Darrell replied, not really knowing what to say.

As Darrell walked toward the warehouse door, he decided that he really did trust Gavril. He was still upset about being lied to for so long but deep down he understood why. Gavril seemed like a really good guy. He believed that Gavril would truly put his life on the line to save Darrell or Marie. He was suddenly stuck on how funny that thought was, since Gavril couldn't really put his life on the line because he was immortal. Darrell refrained from laughing out loud, but it was a struggle to do so. It's weird how sometimes you can have moments of levity in stressful situations.

Darrell pulled the door open and was suddenly struck a little blind by how bright the interior was compared to how dark it had been outside. Only with that realization did Darrell realize that all the exterior lights, including all the parking lot lights were out and Gary must have blacked out the windows. His eyes adjusted quickly and he noticed the big structure in front of him. He was not sure what to make of all the scaffolding but it only took a moment for his eyes to reach the top and notice Marie standing there with duct tape over her mouth. Darrell began running for the structure, while simultaneously looking for a ladder to climb up. He had only made it a few feet when Gary's voice broke the silence.

"That is far enough!" Gary's voice rang out sharply as it bounced around the metal building.

Darrell stopped running and looked for Gary. He looked all around and couldn't see him until a moment later. Gary stepped out onto the top of the structure standing next to Marie.

"Getting your damsel in distress is not going to be that easy. You have to win the game if you plan on rescuing her. If you refuse to play, or try to cheat in anyway, I will be forced to use this," Gary said, as he held out a small mechanical device. "One squeeze of this remote and the little robot arms attached to Marie's neck will inject her with enough morphine to overdose a mule. She will be dead before you could even reach her." Gary's voice seemed different than it had been in the visions. Now it had hint of crazy mixed with joy. Darrell thought he sounded like some sort of TV super villain, but he thought it could be his imagination mixed with his anger. After all nobody really sounded like that in real life.

"Why are you doing this?" Darrell asked. "She is not part of this. We both know you want me. Just let her go."

"That's not going to happen. I have a question for you though. Where is your Overseer? I guess I don't really have one now but when I did it seemed like she was always asking where I was going and what I was doing. So where is yours?"

"Back at home, I guess. He wasn't really onboard with me coming here. As a matter of fact, all he has ever done is try to talk me out of anything to do with my visions, or you. I finally gave him the slip by convincing him that I gave up on you and was leaving it up to the police. He thinks I'm home sleeping," Darrell said, pleased with how well his lie came out. He just hoped Gary couldn't see through it.

"Good. Overseers in general are pretty worthless. I got lucky with mine since she wasn't as stuck up as most, but her boss was a complete idiot. Overseers seem to always have an agenda. They never let you do what you want. They always sit up on their moral high horse and tell you what you shouldn't do. I really wish mine could be here to see this, but alas I had other plans for her."

"Why don't you let her go and we can really discuss our

visions and Overseers?" Darrell asked.

"You really think I'm stupid, don't you? I want you to play the game. Without her, you wouldn't play. Besides, without her, this game wouldn't be complete."

"And what game is that?"

"You haven't figured it out yet? I am truly disappointed. I know the game is before your time and even a little before mine if I'm being honest, but I would have thought you would have recognized it at least. I am quite proud at how it turned out. Mr. Johnson, I present to you, 'Human Donkey Kong'."

Darrell could see it now. The entire structure was built to mimic the first level of the old arcade game Donkey Kong. The scaffolding had been laid out at angles to mimic the bent girders making up the main layout. There were several small ladders around the structure to make shortcuts between the tiers of scaffolding. Then, Darrell noticed that Marie was standing at the top, just like the woman in the game. Gary was standing where Donkey Kong would be. He even had the barrels, or in this case fifty-five gallon drums next to him. Just then, above Gary and Marie, a giant scoreboard lit up that mimicked the score you would see at the top of the screen in the arcade game. Darrell was speechless. He had to admit the structure was impressive but was certainly from the mind of a psychopath.

"Looks like you figured it out. Can I assume you know how to play?" Gary asked.

"You can't be serious with this thing?" Darrell asked.

"Oh, I am quite serious, and if you want Marie to live, you will play," Gary said, waving the trigger mechanism around. "Now, do you know how to play?"

"I'm not sure," Darrell replied. Darrell was suddenly struck with a memory. Since he was so young when he had been adopted, he never really had memories of his birth parents, but now as he stood here staring at the monstrosity that Gary had built he had the very clear memory of a Donkey Kong arcade machine in the living room and his birth father holding Darrell in his lap as he played it. "I think I played when I was a little kid. But I would have been like five or so," Darrell added.

"Is that a yes or no?" Gary asked.

"No, I guess," Darrell said, as he struggled to shake the memory out of his head and focus on the task at hand.

"Jesus, are you always this frustrating? Ok, listen closely as I'm only going to explain this once. Your job is to walk up the scaffolding going from level to level until you make it to the damsel in distress. You can also use the ladders scattered over the level as a shortcut. The trick is that I will be throwing these barrels down at you. You have to jump over them to get past them. You can't go around them, as that would be cheating, you must jump over them. The only exception is to use a hammer. There is a sledgehammer hanging along the way. If you want you can pull it down and use it to smash the barrel. If you smash it you must push it off the edge and then you can go past. If you get hit by or touch a barrel while jumping over it, that will cost one life. You get three lives. If you get to Marie without dying three times, you two get to leave, fair and square."

"And how do we know that you will hold up your end of the bargain?" Darrell asked.

"I guess you will just have to trust me," Gary said.

"Because you have been trustworthy so far," Darrell spat.

"Listen! You don't have much of a choice here, do you? I want to be Donkey Kong and you are going to be Mario, or I'm going to kill her!" Gary yelled. His voice was much stronger now and his rage was showing through. "Now get in place, the game is about to start."

CHAPTER TWENTY-SEVEN - DARRELL

Darrell didn't see any other choice but to play along. He hoped that whatever Gavril's plan was, it was going to work, and he hoped that the plan was going to happen soon. Darrell took his place on the bottom level and got ready. On its surface, Darrell thought the game seemed pretty easy, so he was even more worried. There was no way Gary would go through all of this trouble if it would be easy for Darrell to win. Then again, Gary must have built the structure ahead of time, and maybe he had someone else in mind when he built it. Maybe Darrell would be better at it than Gary thought and could win. Marie looked frightened, but resolute. Darrell tried to give her a confident smile, but he wasn't sure she bought it. Suddenly, the sharp blast of an air horn rang out, which echoed loudly around the building. Darrell assumed that meant the game had started. He began walking toward the opposite end of the scaffolding he was on.

"Was that really necessary?" Darrell asked, though much louder than he meant to, due to the ringing in his ears.

Darrell had taken only a couple of steps when music began blaring from the many speakers that Darrell now noticed were scattered along the ceiling. Darrell assumed it was the music from the video game. Whatever it was, it was exceptionally loud. The volume gave Darrell an immediate headache, and he realized it was all part of Gary's plan. The music made it very hard to concentrate. It was so loud that when he passed under one of the larger speakers it was hard to even keep his eyes open. The music was affecting his concentration and he knew that must have been Gary's plan. He was nearly to the end of the first of the six tiers when one of the drums fell down right in front of him and began rolling toward him. Darrell had only a split second to react, and he had no choice but to jump over it. He wasn't quite quick enough though and his front foot caught the front of the barrel just a little bit. Darrell kept moving a few steps when a loud sound played, Darrell assumed it was the sound the game makes when a player dies.

"Now now. You weren't going to try to cheat were you? We both know your foot touched that barrel. You are dead and that is one life down. Back to the starting place for life number two. I give you permission to sidestep the two barrels that are already heading your way so we can start fresh."

Darrell turned around and walked back to the starting spot. He tried but couldn't find the camera that Gary must have hidden somewhere to notice Darrell hitting the barrel. Darrell moved aside to let the two barrels pass but changed his mind and instead used them to make practice jumps to try to get the timing down.

"Glad to see you are getting in the spirit!" Gary said excitedly. "Get ready for life two." The giddiness in Gary's voice was becoming unsettling. Gary was enjoying this far too much. Darrell was sure now that with Gary enjoying the game this much, there was no way he was going to let Marie go if Darrell won. Unfortunately Darrell couldn't come up with any other solution so he needed to continue to play.

The air horn sounded again and Darrell began walking. When he was about halfway to the end he realized that he was so tall that he could reach up and touch the bottom of the tier above him. He could feel the barrel coming down the scaffolding so he made his way toward the end and quickly jumped over it when it fell. He climbed up to the second tier before the next barrel could make it to him. Safely on the second tier now, he began to walk. A few feet into the second tier he found the sledgehammer Gary mentioned. Darrell didn't have too much trouble jumping the last couple of barrels but thought maybe the hammer was a safer bet. It wasn't long before he got his chance to test that theory. As another barrel came along, Darrell took the sledgehammer and swung it toward the barrel. He was surprised how easily it was crushed. Darrell pushed it off the edge and made his way toward the end. He decided to use the ladder toward the end to avoid the barrel coming down from above.

He waited for the barrel to pass over him and finished climbing the ladder to the third tier. Another barrel came rolling down the scaffolding. Darrell smashed it with the sledgehammer, but he was surprised that the hammer broke right where the handle met the steel.

"This stupid hammer broke!" Darrell yelled as he shoved the broken barrel over the side

"Of course it did. The hammers don't last forever. You really should have played this video game before, you would be more prepared. Especially for what's coming up," Gary said.

Darrell didn't have time to really register what Gary said before he saw what Gary meant. Darrell had been distracted by the hammer so much that he had forgotten to keep checking the ceiling and didn't have much warning for the next barrel. Although, even if he had known the barrel was coming he wouldn't have been prepared for it. Darrell stood, staring at the rolling flaming barrel coming straight for him. Between the hammer and the surprise of the flaming barrel he didn't have enough time to properly react. He barely jumped over it but his pants must have been too close because they caught on fire. Darrell dropped to the ground and began slapping at his pant leg, trying to put the flame out, but there must have been some kind of accelerant on the barrel, though, because the flame was not going out easily. Darrell ripped off his jacket and was able to put the fire out by smothering it.

Just as he put the flame out, the player dying sound was played over the speakers. Darrell looked down at his leg and tried not to freak out. The fire had done a fair amount of damage. As the shock began to wear off, the burn was beginning to really hurt. He pulled the remaining fabric away from the burn and tied it up above his knee to keep it from rubbing or hitting the burn. As he stood up, the pain seemed to grow exponentially. He stood for a moment and focused. He tried to think past the pain. Somehow he was able to focus enough to make the pain lessen. He wondered if it was just the adrenaline from the game and wanting to save Marie, or did he have a secondary power? He silently cursed himself for being obsessed about having another power. Hadn't the first power caused enough trouble already? He forced the thought from his mind, he knew this was not time to worry about it. He still had to save Marie and that meant he still had to play this psychopath's game.

"Back to the start, Darrell. I'm sorry about the flaming barrel."

"You nearly burnt my leg off you maniac!" Darrell yelled.

"Oh, I am not sorry about burning you," Gary said laughing a fairly maniacal laugh. Darrell couldn't help but wonder if once you know you are a maniac you put the effort into learning to laugh like a crazy person, or if having a crazy person laugh was some sort of early warning sign that you would turn into a maniac. "I'm sorry because flaming barrels don't really come down in the game, they catch fire at the bottom and follow you up. I couldn't rig that up in time, so I decided throwing them from the top would suffice. By the way, you are down to your last life. You better make it count," Gary said.

Darrell made his way back down to the starting point. He did a couple of practice jumps along the way to test his leg and see if he was going to be able to do it. He still had a lot of pain but he decided he was good enough to be able to make it through. He was pretty sure he should go to the hospital afterward, but he could power through for now. He had barely made it past the starting line and turned around when the air horn sounded. He was determined to make this last life count and make it to the top. He decided his best bet was to use the ladders as much as possible. Not only as shortcuts but the ladders could help avoid having to jump barrels.

Darrell's plan was working like a charm. He was now on the ladder to climb to the top level. When he climbed high enough to see the top level, he could see Marie standing there strapped into Gary's crazy morphine contraption. She still looked so calm though. Darrell wished he could have her resolve. He felt he was doing a good job of staying calm enough to get through but she was unflappable. Darrell was waiting for the right moment. He was going to jump up there and save Marie. He watched as Gary grabbed a barrel and placed it to roll down the scaffolding. Darrell's plan was to duck down, let the barrel roll over him and then jump up and run to Marie. If Gary could even roll another barrel fast enough he was certain he could jump over it. If not then he would at least be close enough to grab the device and rip it off of Marie.

Darrell climbed down a couple of rungs on the ladder and prepared himself to move quickly. The ladder was so close to the end of the tower that he would only have a few seconds after the barrel passed over him before it fell to the next tier and began rolling toward him, hitting his feet. Darrell looked up, poised to move when he saw the barrel, and everything seemed to move in slow-motion. Right as he saw the barrel, he knew something was different. This barrel was a little smaller than the previous ones which meant that it didn't roll over the ladder hole, it fell right through. Even if Darrell had world class reaction times, which as a decidedly non-athlete he didn't, he wouldn't have been able to dodge the barrel falling down on him. He only had time to think that he really wished he had played Donkey Kong more so he would have known this was possible.

Darrell threw his arms up to block the barrel but moved so quickly that he lost his balance and fell on his back. The barrel landed on his chest, knocking the breath out of him. Time still seemed to be moving slowly for Darrell as he threw the barrel off of himself and struggled to get to his feet while his body struggled to catch its breath. With one hand grasping his chest, his other grabbed the ladder, he heard the player dying sound ring out overhead. Darrell was still determined to get up and save Marie before Gary could get to her. He climbed the ladder with such speed that he surprised himself. He skipped several rungs and launched himself onto the top platform. Marie was only steps away when Gary yelled out.

"Stop!" Gary shouted "That's game over. Don't try to cheat or you know what will happen."

"I played your stupid game, now let Marie go," Darrell said in spurts, still trying to catch his breath. He took a single step forward.

"Seriously, you don't think you can get to her before I can pull this trigger, do you? I have just seen a demonstration of your athletic prowess, and while better than I had expected, it's nowhere near good enough to pull off that feat," Gary said.

Gary reached behind the barrels and pulled up a big box

attached to a thick cable. The box had three large buttons on it. Darrell thought it looked like something he had seen in professional garages to raise the lifts. Gary pushed the top button and smiled at Darrell as the ceiling began to slowly open above them. Darrell wasn't sure what to make of it. Gary hit the next button and the platform containing Marie began to rise toward the new opening. This was Gary's escape plan, and Darrell wasn't sure how to stop it. Gary climbed up next to Marie and gave Darrell another one of his creepy smiles. Darrell took another couple of steps toward him, not knowing what else to do. Gary stopped him by holding out his trigger again as a threat.

Darrell was about to accept the fact that Gary was going to get away, then a loud shot rang out. The noise was deafening, and for a moment Darrell was confused as to what was going on. He saw Gary clutching his hand, blood was pouring out and he had dropped the trigger. Gary had been shot in the hand. Darrell looked around for the source and saw Gavril on the opposite end of the warehouse. He had to be over a hundred feet away on a metal scaffold. Gavril was lying on his stomach with the biggest gun Darrell had ever seen. He figured it was some sort of a sniper rifle based on his Army video game expertise. He looked back at Gary and saw Marie kick the trigger off of the still rising platform.

With Marie safe from the poison, Darrell began running toward the platform. He was about halfway there when another shot rang out and he saw blood spurt out from Gary's arm. Gary was in a full blown panic now. He was bleeding badly from his two gunshot wounds, but it was all too late. The platform rose too quickly. Gary and Marie were already on the roof before Darrell reached the platform. He climbed up the steel rungs to the top of the platform as quickly as he could, hearing another shot ring out just as he reached the roof. He was on the roof quickly, but it wasn't quick enough. He could see Gary throw Marie in the back of a van and jump in the driver's seat. Darrell noticed a zip-line next to him. That must have been how they got down so quickly. Darrell heard Gavril call out from behind him.

"Don't try it, you don't have a good handle, you'll just fall."

"They got in a van and are getting away!" Darrell yelled back, knowing Gavril was right about the zip line.

"Hurry back down and get to the car!" Gavril yelled as he was already running back to where he came from. Darrell ran down through the tower and was on the ground in a matter of seconds. He began running toward the door. He slammed the door open mid-stride so violently he surprised himself, and without looking back wondered if he actually broke it. He was about halfway to the car when he realized Gavril had the keys. He stopped and turned in a panic. He saw Gavril following him, running much faster than a man of his size carrying a case so large should have been able to.

"Get in, it's unlocked!" Gavril yelled.

Darrell did as he was told. He watched in awe at how deftly Gavril opened the trunk, threw the case in and jumped in the driver's seat, in what Darrell swore was one fluid motion. Gavril started the car, jammed it in first gear and tore out of the parking lot so fast Darrell's head was slammed backwards. Gavril was accelerating so quickly that Darrell couldn't pull his head away from the headrest. His dad had always talked about how fast the car was, but Darrell had never seen evidence of it because his dad always drove it so conservatively. Darrell had never really believed him until now, when he could feel the power for himself. For a split second he had a thought about being sorry for not believing his dad. This thought was quickly replaced with a feeling of terror as Gavril turned the wheel hard and pulled the emergency brake, causing the back end of the car to lose control and slide sideways. The car drifted around the corner and just as quickly as it was out of control, Gavril slammed the car into another gear and the car regained traction as it leapt forward, gaining speed. He didn't know what to think about Gavril's driving. In the time Darrell had known him, Gavril had only ever ridden a bike. Perhaps it was because it would be hard to explain being able to drive like you were in a Fast and Furious movie at the age of sixteen. Darrell was jerked back to reality when he saw the van's taillights ahead of them.

"There they are!" He yelled.

"They are too far away," Gavril said, slamming the car into another gear. "Too much of a head start."

Just as he said that the van took a turn and Darrell knew what Gavril meant. The van had quite a lead, and when it took the turn it was a little difficult to see exactly where the van went. When Gavril got to the street the van had turned onto, the van was nowhere to be seen. They could have taken any number of turns in either direction. Just like that, they were gone. Gavril quickly brought the car to a stop, rolled all the windows down and shut off the engine.

"What are you doing?" Darrell asked.

"Shh. Maybe we can hear them and figure out which way they went," Gavril said in a forced whisper.

A few seconds later they heard a loud crash. Gavril started the car up and quickly made his way toward the sound. Darrell was quite impressed at how accurate Gavril was in finding the crash site based on sound alone. They pulled right up to the van and both jumped out. Darrell quickly opened the back of the van and was disappointed to find it empty, except for a lump under a tarp. Darrell's heart stopped as he lifted the tarp to see what was underneath. He was relieved to see that the body underneath was not Marie's. He knew he should feel bad for the man that was obviously murdered by Gary, but he had thought for a moment that it would be Marie and that feeling of relief was hard to shake. A moment later the relief turned into realization. Marie was gone. Apparently Gavril had been thinking the same thing because he seemed to reply to Darrell's thought.

"We are too late," Gavril said.

"We can still track them. Look, he is leaving a trail of blood," Darrell said, pointing to the ground leading away from the crash.

"We really need to get out of here Darrell. We have to get back to HQ and regroup," Gavril said.

"No. We are close, we can't give up now," Darrell said. His anxiety and panic were both climbing at an alarming rate. They couldn't give up. He had been so close to saving her.

"We aren't giving up, but look at the situation. This van made a very loud crash, so police are most likely on the way. When they get here they will find a dead body in the back. They are going to potentially follow the trail of blood to find a man who has been shot twice. Oh, and by the way, they will find a highly illegal sniper rifle that happened to make those gunshot wounds in the trunk of a car that may have been reported stolen at this point. Then they find two teenagers, one of which has forged identification papers. Does that sound like a good scenario to you?" Gavril said, much more animated than usual.

"Okay okay, I get it. I can't believe we are gonna just let him get away with Marie. What if he kills her?" Darrell asked.

"Don't worry about that. He is going be pissed, sure, but he still wants to finish the game and he needs her to motivate you. Now let's get out of here," Gavril said.

CHAPTER TWENTY-EIGHT - GAVRIL

A few minutes earlier

Gavril watched Darrell run to the warehouse door and waited until he was completely inside before he began running toward the warehouse himself, looking for a different entry point. He knew he had the element of surprise in his favor since Gary wouldn't be able to see him in his visions, but if he didn't find the right way to execute his plan quickly and silently, it would all be for naught. Gary seemed to be laser focused on Darrell, but he had to know Gavril existed. Even if Gary didn't know exactly who Gavril was, he knew that Darrell would have an Overseer and he knew Gary would be cautious about how that Overseer was helping Darrell.

Gavril ran all the way around the building, but didn't find another way in. He couldn't exactly go through the front door. He had no idea how long he had. He was nearly back to the front when he found a ladder about eight feet from the ground that he couldn't quite reach. Luckily he quickly found the release to drop it down to the ground. As he stood at the bottom looking up, the ladder appeared to go all the way to the roof. The ladder looked like it was about forty feet high and Gavril couldn't even be sure that there would be a way inside once he was on the roof, but he needed to make a decision quickly and decided that it was worth the gamble, because Gary probably wouldn't think about looking for someone coming down from the roof.

The climb up was very long, very slow, and incredibly painful. Gavril cursed himself again for doing something as stupid as stabbing himself in the heart. It had been a thousand years since he did that, but he still should have remembered how much it hurt. The way he had to twist his body to hold the case and climb up the ladder was putting an incredible amount of strain on his stitches. He knew that regulations were one rung every twelve inches, which meant he was going to have to endure at least forty of these painful steps.

The pain mixed with the cumbersome nature of his large case made the climb take far longer than he anticipated. When he reached the top rung, he swung the case and threw it on top of the roof. He felt a sharp pain in his chest and instinctively grabbed it. He didn't have to look to know he had ripped his stitches open. He could feel the warm blood slowly seeping through his t-shirt. He wiped the blood from his hand onto his jeans and climbed up on the roof. He was pleased to see that only a few feet away was a hatch that led inside.

He hurried over and opened the hatch. Inside there was a small ladder that led to some sort of catwalk about ten feet down. Gavril grabbed his case and carefully lowered it down to the catwalk as he climbed down. Once he was standing on the catwalk, he looked around and noticed the catwalk went around the entire warehouse. This was good, because he could only see the back of Gary standing on top of some huge structure. Marie was next to him in some sort of cage. She seemed to have a contraption attached to her neck that Gavril couldn't quite make out. There was also some incredibly loud music playing that Gavril couldn't quite place.

Gavril, as quickly and as quietly as possible, moved down the catwalk until he could see the front of Gary and the structure. He heard Gary say something about life two and heard another air horn sound. As soon as he turned around and was able to take in the entire structure, he knew immediately what the Donkey Kong game was in reference to and suddenly with context the music and Gary talking about lives made perfect sense. It was the theme song to Donkey Kong and Gary was making Darrell play some sort of human Donkey Kong.

Gavril had been without a Seventh during the video game explosion of the early 1980's and had fallen for those games hard. Donkey Kong hadn't been his favorite, that would always be Tempest, but he had played Donkey Kong quite often enough. As much as he hated himself for even thinking it, as he looked at the giant human Donkey Kong structure, he couldn't help but be impressed. The structure was immense and Gary really had put a lot of effort into the details.

Gavril shook himself out of the surprise of the structure and knelt down to open the case. He heard Darrell and Gary arguing about his hammer breaking. Gavril turned around just in time to see Darrell misjudge a flaming barrel and catch on fire. It was all Gavril could do to not scream out but luckily he could see that Darrell was putting the flame out. He would be hurt certainly, but he would be okay. Gavril went back to the case and unlocked it by putting his eye in front of the scanner and then placing his thumb on a print reading panel. He knew all of the security measures were over the top, but he had seen so much gun violence and death over the years, he didn't want to be the reason someone got hurt just because he left his gun unsecured.

He opened the case and began to pull out the Barrett M82 sniper rifle. He was very intrigued by guns once they came into use, until he saw their destruction up close and first hand. He grew to hate guns after fighting in several wars and seeing how easy they made it to take another person's life. After his stint as a sniper in the Gulf War, he vowed to never use one again. This particular rifle had been put in its case and shoved away for many years. He didn't know why he felt compelled to bring it along when he moved to Junctionville, but when this situation came up, he knew he was destined to bring it to this warehouse.

He assembled all of the pieces together as fast as he could and laid on his stomach with his rifle facing toward Gary. He was in place just in time to see Darrell working his way up to the next to last level of scaffolding. Gavril began to wonder if Gary would actually admit defeat and give up Marie if Darrell reached her, and then he saw it.

Darrell was waiting on the last ladder for a barrel to pass, but Gary had grabbed a noticeably smaller barrel. Gavril knew instantly that the barrel would fall down the hole for the ladder and land right on Darrell which would cause him to lose. Gavril began to look at Marie and Gary through his scope. He had a clear shot at Gary but he was holding some sort of trigger device, and Gavril had to assume that it was set to do something to Marie with whatever the contraption attached to her neck was. Gavril's thoughts proved true when a moment later he threatened to pull the trigger if Darrell came after Marie. He then pulled out a big mechanical box that Gavril knew right away was to make the platform raise.

They began to rise toward the now open ceiling. Gavril could see that Darrell was torn and when he began to get closer, Gary threatened him with the trigger again. He knew what he had to do. He quickly adjusted his scope and aimed on Gary's hand. Gavril's target was moving, not only upwards, but as Gary moved his hand around naturally. Gavril knew he only had one shot so he took a breath, steadied his aim and squeezed the trigger.

He had forgotten how loud the rifle was and with it being fired in a closed area, it rang even louder. Gavril was stunned by the noise and struggled for a moment to regain his focus. Once his head cleared, he looked through his scope again and noticed that he had hit his mark and Gary had dropped the trigger and was now holding his hand, trying to stop the blood. Gavril saw that Darrell had realized Marie was safe and began running toward Marie and Gary. He could tell that Darrell wouldn't make it in time and decided to help again.

He took aim at the mechanical box located on the platform that was making it rise. He thought that if he shot that box, the platform would stop rising. He took aim, but his adrenaline was now soaring and his head was still swimming from the unexpected loud sound. Gavril squeezed the trigger but knew as soon as he felt the rifle recoil, he missed.

He looked through the scope and realized he had hit Gary in the arm and the platform was still rising and it was going too quickly for Darrell to catch. He cursed his aim. All of those years without practice had obviously taken their toll. Gavril grabbed his rifle and case and began running as quickly as he could toward the ladder that led to the roof. He made it faster than he thought he could and thanked his adrenaline rush. He dropped his case and quickly climbed the ladder with one hand, holding his rifle in the other. By the time he got to the roof he saw Gary and Marie sliding down a huge zip line that went from the roof to the street where Gavril could see a van waiting for them. Gary had made Marie go first and she looked terrified as she was holding on to the handle for dear life. Gary was sliding right behind her and looked like he was really struggling to hold on with only his one good arm.

Gavril raised his rifle and took aim at Gary's leg. He didn't want to kill Gary, he had dealt with death enough over the years, but he wanted to make it impossible or at least difficult to get away before Darrell and Gavril could get down to the street. Gavril squeezed his trigger again and missed completely. He decided he couldn't take another shot without potentially hitting Marie in the process.

Darrell appeared from a hole in the roof and saw Gary and Marie landing on the street. Gavril knew what he was thinking right away.

"Don't try it, you don't have a good handle, you'll just fall," Gavril yelled at Darrell, praying that Darrell would listen.

"They got in a van and are getting away!" Darrell yelled back.

"Hurry back down and get to the car!" Gavril yelled.

Gavril began running back to the hole he came from. He needed to get his case from the catwalk. That wasn't the kind of evidence he needed laying around for the police to find. He quickly jumped down to the catwalk, grabbed his case and began his one-handed climb back up. His chest was burning and he didn't dare look down to see how much it was bleeding. He didn't want to know. He was able to disassemble his rifle in a few seconds and shove it in the case. It wasn't in there perfectly, but it was good enough to close. He grabbed the case and ran over to the ladder he used to climb up.

His rifle case was supposed to handle a ton of abuse, and Gavril decided this was a perfect time to test that out. He dropped the case down to the ground and began climbing down the ladder as quickly as his body would let him. He hit the ground a few moments later and was pleased to see the case was still in one piece. He grabbed the case and began to run as fast as he could toward the car. As soon as Gavril rounded the corner he saw Darrell burst through a door. Gavril was shocked to see the door's top hinge break away. Darrell had done some serious damage to that door and Gavril made a mental note to avoid playing football with him. Darrell stopped and turned around, obviously looking for Gavril, or at least the car keys Gavril was carrying.

"Get in, it's unlocked!" Gavril yelled, waving Darrell toward the car.

CHAPTER TWENTY-NINE - GAVRIL

The sounds of sirens were still distant as they pulled away and made their way back to HQ. Gavril knew Darrell was upset about leaving without pursuing Gary and Marie, but hoped he would understand his reasoning. Gavril knew his identification paperwork was pretty good, but unfortunately the Overseer Council being so old, was not exactly skilled in newer technology. The Council always claimed that they never saw the value in technology. Gavril knew the real reason was that they hated change. He figured that technology was just too big of a change, especially changing something that had been in place for so long. Because of this reluctance to adopt technology, the identifications they produced were still old school and rarely went beyond paper. When they did do something electronic it was only to try to hide some major event a Seventh caused, and that was only done out of necessity. The funny thing was that some of the new Overseers were quite adept at technology.

Gavril couldn't afford to have the police looking into his records. If they did, he would certainly end up in some federal facility, and the Overseer Council would have to pull strings to get him out. The last time he knew of that happening, that Overseer was reassigned to translating duty. He had to spend every day copying and translating Overseer journals. Gavril shuddered at the thought of having a real job, especially one so boring.

"How is your leg? Should we go to the hospital?" Gavril asked.

"No, I can deal with it. It hurts like crazy, but if I go to the hospital who knows what will happen. They will call my dad for sure, which will effectively end our ability to find Gary and Marie. I will get it looked at when this is all over. Besides, if you are still going with a giant hole in your chest, I can handle a little burn. Speaking of which, your chest looks like it is bleeding pretty badly."

"I know, I'll deal with it back at HQ," Gavril replied.

"So, where did you learn to drive like that?" Darrell asked.

"Japan. Before I got assigned to you I had a long layoff. When we are not actively overseeing a Seventh we pretty much get to do whatever we want. At least the field Overseers. I have been lucky over the years to have amassed a lot of money, so while others have to get jobs, I get to have fun. I heard about drifting in Japan back in the nineties and decided to give it a go."

"You were amazing," Darrell said.

"Thanks. With over twenty years' experience, I had better be," Gavril said.

"Wait, twenty years? How did you explain to the other racers that you didn't age?"

"That's actually a funny story for another time. I'll just say that over those twenty years I was three separate people. I would move away, change my hair and clothing style, and then move back. Nobody ever noticed. I think a few people had suspicions but didn't want to appear racist by saying all non-Asians look alike."

"That's funny. You're gonna have to tell me about that later. So you speak Japanese too?" Darrell asked.

"When you count dialects, I speak over twenty languages fluently," Gavril replied.

"Holy cow, that's ridiculous. How can you keep them straight?" Darrell asked.

"Practice and immersion. Don't forget, I have nothing but time. I really just put myself into the middle of the country and don't give myself the option of not speaking the language. And of course originally it took a lot of studying. The world is more connected and accepting now, but a thousand years ago I couldn't go into a place like China and get anywhere not speaking Chinese."

"I guess that makes sense," Darrell said. "I'm still struggling to wrap my head around how old you are. You must have seen some amazing things. I mean you have lived through most of recorded history."

"Yeah, but I have seen some horrifying things as well. Those are the things that really stick with you. Those are the things you can't stop seeing when you close your eyes at night. More than half of all Overseers don't make it past three or four generations before they opt out, so to speak," Gavril said.

"Opt out, you mean kill themselves? I thought you were immortal," Darrell asked.

"There are ways, horrible ways, but it is possible."

"You ever think it was too much?"

"A time or two, sure. I have served in eight wars, accompanying a Seventh, and those are never good."

"I guess that explains the gun and how you could hit Gary from so far away," Darrell said.

"I was a sniper in the first Gulf War. I used to be pretty decent but I guess I am rusty. Twenty years ago I wouldn't have missed the second time."

"I thought you haven't had a Seventh in a long time?" Darrell asked.

"I haven't. I fought in that war on my own. Again, that's a story for another time," Gavril said as he pulled into the back parking lot of their HQ and turned off the headlights.

"Is someone still in there?" Darrell asked pointing to a lit window in the law office that was attached to their HQ.

"There might be. If the case was big enough they might pull an all-nighter. It is probably just the security guard though. I have seen them hanging out inside before. They watch TV and stuff."

"I'm torn about that. On the one hand I guess it makes us less likely to get caught sneaking into HQ, but on the other hand it doesn't exactly make this place as safe as I thought it was."

"Either way, let's not get caught out here. Come on," Gavril said as he and Darrell quietly snuck through the parking lot and into their HQ.

"I'm going to call Andrea and see if she has any new insights. You should start working the cameras to see if you can track them. He was injured and in a hurry so maybe he was more careless this time," Gavril said.

"Sounds good. What about hospitals? He seemed like he was losing a lot of blood," Darrell asked.

"That's a good idea, but I'm not sure he would go knowing that they would report a gunshot wound. You think you could hack into the hospital's systems and check new patients?" Gavril asked.

"I'm not near as good as Marie on that front, but she has taught me a thing or two. I'll give it a shot," Darrell said.

"Cool, I'll leave you to it. Here is some burn cream and some gauze for your leg. I'm gonna go out here, stitch up and call Andrea," Gavril said, as he pointed to his chest and walked into the living room area.

Gavril knew Andrea was going to be pretty angry when she heard about what happened at the warehouse, especially about Gavril using his sniper rifle. Overseers were supposed to do just that, oversee. They were never supposed to interfere or take part in visions. The council always said that Overseers were excluded from the visions for a reason. Our job is to observe, guide and record they would say. If the council found out how active a role that Gavril was taking, he was certain they would remove him and maybe even give him a stupid job as punishment. He took a deep breath and dialed her number.

"Are you serious? Do you have any idea what time it is Gavril?" Andrea said as she answered the phone. "This better be important."

"It is Andrea, Sorry for the early call. I just wanted to keep you abreast of the kidnapping situation here," Gavril said.

"Did you get him?" Andrea asked.

"No, not yet. We were close but we had to fallback to avoid the police. I used the fact that he couldn't see me in his visions to my advantage and wounded him, but he got away. Now he knows I am helping Darrell so he will be more careful," Gavril said.

"Wounded him? Do I even want to know?" Andrea asked.

"No, you don't. Let's just move on. Do you have any other information that could help?" Gavril asked.

"I have. I was going to call you later when it was a decent hour. Anyway, I'm not sure Darrell will be able to do it," Andrea said.

"If I have learned anything recently, it is that Darrell can do anything he sets his mind to. What is it?"

"I spoke to one of the seniors and she says that there is no way to combat the pushed visions. She suggested having him force his own vision."

"That is pretty advanced. I had him try to force a vision before and it didn't work," Gavril asked. "Any word one the Council's people getting here?"

"No. it sounds like they don't understand or believe in the severity of the situation. You know they never watch the news so it might be another day or two. Are you sure you still don't want me to come down? I can be there soon."

"I'm sure."

"Okay. Gavril?"

"Yeah?"

"You really need to get this guy. You have to keep

Darrell safe. The council can be forgiving, but if Darrell is hurt, I won't be able to protect you or myself. I don't need to tell you what a catastrophe like that would mean for our careers. We might get some leniency because Gary is a psychopath and the council lost track of him, but it still won't be good," Andrea said. "I'm putting a lot of faith in you and putting my career on the line. I didn't sign up for being immortal to be regulated to pushing paperwork for eternity."

"I know, and I really appreciate it Andrea. Your help and situation doesn't go unnoticed," Gavril replied. He wasn't sure he agreed with the council being forgiving, but he did agree that if Darrell was hurt it would be much worse.

"I am appearing before the council today about the situation we had here. I'll see if I can persuade them again."

"Appearing before the council? It must have been pretty bad if you have to debrief the council in person," Gavril said.

"I predict at least two Overseers being stripped of all duties and rights and who knows what they will do to the three Sevenths," Andrea said.

"Holy cow, I haven't heard of anything that big happening in at least a thousand years. Anybody I know?"

"One thousand three hundred and twenty years to be precise. At least that is what I have been told. Several times. I'm sure you know them or at least know of them, but I'll wait until their trial is over before I tell you who they are. Anyway, if you don't need me I'll get some more sleep so I can function better. Call me when you have more updates and please take care of Gary Franks," Andrea said.

"I will," Gavril said. Unfortunately, Gavril wasn't sure that Gary would allow himself to be caught alive. Gavril headed back to the kitchen to get the first aid kit to patch himself up.

Once he was clean and bandaged, he went back into the conference room to find Darrell working on the traffic cameras.

"Any luck with the hospitals?" Gavril asked.

"No. I was able to get into all three of the closest hospital's computers, but none of them had anyone come in with gunshot wounds. It really is concerning how easy it is to hack into the hospitals. I'm working on the cameras now. It doesn't look like that part of town has many cameras so I'm not having any luck here either. How about you, any luck with your mom? I mean Andrea. That's still weird," Darrell asked.

"Maybe. She says you should try to force a vision," Gavril said.

"I tried that before and it didn't work," Darrell asked.

"I know, but you were distracted. You just need to focus," Gavril said. "I wish I could give you a more technical explanation, but that is all I have. I know you are powerful enough to do it."

"What do you mean powerful enough? Why would I be more powerful than someone else? Gav, are you sure that you're telling me everything you know about Gary and this situation?" Darrell asked.

"Not exactly. I know that this may come as a shock, but-"

"Gary is my birth father," Darrell said, finishing Gavril's sentence.

"You knew?"

"I guessed. The Donkey Kong game stirred up an old memory that I didn't even know I had. In the memory I saw my birth father and he had different colored eyes, just like Gary. I looked it up and apparently that is pretty rare. Couple that rarity with the weird Donkey Kong obsession and I just guessed."

"Wow, that's pretty good deductive reasoning. Your father left your mother-"

"I don't care," Darrell said cutting him off.

"What?"

"I don't care about my birth father and why he left. My real father is at home asleep. He may have his faults, but he takes care of me the best he can and always has. Also, he doesn't kidnap people and isn't a psychopath. So as far as I'm concerned I don't really want to talk about Gary being my father anymore and I would prefer we don't tell Marie."

"If that is what you want," Gavril replied. Gavril wasn't sure what to make of Darrell's reaction. He had expected Darrell to be angry. Gavril knew it was a lot to process, but it wasn't healthy to bottle up all of those emotions. He knew that now wasn't the time to talk about it though, so he would leave Darrell alone about it.

"One thing I am interested in though is why you say we are more powerful than others."

"The power of a Seventh grows with each generation. Nobody is sure why, but it can't be denied. So the farther back the birth line goes, the more potential power the Seventh possesses. You happen to be a direct descendant of the very first Seventh. At least that is what the experts think. So your potential power is higher than anyone else really. Including Gary, by the way. That means that even though you don't have a lot of experience, there is no other Seventh in the world more capable of stopping Gary and saving Marie than you."

"I feel like I'm flying by the seat of my pants here, so I'm not sure I believe you, but I appreciate the vote of confidence," Darrell replied.

"Try to force a vision now," Gavril said.

"Okay."

Darrell concentrated as hard as he could for what seemed like minutes but nothing happened. He hadn't really expected anything, but he was disappointed none the less.

"Nothing," Darrell said.

"Damn. Don't beat yourself up about it. It is pretty tough to do and most people have to work on it a while before they get it to work."

CHAPTER THIRTY - DARRELL

Darrell had known as soon as he had the memory about the Donkey Kong game, but to have it confirmed hit Darrell like a punch in the gut. Gary really was his birth father, which meant that they shared the same genetics. Was Darrell going to go crazy like Gary? Gavril and the other Overseers seemed to think that getting his powers early was bad. Was that going to affect his brain and make him a lunatic too? The things he had already seen in his visions were haunting enough and it had only been less than a year. How would he handle the accumulation of those horrible things over the next twenty years? The past year was almost too much for Darrell to handle. He had lost his mother, developed the power to see the future, gained a good friend that turned out to be an immortal that lied to him, been partly responsible for getting his best friend kidnapped and hurt, and found out that his birth father was a lunatic, hell-bent on playing some sadistic game. The worst part was that he didn't think he could really talk to anyone about how he felt. He was too angry at Gavril, and Marie would be too emotional for sure. If he tried to tell anyone else, he was sure they would have him committed. In any event, this wasn't the time to reflect on his conflicting emotions. Marie was still in danger and he needed to save her.

As time wore on, Darrell was becoming increasingly frustrated. He was stuck and he didn't know what to do next. He had checked the hospitals, reviewed all of the traffic cameras in the area and had been listening to the police scanner for the past four hours with no luck. He hated to admit that he was out of ideas, but he had no clue how to save his best friend, and it was eating him up inside. He couldn't bear to think about what Gary must be doing to her and he had no way to stop him.

Darrell was staring off into space, lost in thought, when the vision hit. He knew right away it came from Gary and was surprised at how basic it was. Gary must be in real pain to not be able to give more of a vision. All Darrell saw was a few quick visions of Gary's old house and the basement door. It kept repeating, as if those weren't the only important things but he couldn't send more. The entire vision only lasted a few seconds.

Darrell was frustrated because the vision didn't give enough info. He figured that they went to the house, but it was certainly a trap. How were they supposed to save her?

Darrell decided he needed to try to force a vision again. He figured that he needed to try something different so he focused on the crown of his head, where the visions came from. He focused as hard as he could. He swore he could feel something in his brain, almost like flexing a muscle. It was extremely disconcerting. He began focusing on Gary's face, hoping that the combination would trigger something.

He was surprised when after a few moments, something began to form. He could see Gary and Marie running through an undeveloped lot. Gary was still clutching his hand and holding his arm close to his body. Darrell could see that both were still bleeding pretty badly. This must have been after the van crashed. Next he could see them in a parking lot. Darrell was able to look around and noticed that it was the parking lot of a hospital. Gary pushed Marie down on the ground and squared himself behind a parked car. A man in scrubs walked past and Gary reached into his jacket and pulled out a pistol. He pointed the pistol at the man and told him to go back to his car. He forced Marie in the backseat and the guy into the driver's seat. Gary got in the backseat behind the driver and made him start the car.

Next, Darrell saw Gary forcing the guy into Gary's house. He forced the man down into the basement with the gun at his back. Once in the basement, he handcuffed Marie to one of the columns that ran from the floor to the ceiling. He made the guy pull two chairs together and then get a first aid kit from one of the shelves. He then made the guy tend to his wounds. The doctor was able to stitch up Gary's arm and it seemed to be relatively okay, but when he began to clean up Gary's hand, it was obviously in bad shape. Gavril's shot had taken off the pinky and ring fingers completely and then gone clean through the palm of the hand. Darrell was no expert but he knew it must have been a pretty big bullet to put a hole that big in his hand. When the doctor began to clean it up Darrell could see right through it. The doctor told him that the only thing he could do was put gauze on it. He said the wounds would need serious medical attention to stop the bleeding and that Gary really needed to go to the hospital. Gary argued with the doctor and told him that he needed to fix it, and that going to the hospital wasn't an option. The doctor insisted he couldn't do anything more. Gary then told him that if he couldn't do anything else for him then he was of no more use. Gary shot him in the head, killing him instantly.

Marie yelled out. Gary pointed the gun at her, and told her that if he had to he could do the rest of the game without her and she stopped yelling. Gary then went on a diatribe about how he was going to make Darrell and his Overseer pay. He went to one of the walls and pushed a hidden button which opened a secret panel. He began to pull out several packets of explosives. Darrell didn't know much about explosives but they appeared to be some form of plastic explosive. Gary rigged both basement entrances with the explosives. He told Marie it was nice knowing her and knocked her out with the butt of his pistol. Darrell was so angry that he could feel himself losing control of his vision. It took everything he had to remain focused. Gary slowly left the basement, carefully making sure that both door's triggers were set. He ran across the street and hid in the bushes. Darrell snapped out of his vision and shocked to see Gavril looming over him.

"Did you get it to work?" Gavril asked.

"I sure did. At least I'm pretty sure it did. It felt like a vision," Darrell said. "It actually worked much better than I expected. I didn't just see one thing. I saw all the events since the crash."

"Really? That's impressive. Okay, so what are we up against?" Gavril asked.

"For starters, He fed me a vision first. It wasn't much but he showed me Marie and the basement in his house. When I got my vision I saw why he didn't go the hospital. He kidnapped a doctor and made him patch him up, and then Gary shot him. He does have Marie in the basement of his old house. He knocked her out. He also rigged the doors to explode, and it seems like he is waiting across the street in the same bush we used before. I'm not sure how we are going to get her."

"Talk to me about the explosives. How did he rig them up?"

"It seems like when you pull the door it has a wire that pulls a trigger. That would, I guess, make them explode. Maybe I could cut the wire."

"No, I'm sure there is a switch that goes off if the wire is cut. Probably has an electric current that can't be broken or something like that. He is too smart to make it as easy as cutting the wire. Don't worry though, I have an idea that I'm sure will work. Let's head to the twenty-four hour hardware store and I'll go over it with you, but first I need you to try to push a vision to Gary, showing him you and Marie blowing up."

"What? I have no clue how to do that," Darrell replied.

"Me either, but I suspect it should be similar to how you

forced your vision. Maybe if you build the images in your mind then concentrate on sending them to him it will work."

"I don't know. I may have just gotten lucky before; what if it doesn't work? Besides, wouldn't he know I was pushing them to him?"

"Like I said before, pushing visions is rare so it would be extremely unlikely he has ever felt it before and with him getting shot he is already in pain and hopefully won't know the difference."

"If you say so. It seems like a big risk."

"That is a risk we will have to take. We need the element of surprise and if he thinks that his plan works, that will give us the leverage we need. Remember what I said earlier. You have more potential power than anyone else on the planet, in the history of the planet for that matter. You can do this. I know you can."

CHAPTER THIRTY-ONE - GAVRIL

Gavril pulled the car over about a block away from Gary's house and shut the engine off.

"We should go on foot from here," Gavril said.

"Okay, so I'll go to the house and rescue Marie and you'll take care of Gary?" Darrell asked.

"That's the plan."

"And you don't think me knowing about your plan will tip him off?"

"It might, but we didn't have time to do it the other way. He is getting desperate and that worries me. Not to mention that he has already left a trail of bodies in his wake and the explosives show that he is planning on killing everyone. Just remember what I told you about getting past the bomb and we should be okay. It is probably a good idea to try to force visions while touching something near the area you would like to have a vision of, like you did before. Hopefully you can make sure nothing is going to go boom, if you know what I mean."

"Gotcha. Let's do this," Darrell said, getting out of the car.

Gavril got out and watched as Darrell made his way toward the house, trying his best to stay in the shadows and not be seen. Gavril went in the opposite direction, also trying to stay in the shadows. It only took Gavril a few minutes to make his way around the last house and come up behind Gary. He could see Gary squatting behind the bushes, watching his old house. From Gavril's point of view he couldn't tell if Darrell had made it in or not, so he decided he would just have to go for it. He crouched down in the shadows and began slowly making his way behind Gary. He had trained for stealth maneuvers when he was in the army and was pretty confident in his skills, but this was the most nervous he had been in a very long time. Gavril knew Gary couldn't see him in a vision, but that didn't necessarily mean he couldn't see something alluding to Gavril sneaking up on him, not to mention, he was surely expecting one of them to come for him. Gavril was about ten feet from Gary when Gary spoke.

"That's about far enough don't you think?" Gary said, holding out another detonator in his only good hand.

"Really? Again? That didn't go so well for you last time, did it?" Gavril said.

"A sense of humor? I can't say that your Overseer brethren would approve. They all seem very uptight. Regardless, I changed this one up a little. This one explodes if I let go of the button, so if you make me drop it the entire house goes boom and your little friends are barbecue," Gary said with a laugh.

"You really are a piece of work, you know. The visions are a gift. Why would you choose to use them for evil?" Gavril asked.

"Evil? Little bit of an exaggeration don't you think? I'm not in the mood for more lectures from an Overseer, so you can keep it to yourself. Besides, this will all be over soon. Now, we are going to get on the other side of the bushes so we have a nice unobstructed view of the evening's main event. Don't try anything stupid," Gary said.

The two men walked around the hedges, with Gary following Gavril from behind. Gavril kept glancing behind him to try to find an opportunity to attack but Gary was being overly cautious and was following too far behind for Gavril to grab the detonator before Gary could let it go. Once they got around the hedges, Gary moved to position himself so he was facing the house but also facing Gavril. Gavril stood there staring at Gary, seething. Gavril was already angry at himself for missing his shot in the warehouse, but now that he was here, helpless, watching this psychotic man get his jollies waiting for two teenagers to blow up, made his blood boil. He stared at Gary, growing angrier by the minute. All he needed to hear was the air horn signaling that Darrell had gotten Marie out of the house and they were safe. Once he heard that horn, he was going to take Gary down.

Several minutes had passed as the two men stood watching. Gary watching the house and Gavril watching Gary. The explosion startled both men but Gavril much more so. Gary had been waiting for the explosion, so while it made him jump a little, he stood straight, watching the flames erupt into the sky. Gavril had truly believed his plan would work, so he was completely shocked by the explosion. He instinctively crouched down covering his head and turning to see the source of the explosion. Gavril was overcome with emotion. His plan didn't work and he sent his friend to his death. Had Darrell's vision been wrong somehow? There must have been a second trigger that he didn't see. Gavril stood up and turned to look at Gary. Gary stood, watching the house with a huge smile on his face. That was too much.

Gavril swung so hard on that first punch that he even surprised himself. The punch was meant for Gary's nose but as is often the case when you fight with too much adrenaline, he missed his mark. Gary was not as tall as Darrell but taller than Gavril. None the less, Gavril had jumped to make sure he hit the mark. It was known as a Superman punch, but he had jumped and swung too high. Gavril's punch landed squarely on the top of Gary's forehead, one of the hardest parts of the skull. He did manage to knock Gary down though. Gavril wasn't sure how many of his bones broke on that punch, but he knew it was several. It hurt exponentially more than Gavril would have thought a broken hand could, coupled with the renewed searing pain from his chest and Gavril was really hurting.

Gavril fell to the ground clutching his hand. He looked down and was a little nauseous at what he saw. His hand had already swollen to at least three times its normal size. His pinky and ring finger were bent in ways they were never meant to, and his middle finger had a bone sticking out of the skin. Gavril looked up and saw Gary standing back up still smiling. He was rubbing his forehead where a giant knot was already taking shape, but otherwise he seemed okay. Seeing him so happy was enough to give Gavril a second shot of adrenaline. He forced himself to stand up and move past the pain in his hand. Gary still needed to pay, and Gavril was determined to collect that debt.

"Wow. That looks like it really hurts. I wasn't aware that fingers could even bend that way. I guess this makes us even," Gary said, raising the hand that Gavril had shot.

Gavril wasn't in any mood to talk. All his brain could think of was inflicting damage. He swung with his left hand and it landed right on Gary's jaw. The punch seemed to snap Gary out of it. Gavril thought the punch was a good one, but it didn't even knock Gary down. He decided he needed more power and would have to use his legs. He swung his right leg right toward Gary's midsection and was shocked when Gary caught it. In a move far too quick for Gavril to do anything about, Gary held on to Gavril's leg and bent over, putting his shoulder in Gavril's stomach. Gary then reached down and picked up Gavril's other leg and drove him to the ground. Before Gavril knew it, Gary was punching him in the face. Gary began throwing punch after punch. Gavril was blocking most of them as he put his arms over his face, but he knew he wasn't going to be able to take it for long.

"High School wrestling champ." Gary said as he continued to rain down blows.

CHAPTER THIRTY-TWO - DARRELL

A few minutes earlier

Darrell slowly made his way around the back of Gary's house to the back door. Just to be safe, he grabbed the doorknob and began to concentrate. He had seen Gary rig that door but he didn't want to chance anything. After a moment with no visions, he decided to go in. He went through the back door, and headed toward the basement. Once he was in front of the door, he took his backpack off and put it down in front of him. He pulled out some wire and wire trimmers and took a deep breath to try to relax. Gavril's plan seemed simple enough, and he was pretty sure it would work, but that was only if he could be careful enough to execute it properly.

Darrell slowly twisted the door knob and gently pulled on the door. He was able to get the door open a few inches when he felt the wire get tight. He looked up and could see the wire near the top of the door. The door didn't open as far as he had hoped. He wasn't sure he had enough room to execute the plan but knew he had no other choice. He slowly closed the door to regroup. He realized he would need both hands, so he took off his shoe to hold the door open. Darrell slowly opened the door again, this time placing the toe of his shoe in the gap to hold it open.

He began working on the wire so carefully and slowly that he was sure his muscles would cramp soon if he continued to keep them so tense. He took one end of his long piece of wire and began to wrap it around the trap wire near the door jamb. He wrapped it several times, slowly and as tight as he could manage without pulling on the trap wire. Once he was satisfied that his wire would hold, he began to wrap the other end around the wire near the door, with the same carefulness. Once he was finished, he stepped back and looked at his handiwork. He decided it was as good as he was going to be able to get it and it was going to have to be good enough. He picked up the wire cutters and prepared to cut the trap wire. He decided to try to force a vision once more and began concentrating. No vision came. He wasn't even sure he could really force a vision in this situation, or even if he was doing it right, but he decided that it was now or never. Either the plan was going to work and he was going to save Marie or this was the end, and he would see Marie in heaven, or whatever the after-life was. Darrell was never big on religion, but considering he had an immortal friend and had apparently been given psychic powers by God or whoever the higher power was, praying seemed logical. Darrell quietly said a prayer to request that everyone get out of the situation safely. Darrell closed his eyes and slowly squeezed the wire cutters. He heard the snip of the wire being cut and opened his eyes. The wire was cut and there was no explosion. Gavril's plan had worked so far. Had Darrell's pushed vision really worked? He thought it felt like he was in Gary's mind when he tried, but he was worried that his mind might have been playing tricks on him.

Darrell put his shoe on and slowly pushed the door open, still waiting for the coming explosion that never came. The new wire that he had put in place was long enough to open the door about 3/4 of the way but he decided to not open it more than halfway. He didn't want to test the strength of his wire wrapping, and halfway was enough to walk sideways through. It was a tough fit for Darrell because of his size but he was able to squeeze through without pushing the door or hitting his hanging wire. However, the way he needed to maneuver his body to make it through the door was especially hard on his burnt leg. The leg was throbbing and the pain was growing again. He forced himself to focus on his task at hand in an effort to forget about the pain, but that was no longer completely working. He was in a lot of pain and he was just going to have to deal with it. Once he was inside, he found the light switch and flicked it on. He slowly made his way down the staircase and there she was. Marie was handcuffed to a column in the middle of the basement with duct tape over her mouth. Darrell felt a wave of relief pour over him as he ran to her, and pulled the tape off of her mouth.

"Darrell! Thank god!"

"You are surprised," Darrell said in a mock hurt tone.

"I knew you'd try but this guy is seriously sick. Let's hurry up and get out of here before he remote detonates the explosives," Marie said.

"Damn!" Darrell said, looking at her handcuffs. "I didn't bring a way to get these off."

"Are you freaking kidding me? You can see the freaking future! You obviously knew I would be handcuffed. You didn't think to bring something to get them off?" Marie asked.

"Hey! I was more worried about the explosives, which I just got past by the way. There has to be something in here we can use," Darrell replied as he began to look around.

"Check over there near that workbench. I saw him using some tools over there," Marie said, nodding her head in the direction of the workbench.

"These should work," Darrell said, holding up a pair of bolt cutters.

"Perfect, now hurry," Marie said.

"There you go," Darrell said as he cut the chain on the handcuffs. "Follow me."

"What about him?" Marie asked pointing at the poor surgeon's dead body.

"It's not really possible for us to get him out right now," Darrell replied.

"We can't leave him here, what if the house blows up? His family deserves to have his body."

"Okay, we can try, but we need to be very careful." He knew trying to carry the body would be really risky, but he also knew Marie was right.

Darrell picked up the body and led Marie back up the staircase and held the door in place.

"Be careful going through, and try not to hit the door or catch on the wire. Once you get through you can hold the door open and I'll try to slide his body through," Darrell said.

"Okay," Marie said, having no problems squeezing her tiny frame through the door opening.

Marie held the door and Darrell carefully slid the body through. Darrell was glad the guy was a very tiny man, but it was still quite difficult. Once the man's torso was through, Marie helped by slowly pulling from the other side. Once the body was safely out, Darrell followed. He slowly maneuvered his body through the opening. His heart was beating out of his chest. The first time was tough, but now his adrenaline was pumping even harder, making it difficult for him to keep calm and move slowly. Finally he was able to make it through without tripping the explosives. Once they were both out of the basement, Marie began running and Darrell picked up the body, threw it over his shoulder and followed suit. They ran out of the house and were about halfway through the yard when Darrell reached out and stopped Marie.

"I need to go back," Darrell said, carefully putting the body down.

"What do you mean you need to go back? We are free, let's get out of here," Marie said, confused.

"I need to do one more thing."

"You have to be kidding me!"

"Okay, you wait here. I'll be right back," Darrell said, already heading back to the house, not giving Marie a chance to respond.

Darrell ran back to the house and to the basement door. He again squeezed through the door, wondering if he was crazy for doing this again. Once past the door he ran down the stairs and toward the workbench. He grabbed the giant ball of twine he had noticed earlier and headed back up the stairs. Squeezing through the door for the fourth time he decided he was indeed crazy and that this was by far the dumbest thing he had ever done. He couldn't say why exactly, but he felt compelled to do it, like he didn't have a choice. Once he was back out of the basement, he unrolled several feet of the twine and tied the end around the wire that he had connected to the trip wire. He walked toward the back door and out of the house, unrolling the twine carefully behind him. He got to Marie a few moments later, still leaving the trail of twine behind him.

"You went back for twine?" Marie asked, even more confused.

"Yeah, watch this," Darrell said.

Darrell began to pull the twine, slowly taking up all of the slack he had left behind him. Once he felt the twine get tight, he stopped and looked at Marie. He thought she was starting to get it. He smiled and pulled the twine as hard as he could.

The explosion was far bigger than he thought it would be and they were not far enough away. As he flew through the air, the old quote 'the best-laid plans of mice and men/often go awry' kept going through his mind. He landed on his wrist and was pretty sure he broke it based on the pain that began shooting up his arm. He got up as quickly as he could and ran around the body, which thankfully seemed okay, to Marie who was face down and not moving. He rolled her over, and began shaking her to get her to wake up.

"Would you stop shaking me?" Marie said, opening her eyes.

"Thank God. I thought you were dead."

"I'm not dead, but you are going to wish you were when we get to safety," Marie said, getting to her feet.

"If it makes you feel better, I'm pretty sure I have a broken wrist to go with my severely burnt leg," Darrell said, holding up his now swollen arm.

"It does, actually. What in the hell were you thinking? You almost got us killed right after saving me."

"I don't know. I thought if Gary thought we were blown up it would help us escape."

"And Gavril thought this was a good idea?"

"He didn't know. I improvised when I saw that twine."

"Where is Gavril?"

"He was supposed to capture Gary across the street."

"Wait, so he is here? He just saw the house blow up and thinks we are dead? Nice plan dummy, who knows what he will do now. Let's go find him."

They ran around the house, having to give the now giant fire a wide berth. As they rounded the house they saw two figures fighting. As they got closer they realized that Gary was the one on top. He was throwing punch after punch down on Gavril. Marie wasted no time, and ran right up to them. She kicked Gary so hard in the face that Darrell thought for a moment that she may have killed him. Gary flew back, landing hard on the concrete with his head bouncing off the ground as he hit. Marie immediately jumped on top of him and began to punch him, much like Gary had been doing to Gavril. Darrell quickly grabbed her and pulled her off of him.

"He's unconscious, that's enough," Darrell said.

"It's not enough! I'm going to kill him," Marie said, trying her best to get away from Darrell.

"No! Killing him makes us no better than him. That isn't something you want to have to live with. That is a bell you can't un-ring. I know you. It would haunt you every day," Darrell said, surprised at how hard it was to hold her.

"He deserves it!" Marie yelled, her resolve beginning to wane.

"You may be right, but that isn't for us to decide. The police will handle him," Darrell said. "Now can I trust you if I put you down?"

"Fine, I'll leave him alone," Marie said as she stopped struggling.

CHAPTER THIRTY-THREE - MARIE

Darrell put Marie down, and she took a last glance at Gary, fighting the desire to go after him again. Once she saw Gavril lying on the ground, and how badly he was hurt, the desire left. All she wanted to do now was help her friend. She knelt beside him, and tried to assess his wounds. She could see that he had taken several punches to the face, as his right eye was swollen shut. He had several cuts to his eyebrows, forehead and mouth. Then she noticed his hand, and swallowed a cry of shock when she saw how badly it was broken.

"Gavril, can you get up?" Marie asked.

"I'll be okay," He said as he began to sit up "Wait! I thought you guys were dead!"

"No. Mr. Moron over here decided it would be a good idea to make the house explode on purpose."

"Admittedly not my best idea. Sorry to scare you Gav."

"No, it wasn't. You had no idea how much explosive was in there, you could have killed us all," Gavril said, getting up to his feet.

"Not all of us. You're immortal aren't you?" Marie asked Gavril.

"Um, I am, but how did you know?" Gavril asked, obviously shocked.

"Gary was telling me about how all of this works and mentioned something about an immortal called an Overseer or something sent to look after people with the powers. I just put two and two together and assumed it was you."

"Aren't you clever? We can talk more about that later. Right now, this isn't quite over yet. You hear that?" Gavril asked as the sounds of sirens got closer. "The police will be here soon and there will be questions to answer."

"We can deal with them. You need to get out of here. Take the Mustang, go to the hospital, and get patched up," Darrell told Gavril.

Gavril nodded and took off down the block. He was moving surprisingly well for a person in his condition.

"What is that about? Why did he need to leave?" Marie asked. "There will be ambulances."

"I'll explain later. You think we are okay to talk to the cops? What are we going to tell them?" Darrell asked.

"I guess we just tell them the truth as best we can. We leave out your visions and any illegal hacking, and tell them the rest. They are already looking for him so it shouldn't be too hard," Marie said.

She looked over at Gary and noticed he was starting to

stir, so she walked over, bent down and punched him as hard as she could in the face, knocking him unconscious again. It felt so good. She was a little ashamed of herself, but only a little.

"Marie!" Darrell yelled.

"What? I didn't want him getting away before the police get here," Marie said with a smile on her face.

"Let me see your phone," Marie said.

"Who are you calling?" Darrell asked.

"My dad. He must be worried sick. I need to let him know I'm okay."

"Good call; I talked to him earlier and he is pretty stressed out," Darrell said, handing her the phone.

Marie decided to not go into much detail with her dad. She just told him that she was okay, and where she was. They sat on the curb and waited for the police to come, which didn't take long.

Three police cruisers pulled up, sirens blaring, followed by two firetrucks and two ambulances. The Firefighters wasted no time in working on the still roaring fire that used to be Gary's house. Marie was quite impressed in how quickly they were able to get the hoses rolled out, attached to the fire hydrant and pumping water at the blaze. It took the police a few moments to notice Marie, Darrell and Gary, but once they did they didn't hesitate to pull out their guns, and point them at Marie and Darrell.

Marie did most of the talking. She was trying her best to be patient but she was growing frustrated. When she told him who Gary was they reacted quickly. They had him handcuffed to one of the ambulance's stretchers as the paramedics looked him over. Another pair of EMT's began working on Darrell's burn and wrist.

The main thing frustrating Marie was the fact that they wouldn't accept what Marie and Darrell were telling them. Marie had thought she had done a good job at recounting the story with all of the pertinent information to let them know what had happened over the last few days. She left out the Donkey Kong incident because nobody in their right mind would believe that, not to mention there might be evidence of Gavril's sniper rifle. She also left out the stuff that might get them in trouble, but the story made sense and fit all the timelines. They just wouldn't accept it. They kept asking her the same questions over and over, or sometimes a different question that was trying to get the same information. When she was just about at the end of her rope, her dad showed up.

She felt a little sorry for the police officers that were manning the police tape perimeter, because as soon as he saw her he plowed right through them, tossing both of them aside like rag dolls. It may have been twenty years since he was a star college fullback but she had to admit that he could still bring it. Several of the officers pulled their firearms when they saw it happen, but as soon as the captain realized it was her father he told them to stand down.

Marie's father was never an emotional man. She could recall only a few occasions of him telling her that he loved her, and he hadn't given her a hug in at least ten years. He made up for it all in that moment as he picked her up and gave her the biggest hug he could muster. As her cheek pressed against his, she could feel the tears running down his face. She had never seen him cry in her entire life and she wasn't sure what to make of it. The sudden burst of emotion made her slightly uncomfortable because she didn't know how to react. She decided to just hold on and let him get it out. It didn't take long, however, before she was crying herself. She had often been hard on her father but she knew he had really tried his best. She hated his prejudices but she always believed in her heart that he was only regurgitating what he heard growing up. She still believed that someday, he could realize he was wrong on that front. She also knew that he was just never equipped to be a single father, but at that moment she realized how much he really loved her. After a few moments, her father put her down and quickly wiped his tears. She knew he would never admit that he had cried.

"I'm taking my daughter home now," Mr. Clarkson said.

"I'm sorry, but we still have questions," the Captain said.

"Is she under arrest?" He said a little more forcefully than she wished he had.

"No, we just need to understand what happened here."

"You seem like a great detective. I'm sure you can figure it out. In the meantime, I am taking her home. She has been through a lot and doesn't need you making it worse," Mr. Clarkson said.

"Darrell too," Marie said.

"Yeah, and I'm taking Darrell too."

"He needs medical attention," The Captain said.

"Then I'll take him somewhere he can get that attention without being bombarded with questions. If you want to ask him something, you can go through his father. Now if you'll excuse us. You can come by and ask your questions tomorrow," he replied, and began leading Marie and Darrell away before the captain could even open his mouth.

"Thanks dad," Marie said, grabbing her dad's hand.

"Let's just get you home and safe," Her dad said, squeezing her hand in a last show of emotion.

CHAPTER THIRTY-FOUR - MARIE

Two weeks later

Marie was really looking forward to going back to school. She was especially glad to see Darrell and Gavril again since her dad had not let her out of his sight since that night. He finally agreed to let her go back to school but it was not easy. She thought that having the rest of winter break off would have been enough for him, but when everyone went back and he wouldn't let her, she knew he was taking it too far. She finally convinced him that missing too much school would make her fail and have to repeat the eleventh grade, so he relented, and she only ended up missing a couple of days.

Now that she was here though, she knew she was going to be the center of attention, which is something she always hated. It seemed to her that the news had reported nothing but Gary's story the entire past two weeks, and her face had been all over it. The reporters had camped outside of Marie's house for the first week or so, until her dad began coming up with ingenious passive aggressive, and a few not so passive, ways to get them to leave. First he just did things like turn on the sprinklers. When that didn't work, he bought a bag of gravel, tossed it all over the yard and proceeded to mow. The rocks went everywhere, hitting a few cars, but thankfully not any reporters, although she was sure he wouldn't have cared if he did. He also broke three of his own windows, but it had worked. The reporters never came back after that. The police came after one of the reporters filed a complaint for the gravel incident, but the police captain didn't like the reporters acting like vultures either, so they didn't file charges.

She spotted Darrell and Gavril waiting for her in front of the school and noticed how pathetic they looked. They were both in casts and Darrell had some sort of thing on his leg because of the burn. Darrell noticed her and began waving out of control. If she wasn't so happy to see him it would have been quite embarrassing. She walked over to them and gave them both big hugs.

"God, I'm so happy to see you guys. You guys look pathetic. How are you doing?" Marie asked.

"We are fine. My wrist is no big deal. My leg still hurts but luckily I don't need skin grafts. The doctors say I will still have some bad scars, but hey chicks dig scars right?" Darrell asked, but Marie didn't give him the satisfaction of a response, but she knew if girls really knew what he had done they would have been all over him. "Anyway, Gavril heals really fast and could have taken the cast off a week ago, but he thinks it looks cool."

"No I don't. I just am too lazy to cut it off."

"How are you? We tried calling, but your dad always said you were resting," Darrell said.

"Yeah, he was a little out of control for a while. It took days of begging for him to let me come back to school."

"I can imagine," Gavril said.

"Hey Gavril, since I was cut off from the world for the past two weeks, I never got to ask you. Why did Gary kidnap those kids? He said he wanted to punish the parents, but he never said why," Marie asked.

"I figured you would have just looked it up," Darrell said.

"My dad also took my computer. He said he didn't want me focused on what people on the internet were saying about me."

"Wow. He really was being over-protective. I guess that explains why you never replied to our emails either. The boy was the son of the District Attorney that prosecuted Gary on one of his convictions," Gavril replied.

"How didn't I see that before?" Marie asked.

"The child was born out of wedlock and had a different last name. Also in the news reports, it always mentioned the boy's stepfather as his father, most likely to keep the DA out of the news," Gavril said.

"And the girl?" Marie asked.

"She was the daughter of the judge that convicted Gary when he was a juvenile," Gavril said.

"Man, I can't believe I missed that too," Marie replied.

"It's not like there was much time between him taking

her and taking you," Darrell responded.

"Plus she had a very common name," Gavril added.

Just then, Marie felt someone grab her butt. She jumped and turned around to see Eric Snow, one of the biggest jerks in school.

"You are so fine Marie. Maybe I should kidnap you too," Eric said.

"You are going to regret that," Darrell said as he and Gavril began walking toward him.

"Relax, she probably likes it," Eric said.

Marie reached out and stopped them. She kicked Eric in the crotch. Eric doubled over and she punched him as hard as she could in the jaw, sending him sprawling to the ground. There was a small moment of silence as those watching took the scene in, and then there was a smattering of applause. Marie was suddenly embarrassed as she realized everyone was watching her. She quickly looked around, and breathed a sigh of relief when she realized that nobody of authority was there to see it. Her dad being called within minutes of her finally going back to school would mean she would end up being home-schooled for sure.

"Wow, you are almost as scary as you are beautiful. Come on, let's go," Darrell said, grabbing her arm and leading her toward the school.

"Good idea," Gavril said.

"Here take this," Darrell said, taking two sheets of paper out of his backpack and handing one to each of them.

"What's this?" Marie asked.

"Those, my dear, are the answers to the pop quiz in

Earth science today," Darrell said.

"Now these are the types of visions I could get used to," Marie said.

"You got that right," Gavril said.

"Hey guys. Something else was nagging at me recently." Marie said.

"What's that?" Darrell asked.

"That lady that was at Gary's house when you first went there. Who in the hell was she, and what happened to her?"

ABOUT THE AUTHOR

Elvis Lawson has had a variety of jobs over the years including the USAF as an avionics technician, selling music (best job ever) and most recently as a business planning analyst. His passions include movies, music and video games. If it is geeky, he is probably into it. He lives in Frisco, Texas with his wife Crystal. He has three wonderful kids, Tyler, Ivan, and Odin as well as an amazing grandson Grant.